ALL SAINTS

ALL SAINTS

stories

K. D. Miller

BIBLIOASIS
WINDSOR, ON

FIRST EDITION

Library and Archives Canada Cataloguing in Publication

Miller, K. D. (Kathleen Daisy), 1951-, author
     All Saints / written by K.D. Miller.

Short stories.
Issued in print and electronic formats.
ISBN 978-1-927428-63-4 (pbk.).-ISBN 978-1-927428-64-1 (epub)

     I. Title.

PS8576.I5392A45 2014   C813'.54   C2013-907290-X
                                           C2013-907291-8

F
MIL

c²

Edited by Dan Wells
Typeset by Chris Andrechek
Cover Designed by Kate Hargreaves

Biblioasis acknowledges the ongoing financial support of the Government of Canada through the Canada Council for the Arts, Canadian Heritage, the Canada Book Fund; and the Government of Ontario through the Ontario Arts Council.

PRINTED AND BOUND IN CANADA

Contents

For John Metcalf, with gratitude and love

BARNEY

BEST THING YOU'VE EVER DONE, this room. Better than the deck out back, and that was pretty damned good. But this room? Leaps and bounds. Every time you come down here, every time you start pacing it off, something new comes to mind.

Take the walls. Case in point. First off, you figured beige. Kind of colour goes with anything. Never get tired of looking at it. But tell the truth. Didn't feel right. Felt more like something she'd go for and you'd just go along with. So you let it be. Didn't worry it. Didn't bring home a wad of beige paint chips and go nuts trying to see the difference. And sure enough, while you were busy sanding a cut end, it came to you. What you really wanted. Green. Kind of a khaki green. Shade that takes you back. Hardly seen it since the war. Made so much sense you damned near laughed out loud. And next thing, you did laugh. Because you thought, wainscoting. Well, why not? Not too small a room for that. Nice dark woodwork up to maybe waist height. Bit of moulding, stained the same. And topping that, the khaki green. Colour you and Barney were kitted out in, last time—

Ga-a-rth?

Ah, Christ.

Ga-a-rth?

Way she drags your name out. When she wants something.

You yell up that you're in the basement. Working. So she yells down that she needs a jar of this or a bottle of that from the shelf under the landing, and could you bring it with you when you come? Except that's not what she means. Oh no. She means right bloody now. But she won't say it. So when you do bring it with you once you're ready to come up, like she said, you'll get that pinched little, hurt little look that says, *Took your time, didn't you?*

Yeah. You did. You will, too. Take your sweet time. Things to do down here. Barely got the joists laid for the floor. Still have to measure for the uprights. So you'll bring whatever it is with you when you come up. When you're damned good and ready.

What was it she wanted, anyway? Needs it that bad she can come down the steps herself.

Where were you? Khaki? Wainscoting? Joists? Floor! Hardwood, it's going to be. In that fancy criss-cross pattern. What's it called? Starts with P. Parkerhouse? No, that's buns. Damn. Tip of your tongue. Well, don't worry it. Just think about something else, and it'll come.

Way this whole thing came to you. Just when it looked like all you were allowed to think about was the sixtieth—hers and yours—coming up. All you had to look forward to, too. Not that you were exactly looking forward to it. More like it was coming at you. Her making her plans, all year long. On the phone to the kids, racking up the bill. Calling up the members of the wedding, them as are still alive. Hauling down the photo albums. Looking at the old snaps. Going, *remember, Garth? Remember?* Over and over.

And all of a sudden, you did. Not whatever she was pointing at, though. No, you remembered waiting with Barney. In the station. You were practically home by then, but you were staying a while with him till the train came that would take him the last leg of his own journey. His girl was waiting for him, just like yours was for you. All full of their plans. It was one of those times when you can't really start in talking about anything too big. It'll just get cut off. So you kept it small. Sports. Job prospects. But all the time, it was right on the tip of your tongue. *Barney? Would you stand up for me?*

Train came and he was gone. Just as well, you figured. Family would have been up in arms about how you had to have your brother—your own brother, your only brother—as your best man. So there was your own and only brother on the day. Already half-cut. Damned near dropping the rings when he had to hand them to the rector to bless.

Remember, Garth? Remember?

How could you not? Say goodbye to your best friend, say hello to your wife. Hardly time to get out of uniform and into a suit.

Ah, but she's looking forward to it. It's all for the women, these things. Weddings. Marriage, even. Start of everything, for her, that walk down the aisle.

Going to be an announcement in church on Sunday. *Sixty years ago today, right here in All Saints.* Christ, will we have to get up on our feet? Get clapped for? Bad enough the cake in the parish hall afterwards, and having to hang around and smile and crack jokes and pretend to give advice. People congratulating you, like you've just climbed Everest. Dug down to China, feels more like. And all the time, just wanting to get back down here. Strip off the glad rags. Get to work on the room.

You did put your foot down about having the bloody rings blessed all over again. What, you said, the warranty's run out? Batteries need recharging? She sulked a bit. But you'd given in about the announcement and the cake, so she couldn't complain.

You've given in about a few things, over the years. And that's what came to you, when she was going through the wedding album with her *remember, remember.* Almost said it out loud. Be hell to pay if you had. But it came to you. How you'd spent sixty years doing something else. Talking about something else. Thinking about something else.

Maybe once a year or so, you'd give Barney a thought. Around Armistice. Veterans. Remembrance. Whatever they call it now. Wonder how he's doing. If he's sometimes maybe thinking back at you.

Who was his girl again? Shirley? Barney and Shirley. Sounds right. And where did they settle? Grimsby? Think he said they were aiming for Grimsby. Not so far from here. Nice little junket, it could have been. Once a year or so. Not so as to be in each others' pockets. But once a year would have been all right. *Off to see Barney and Shirley for the day.* Or, *Like you to meet Barney and Shirley, in for the day from Grimsby. Barney and I go back, you know. In the war together, weren't we? Got some stories, don't we?*

Shit. Was it Grimsby? And was his girl Shirley?

You say you'll stay in touch. Still in your fatigues, at the station, your duffel over your shoulder. Shaking hands. Hard. Looking into each others' eyes. Then away. You say you'll write. You say you'll get together.

What the hell is the name of that criss-cross hardwood pattern? Not going to come to you after all. Going to drive you nuts, all bloody day. Porterhouse? No, that's steak.

She'd know. Upstairs. Waiting for her jar of this or her bottle of that. But damned if you'll ask her. She hates the room. Says it's a waste of time. Kill yourself down there, she says. Man your age. Lugging two-by-fours. Hammering nails.

We can rent it out, you keep saying.

To who, she says.

Make some extra money, you say.

For what, she says. We're old, Garth. The mortgage was paid years ago. We don't need extra money. And we don't need an extra room. Who on earth are you building it for? The kids are grown and gone. The grandkids won't even be coming here. Not to stay, anyway. Nobody's coming here. What we need is to start thinking about selling this place.

Right, you say. And when we do, the room will increase the value.

There. That's your trump card. Stops her noise for a while. For all it's a lie.

Parquet! There. See? Just think about something else. Parquet. That's what it's called. And you can get it in squares now. Tack them down onto the plywood underlay. Make a parquet floor. Square by square. For Barney. Hell with selling the house. Hell with her. *Could you lift this and could you reach that and just look at the spot on your nice clean shirt and when am I going to get a new washer-dryer and and and.* And talk? Jesus. Not like she's trying to tell you anything. Not like she's got something to say. More like her heart's in her tongue and if she ever stops for one blessed minute that'll be it.

Not that you and Barney didn't talk. Probably talked more to Barney than you've ever talked to anybody. In your life. Those weeks before you got sent over. And then once you were in the thick of it. When every word might be your last, so you made it a good one.

It wasn't just noise, though. Just talk to fill the nothing. The words—if you added up the words, they wouldn't come to much. Not yours, anyway. But Barney? He could ask you a question—*You ever get up real early, Garth, and see a lake like glass before the first wind's ruffled it, and the reflection of the far trees so perfect you don't know which is water and which is sky, and it makes you wonder if you've been upside down all your life?* If things were quiet, it would sound like the damnedest fool question you'd ever heard. But then all the hell would start up. And at the end of it, when you were just getting used to not being dead, you'd find that question still in your mind, and it would be the only thing in the whole universe that made any sense. So you'd say, *Yeah. I've seen that. Once or twice.* And Barney would smile like he'd known all along you had, like that question was the one he'd been saving up just for you. Like the two of you hadn't just come close to being blown to bits, and that lake was right there in front of you both, in the early morning, with the first wind yet to ruffle the surface. And soon—

Ga-a-rth?

What! What! What! You're down here! Working! And whatever she needs she can come get it for herself!

Silence. Oh, right. You know how it's going to be now, once you do go up. She'll put your lunch down in front of you without a word, then sit across the table from you not eating. Not talking. For once. And you'll try. Try a little joke. Call her one of the old names. Say, How about supper down at the Legion tonight? Save cooking? No dishes? Still nothing. So finally you'll say, All right, what is it then? And she'll be all tears, blubbering on about the jar of pickles or whatever the hell it was that you wouldn't bring up. Except it's not the jar of pickles. It's never the bloody jar of pickles.

Makes you wonder how the human race ever managed to get a toehold.

Things you can't tell a woman. A woman's forever waiting for you to come back home. From the war. From the job. Sees you off in the morning. Thinks you're the same man at the end of the day. Can just get on with the plan. Like the day never happened. But every day takes something away from you. Or hands you something to take, whether you want it or not.

And then there are the things you see. Can't talk about them either. Like remembering a dream, some of them all in flashes, like lightning. And thunder—worse than any you've ever known. But not thunder. Guns. Men. No. Boys, most of them. Just boys. Cold. Scared. That's what you tell yourself after. About what you see in that one flash. Think you see. Two of them. One holding the other because he can't stop his noise. Unbuttoning his tunic. Giving the kid the nipple, hair and all. And after, it's like you did it. Except you didn't. Or it's like it happened to you. Except it didn't. All you know is you can sleep. Sleep like a baby. First time in—

Shutters. God, yes. Just came to you. Shutters. For the window. Stained to match the wainscoting. Not curtains. No. Not bloody curtains. Shutters that he can fold open, if he likes, or pull closed. With little visors so he can adjust the light. You're starting to see it. Really see it. Bed over there. Dresser up against the other wall. Desk in the corner. Shelves. Oh, you'll be fine, Barney. I'll look after you. You'll see. You'll see.

Which of us said that? *I'll look after you. You'll see. You'll see.* Was it you? Or him? It got said. One way or the other. Sixty years ago. Could have been yesterday.

Not that you were. You and Barney. No. Not like that. You'd both been engaged to be married when you were sent over. And you and her. You already had. Twice. And it had been all right. It had been fine. For you. Maybe for her too. But she would never say, and you don't ask a girl about a thing like that. Not the kind of girl you'd think of marrying.

You were pretty sure Barney had, too. With Shirley. He hinted as much, once or twice. But you don't come out and ask a man about a thing like that either. Not even your best friend. Not even in hell.

Better go up soon. Face the music. Maybe ask her about the grandkids. Any of them coming on Sunday? She told you, but it's hard to keep them straight, where they are, what they're doing. Well, just ask her again. Break the ice. Can always get her talking about the grandkids.

Wonder if Barney has any. Grandpa Barney. Grandpa Garth. Strange, that. Can't get used to it, for all the youngest is in high school and the oldest going to be married. Could never get used to being Dad, either. Or even Garth, the way she says it. Wake up in the middle of the night and wonder where your boots had got to. Reach for your rifle, and there's your wife.

You get lodged. Things take. You're here, but you're still over there. And nobody can know what that's like, unless they were with you at the time. Unless there's a part of them that never quite made it home, either.

Parquet floor. And wainscoting. *My God, Garth*, he'll say, once he's dropped his kit bag on the bed and taken his first look round. *You wainscoted the walls!* And you'll kind of smile down at your feet, like it's nothing. And just when you're wondering when he'll notice the shutters, he'll say, *Shutters!* And he'll try them out, folding them back, working the levers. And all the time you'll be keeping it small, just shrugging and saying something like, well, you guess you'll let him alone to get settled in. And maybe in a little while—

What? What's she doing on the stair? Coming down here? Stepping harder than she has to? Oh, right. Making a big show of getting the pickles or whatever it was from the shelf under the landing. Back up now, stamp stamp stamp. *Didn't exactly kill you, did it?* you want to call after her, but don't. One thing marriage teaches you. When to hold your fire.

Where were you? Barney. In the room. The way it'll be. When he comes. Come on. You can remember. Don't let her take it away from you. Get it back. Try.

Ah, Jesus Christ.

Is he even still alive? And how are you going to finish down here? All you've got is the joists laid. Like a honeycomb on the floor. Not even plywood over them yet. And the lumber for the uprights stacked but not cut, not even measured. And don't even think about the batts of insulation for the outside wall, and then the bloody drywall over that. Then the prime. Then the paint. And wainscoting? You've never installed wainscoting in your life. Parquet floor? When you've barely laid the joists? Man your age. Stupid bloody waste of—

All right. All right. All right. Enough of that. Take yourself in hand. Lay down the law. Way you did with the kids if they got lippy at the table. There'll be no more thinking that way. No more thinking it's hopeless. It's not. You'll do it. It'll happen. Just don't worry it. You start to worry a thing, you'll worry it down to nothing. So keep your eye on the way it's going to be. Not the way it is now.

Try to see it the way Barney would. Way he looked at things. *Think of Stonehenge, Garth*, he said to you once. *Think of it brand new. Or even not quite finished. Think of the sparks jumping from the stone masons' mallets. Those sparks are still burning, Garth. Dimmer and dimmer. But never out. Never completely out.*

Thing about Barney was, you could believe him when he said something like that. While he was saying it, that is. If you wrote it down after and tried to say it yourself, it'd be so much drivel. But if you put the words back in his mouth, heard them in his voice and watched him saying them—that little smile he always had no matter what—then, yeah. You could believe. And you would believe. Keep coming back to those words, crazy as they were. And after a while they wouldn't be crazy any more. Everything else would be crazy. But what Barney said would be the only thing that made any sense. More sense than anything you've heard in church week after week, sitting beside her in your suit. All of it worried down to nothing. Son of God? Holy Ghost? Never met them. Never shaken their hands. But Barney? Been to hell and back with Barney.

So you just think about making that first call. Hearing the phone ring in Grimsby. Once. Twice. Maybe three times, if he's out back or down in his own basement working on something. Now he's picking up. *Hello?* The voice doesn't change. *Barney?* you say. And you're all set to go on with, *It's Garth* when he cuts you off with his own *Garth! My God! Garth! What the hell took you so long?* And now you're both shouting and laughing. *Well, I had to finish the bloody room, didn't I*, you say. *So you just get your kit together and get your backside down this way before I rent it out. Before I—*

Oh, bloody hell. What does she want now?

Lunch. Has your lunch ready for you. Well, it's a peace offering. Better go up. Marriage. One ceasefire after another. Potshots in between.

Need your lunch, anyway. Keep your strength up. Might not be able to get through to Barney by phone. Might have to go to Grimsby. Take the bus, now that your night vision's shot and she has to do the driving.

Try the Legion first. If he's kept up with the Legion. Then make inquiries at the Chamber of Commerce. Man like Barney, he'd have made a name. Or if not, try the local churches. What was he? Catholic?

All else fails, go door to door.

You'll know him, even through the screen. The eyes don't change. And he'll still have that smile. *Garth!* he'll say, and open the door and pull you in. And then—

Oh, here's a thought. Amazing what comes to you.

What if Barney's been building a room too? All this time? For you? *Place you could come and just be, Garth. Figured it was time to put my money where my mouth was. After sixty years. Time to make a place for Garth, I said to myself. Time to bring Garth home.*

Christ. What a thing to happen. Make you laugh, it would. Laugh till you cried.

STILL DARK

SIMON CLOSES THE DOOR of his office behind him. Locks it. Checks that it is locked. Turns and wades through the dark until he nudges the edge of his desk. Works his way around to his chair and sits.

He pulls open the bottom left drawer, bunches the hanging files together and reaches into the cavity at the back. Touches a softness that always surprises him, like the fur of a sleeping animal.

While his eyes adjust to the dark, he lifts the sweater out, holds it up and shakes it gently. Telling himself again that he should be keeping it in a plastic bag. Telling himself again that he shouldn't be keeping it at all.

"Simon? Hi. It's Kelly again. Sorry to bother you, but I was wondering if I left my sweater in your office this morning."

She had. She had been wearing it when she arrived to interview him for *Saints Alive*. "Hot for September," she had murmured halfway through, unfastening the top button and pulling her arms out of the sleeves. She was wearing a white shirt underneath, tucked into jeans. The sweater had slipped down behind her on the chair, and she must have overlooked it when she was gathering her stuff to leave—purse, pen, notebook, hat.

"I don't see it, Kelly," he said into the phone. Which was technically true, if not the truth. He had spotted the sweater—a small black bundle on the chair seat—the second he returned to his desk after seeing her out the door. He had picked it up, thinking to call her back. But then he had just stood, holding the thing in his hands.

"Is there any chance you left it in the ladies' downstairs?" Compounding the lie, now. "I can ask Gail to have a look." Implicating his secretary.

"No, that's okay. I've been all over the place since I left the church, so it could be anywhere. I'll just have to retrace my steps. Thanks anyway."

"I—" He what? Had just told an untruth, in addition to committing theft? Two out of ten. Not bad for his first week. "I enjoyed our chat this morning, Kelly."

"Me too. You're an easy interview. Well, I guess I'll see you Sunday. Bye."

Simon lifts his face. There's a warm patch near the neckline from his breath. And still that hint of Ivory soap, after—It's the middle of November.

How much longer is he going to do this? Try to do this? He should just give up. Have the sweater cleaned and give it back to Kelly.

And tell her what? And what, exactly, would he be giving up?

Easier just to get rid of the thing. Right now, while the place is empty. Sneak downstairs and slip it into the donation box in the hall outside the sanctuary. A classic, unadorned black cardigan. Chances are not even Kelly would recognize it if she came across it at the rummage sale or saw it on one of the neighbourhood's homeless.

But what, exactly, would he be getting rid of?

He has this argument with himself every morning.

When he can see well enough, he gets up and goes around his desk to the facing chair. Drapes the sweater over the back and arranges it so the button at the neckline is centred. That's

important. It gives the garment a presence, a sense of awareness. And there is something sweetly composed about the
curves of the fabric joining at the button.

He sits back down at his desk. Looks for a long time at
the dim shape of the chair, the dimmer outline of the sweater.
Imagines Kelly sitting facing him.

"This is beautiful."

She had arrived early for the interview. He'd had some
forms to deliver to Gail downstairs, so he'd asked her to make
herself comfortable. When he came back up into the office, he
found her looking at the cross hanging on the wall above the
bookcase. It was one of the first things he'd unpacked when he
arrived the week before. It's so fragile.

"My wife made that," he said, coming and standing beside
Kelly. He hadn't realized how short she was. Her head barely
reached his shoulder.

"I don't know why the paint brush is so right," she said.
"It just is."

It was an old brush, the kind a house painter would use,
all splattered and stiff with dried paint. Ruth had wired twigs
across the handle to make a rough cruciform shape, then had
hung trinkets from the twigs. There was a blue beaded book-
mark she had picked up in a gallery gift shop. A pink heart-
shaped pendant she had worn as a girl. A round white shell she
had found on the beach, with a convenient hole in it for the
wire to go through. A brass Buddha pin she had worn in university. A jade pendant in the shape of some Maori god that a
childhood pen pal had sent her from New Zealand.

"It's probably the best thing she ever did," he told Kelly
now, as they stood looking at it together. *And one of the few
things she ever managed to finish.*

It helps, in this new place, to look up from his desk and
see it on the wall. It helps to imagine Ruth working away at
it, her lip caught between her teeth, her braids—she would
have braided her hair to keep it out of the glue—swaying
back and forth. "It was BYOJ," she had told him, flushed and

bright-eyed. Simply happy for once. "And there was this big communal pile of junk in the middle of the floor that we all got to pick through." She was always starting some course or other—yoga, watercolour painting, meditation, collage, acting, creative writing, and now junk sculpture. The workshop had been a one-day affair, and had coincided with one of her good days. "Trust me—you haven't lived till you've watched two grown women in a tug-of-war over a headless Barbie doll."

"So she's not doing this kind of thing anymore?" Kelly asked.

"No, she—" Surely his story would have preceded him? Churches are such gossip centres. "I'm sorry. I should have said something. Ruth—my wife—died. About a year and a half ago."

Kelly turned and looked up at his face. He braced himself for the *I'm so sorry to hear that* or the *My condolences on your loss* or even the *What did she die of?* that had long since ceased to shock him. But she said nothing. Just gazed at him gravely for a moment, then turned back to the sculpture.

"See how it moves," she said softly. "See how the bits of it are swaying back and forth, just with our breath."

"Bless the Lord who forgives all our sins."

Simon keeps his eyes on the sweater, hearing the words in Kelly's voice. Then he whispers the response: "His mercy endures forever."

He imagines her saying the first line of the psalm: *"Have mercy on me, O God, according to your loving-kindness;"*

He whispers the next line: "In your great compassion blot out my offences."

"Wash me through and through from my wickedness;"

"And cleanse me from my sin."

It's been years since he's heard a confession, much less asked anyone to hear his own. The Reconciliation of a Penitent is there in the prayer book, available for anyone who wants it. *All may, some should, none must,* as the saying goes. People confess to their psychiatrists now, or to the Internet. Words like *sin* and *mercy* and *wickedness* strike them as quaint at best, more often baffling or even offensive.

But the lofty language serves a purpose, as he's tried to explain, the few times he's gently urged a parishioner to consider confession, even just as a way of offloading some guilt. It helps both confessor and penitent to focus. It maintains a boundary between them, and preserves the dignity of both. It—

Who is he preaching this sermon to?

After a couple of abortive attempts in the pool of light from his desk lamp, he committed the rite to memory. He needs to get through it without having to see the page. He needs to start in the dark, to come gradually into the light. Otherwise, he's just reading to a sweater.

Simon hadn't felt much of anything in months. His body had become a thing to feed and wash and clothe. It got him wherever he had to be and anchored his floating mind. Then Kelly said what she did about them breathing on the sculpture and making it move.

He took a step away from her. Turned and headed for his desk. "Do you mind if we get started?" Even to himself he sounded abrupt. "I have quite a day ahead of me."

A few hours later, he lied to her and stole her sweater.

"May God, who enlightens every heart, help you to confess your sins and trust in his mercy."

Kelly has a slight lisp. Simon smiles, imagining her damp delivery of those last few phrases. He whispers the response: "Most merciful God, have mercy upon me, in your compassion forgive my sins, both known and unknown, things done and left undone."

He pictures the word *especially* as it appears at this point in the prayer book, italicized and followed by an ellipsis. In seminary, it had been a running joke: *Especially*... the toenail clippings down the back of the chesterfield. *Especially*... the crusted Kleenex under the mattress.

"Especially … " he whispers, then stops, as he always does. The sweater waits. It is easy to read patience into its silence and stillness.

He recognized Kelly, that day in his office. Knew her instantly—as his confessor and more—and had to get away from her. Right then and there. His arm was too ready to lift, reach, pull her to him.

Something they weren't taught in seminary is how erotically charged the confessional can be. A secret will wait for years, decades, until the right pair of ears comes along. A new priest, maybe. Or a stranger on a bus. Or a woman making an innocent remark about breath. He was so close, that day. If he had let himself, he could have dissolved into her. Soaked his tears and sweat into her, and the spit from his bawling mouth.

And then what? Would she have run screaming from his office? Or would she have stayed and received him—all of him—in her arms?

It's still dark in the office, but not as dark. The window behind him will soon start to turn pale. And Gail gets in at eight-thirty.

"Especially … " he whispers, then stops again. Every morning for weeks, he has gotten this far, then has stopped.

"So did you always want to be a priest? Or, deep down, do you still wish you were a fireman?" Kelly clicked her pen and waited, notebook open on her lap.

Safe behind his desk, Simon let himself take a good look at her. He wouldn't call her pretty. Certainly not beautiful in the classic, patrician way Ruth had been. With her big eyes blinking behind those glasses that managed to stay perched on the bridge of her small nose, she was more like a friendly alien. A Disney-drawn bug.

"Some people would say that I *am* a fireman, Kelly. Or maybe that I sell fire insurance." Oh hell. She was writing that old chestnut down. "What I remember is wanting to be anything but an Anglican priest. Probably because my father was one. Typical rebellious son. Then one day, well, I won't say I heard a voice, exactly. But something in me did seem to be telling me to grow up."

"What is a priest?"

Hello. He wasn't expecting that one. "Good question. Okay. Let's see if I can remember my own job description from seminary. I think the formal definition is 'one who is set apart by the church to preside over the sacraments and minister to the community.'"

When she stopped writing, she sat looking down at her notebook for a moment. He wondered if she was disappointed in his answer. Maybe she was expecting something more poetic. Personal. She looked up again and he had to smile. She *was* kind of buggy, with those spiky bangs. And so unlike Ruth. Odd he would have felt—

"Do you believe in God?"

"Especially ... "

He's confessing to a sweater. A woman's sweater. Every now and then the weirdness of what he's doing hits him. He imagines the sexton walking past the office on his rounds some morning. Hearing something. Using his pass key to open the door. He can just see himself trying to explain that it's not the way it looks.

Or is it?

Okay, he's been friendly with Kelly. But he's always maintained a pastoral reserve. And he's only had lunch with her a couple of times since the interview. Three times. But eating with parishioners and getting to know them is part of the job.

She's a year younger than him. Single. Works in a library. Not a cradle Anglican. Wandered into All Saints about fifteen years ago, in the wake of a divorce. He was at St. Tim's fifteen years ago. What if she had wandered into St. Tim's?

He never cheated on Ruth. Never seriously wanted to. Not even during those long stretches when she couldn't stand to be touched. He could have. There were always women who were attracted to the collar he wore and the rituals he enacted. He did sometimes get a certain look over the rim of a communion cup. And he would probably have been more pitied than blamed, by anyone who knew Ruth. Knew about Ruth.

He wasn't a saint or anything. He just could never stop hoping. Whenever she was coming down from a high or up from a low, he would see again that girl standing in the middle of the student centre, a rubble of dropped books and binders and papers at her feet. His first week of university, and here in front of him was this unbelievably beautiful blonde girl. And when he asked if he could give her a hand, she laughed and said, "I'll take two if you can spare them."

He needs to focus. "Especially ... "

The dark is starting to lift. He can see the holes in the top button of Kelly's sweater, and the criss-cross of thread.

Is he flirting with professional suicide? Is that what this is about? The church's policy is clear about clergy not entering into relationships with parishioners. He appals himself sometimes with the silly risks he takes. Walking into her library that Monday morning. Pretending he didn't know it was the branch where she worked. Suggesting oh-so-casually that they go for lunch. And then that Sunday afternoon when he phoned her about a change to the proofs of the October *Saints Alive*. He didn't need to consult her. He just wanted to hear her voice. They got going about movies and books and things, and he heard himself say, "I could talk to you all day." He tacked on an awkward, "But I'm afraid I have to go. Thanks so much for your time." When he hung up, his heart was banging like a boy's.

"I'm sorry," she said. "I crossed that question out, then put it back in, then crossed it out again. See?" She held up her notebook to show a page of scribbles, ending with the words *Do you believe in God?* "It's just, I've never asked one of you guys what you actually think about things. And sometimes I wonder. Because some Sunday mornings, I sit there in the pew and it all seems like a bunch of hooey. Sorry."

"No. Don't be sorry," he said automatically. The standard pastoral response when somebody blurts out an awkward truth, then apologizes for it. As if they think his collar is there to shield him from anything controversial. "It's an excellent question. The best possible question. And I'm very glad you asked it."

So how in hell was he going to answer it?

He hadn't prayed since Ruth's death. He had conducted services, had mouthed the words of rituals. But when he tried to open himself and wait in silence, now that he had the time, now that he had so much less to worry about—

He used to pray constantly. For Ruth. About Ruth. In spite of Ruth. When she was happy, she sucked up all the happy air in the room. When she was sad, she sucked up all the sad air. There were times when he could hardly breathe, when he would beg God to help him remember that it wasn't her fault. That he must not blame her for sitting in a chair day after day, staring at the floor. Or for going off on one of her mad quests, maxing out their credit card on junk from the hobby store because she was going to make some marvellous, magnificent *thing* that was going to be worth millions and make them both rich and famous and—

Help me to remember was his mantra. *Help me to understand.* That it was an illness. That she was not playing some fucking game. That he must not lose his temper and yell at her to stop. Just stop. Please. Just put a stop to it. The cycle. The never-ending up and down.

Ruth Ascended was a fearsome creature—eyes preternaturally bright, a crackle of energy around her like a halo. Ruth Ascended had no tolerance for ambiguity. Demanded to know what exactly he believed, and what exactly he expected her and everybody else to believe. Insisted on a clarity, an integrity, a sharpness of vision he could not give her. "You should have married a fundamentalist," he joked once, in the early days before he understood. Before he had any idea.

Ruth Descended was not capable of belief. In anything. He begged her once, when she was on her way down but still reachable, to tell him what she saw opening up beneath her. Share it with him, so that he could pray into the void. Fill it up with God. She couldn't. One thing the descent robbed her of was coherent speech. Her words would get fewer and shorter, the sounds moving further back in her throat, becoming guttural, almost inaudible. A linguistic devolution. This time, when he asked her to tell him what she was seeing, where she was going, she rolled lightless eyes to meet his and opened her mouth. No sound came. No words. Just those eyes, and that mouth hanging empty.

But then, in between the highs and lows were those precious, fleeting bits of time when she was Ruth. Dear, funny Ruth. Neither dead cold nor white hot. Ruth he could touch and hold. And he would convince himself all over again that he could hold her and he could keep her and she would stay.

Did he believe in God?

At first, he had thought he must just be angry. He had counselled enough bereaved people over the years to know that anger with God had to be indulged before anything could heal. So he had waited for the hardness inside—so much like an adolescent sulking behind a slammed door—to soften. But it had not softened. And as the weeks and months went by he had begun to wonder if a door had even been slammed. If there was a door to slam. A face in which to slam it.

Kelly was waiting, pen poised over page.

"I find that, as I get older..." he began. He would have to word this carefully. He was, in spite of everything, the new rector of All Saints. Whatever he said would serve to categorize him in the eyes of each member of his congregation. The one who took every word of the Bible literally and was anxious to know that he did too. The one who subscribed to a New Age Jesus that morphed conveniently into Buddha or Krishna or any other spiritual flavour of the month, and was anxious to know that he was just as laid back. And this one in front of him. An old hand who edits the newsletter. In the pew every Sunday. Yet possessed of enough negative capability to see it all sometimes as so much hooey.

" ... as I get older, I believe fewer things. But I believe them more deeply." He paused to let her write that down. When she was finished, she looked back up at him, waiting. Giving him that grave, silent gaze he had seen when he told her his wife was dead.

"And I'm starting to wonder if the word 'believe' shouldn't be retired in favour of the word 'belove.' I didn't make that up, by the way," he said, watching her scribble. "More than one theologian out there has written it far better than I can say it. But the idea of beloving, rather than believing. It gets you over that whole literalism hump which is so difficult for so many people, one way or another. And it captures the idea of relationship. Because it is an ongoing relationship. With its ups and downs, like any other. Its periods of anger and silence, followed by periods of intimacy and joy."

"Especially … turning off my cell phone."

He always comes round to that. The default detail. But better than nothing. How often has he said to a parishioner who was struggling with words, "Just tell me one thing. One small thing. Doesn't matter what it is. Just anything at all." He remembers a woman finally bursting out, "I forgot to feed the cat this morning!" And from there they worked it round to her husband's affair with his dental assistant.

Now, as always, he imagines Kelly nodding and saying, *Okay. You turned off your cell phone. Then what happened?*

"I took a nap." He always comes round to that, too.

"All Saints is my first incumbency, Kelly." *And it will be my last.*

He had watched her putting the pieces together. She had asked him about his previous churches, and he had listed them for her—curate at St. Philip's-On-the-Hill, then associate priest at St. Paul's, then associate at St. Tim's and lately associate at St. Mark's. She had scribbled it all down then flushed slightly, looking at her notes. Obviously wondering how to frame the next question. Or whether to ask it at all.

"Most first-time rectors are a lot younger than fifty-eight," he said, smiling as she visibly relaxed. "But I've no regrets.

My talents and inclinations were always more pastoral than administrative. And I've worked with some wonderful clergy around the city. But I guess if you hang in long enough, eventually you get kicked upstairs."

That was the official story. That, and his alleged lack of ambition. The truth of the matter, which everyone knew and no one spoke, was that if you were going to run a church, you'd better have the right kind of partner. A sturdy, reliable helpmeet. Who would neither chatter a mile a minute at parish events while people exchanged looks, nor slump in a chair, vacant-eyed and all but drooling, stoned on her latest medication.

The only one who ever wanted to talk about it, and once actually tried to talk about it, was Ruth. It was during one of her sweet, short respites from highs and lows. She sat him down. Calmly and gracefully, she started to apologize to him for wrecking his career. He cut her off. Would not hear what she was saying. Repeated the cant about his pastoral skills. His lack of ambition. Blamed himself for being timid. Lazy. Stupid. Lacking the balls for the job. After a while, she bent her head and stopped trying to protest. And she never brought the subject up again.

Turning off his cell phone. Lying down on the hotel bed for a quick nap before the evening reception. Not crimes. Not sins. But what he keeps coming back to. Probably because they are neither crimes nor sins.

"I left her alone?" he suggests to Kelly's sweater. "I cut myself off from her?" No. A step. Furthest he's gotten so far. But still not the essence. "I shouldn't have believed her? When she said she'd be all right? I should have insisted she come with me?"

The sweater still waits. He can see the pattern in the knitting round the collar now. And on the far wall, above the bookcase, the shape of Ruth's junk sculpture cross is dimly visible.

He went away for a weekend. One of those increasingly common—and increasingly desperate—"Whither the Church" conferences that are scheduled into the gap between Christmas and Lent. As a career associate, he was always the one who had to go to these things and take notes, sparing the rector to stay behind and do the real work. So, as he always did, he asked Ruth if she wanted to come. Preserving that courtesy between them—the illusion that her staying home alone was a real option.

For once, she said no. Stood her ground when he tried to argue with her. Insisted that he go without her. That she would be fine by herself for two nights and a day.

She was on new medication. It seemed to be working, but without the zombie side effects. She was as stable as she had been in years. Maybe because she was past the worst of menopause. They'd been told things might settle down once she was in her late forties, her early fifties. (They'd spent so much of their marriage sitting side by side on hard chairs in doctors' offices, being told what they could or could not expect, could or could not hope for.)

It was a long drive to the conference centre. The cold was so sharp he kept expecting the windshield to shatter with every gust of wind. In his room he unpacked and looked over the weekend agenda. A reception that night, followed by an open discussion about youth—"Cyberspace to Sunday School—Is There a Bridge?" He almost wept. He couldn't face it, after that drive. Not right away. So he turned off his cell phone. Just for a little while. Ruth would be fine. She had said she would be fine. Then he lay down on the bed for a nap. Just half an hour or so. That was all he needed.

A crescent of light is edging round the top button of Kelly's sweater. "It's not about leaving her alone," Simon tells it. "Or the cell phone. Or the nap. Is it?"

No, the sweater seems to agree. *It isn't.*

They are all red herrings. They do not constitute his original sin.

"So what are your plans, as rector of All Saints?"

Do my time and get out.

31

The facts, as he had explained them in his mind to his dead wife while he was packing, were these. Yes, he was moving up from associate to rector. Finally. But it was only happening because yet another priest had burned out, leaving an opening that had to be filled quickly. Yes, he would have his own parish. Finally. But it would be creaky old All Saints which was tiny and getting tinier by the Sunday. He doubted the bishop actually thought he was going to revive the place with his innovative ideas and commanding presence. More likely, it was a relatively painless way of getting rid of them both. Five or so years of ministering to a dwindling congregation would serve to end his career. And his retirement would make it easy for the diocese to turn a cool eye on All Saints, with its empty pews and emptier collection plates.

But that wasn't the right answer for the newsletter.

"My plans, Kelly, are first to touch base with each of the Sunday morning regulars. Ask them why they come, what they want and need from All Saints, how much of it they're actually getting, and how we can work together to build on that."

Not exactly inspiring, he thought, watching her write. *But doable.* The touching base business wouldn't take long. According to the records, Sunday numbers had rarely topped one hundred in the last five years and tended more often to hover around seventy-five.

There were no children at All Saints, and only a handful of teenagers. The biggest group were the old guard, the ones who had been baptised in the font some eighty years ago, confirmed on the chancel steps, married at the altar, then had followed their spouses' coffins out through the nave. They showed up every Sunday without fail to complain if the candles weren't lit or if the word *people* was substituted in the liturgy for the word *men*. Little changes terrified them. They were so close to the big one.

The only incoming were the so-called seekers. Late thirties and up. Just as terrified as the old guard, but for different reasons. They had stepped through the door of a church, some of them for the first time in their lives, because something had happened—a death, a divorce, a diagnosis, a downsizing. All of a sudden they were on their own, with no context, no frame of reference, no way to make it all mean something. Most of them disappeared after a few Sundays, as mysteriously as they had come. A few stayed on. The way Kelly had.

"I lied to her," he says to the sweater. "That's it, isn't it? I should have told her the truth when I had the chance. But I didn't."

You can tell her the truth now. It's still dark. There's still time.

He woke up to the sound of someone knocking on the hotel-room door. He was still fully clothed, lying on top of the spread. He got up, confused by the light coming through the window. Stumbled to the door and opened it. It was the maid. Wondering if he was going to go down to breakfast, if she could come in and do up his room.

He grabbed his cell phone and turned it on. Ruth had called at six the evening before. Called and left no message. Six. Just when it would have been starting to get dark.

He gets up from his desk. Walks past the chair with the sweater on it. Goes to the bookcase. In the dim light the junk sculpture cross looks like a black and white photograph of itself. He puts his palms on the wall to either side of it and braces himself, leaning forward and hanging his head.

"Ruth," he begins, "that time, when you tried to tell me you were sorry for screwing up my career, I should have let you talk. I should have heard you out and accepted your apology. And then I should have said, You're right, Ruth. You did screw up my career. You screwed it up good. Best thing you ever did, matter of fact. But you know something? It's okay. Because if it was between the church and you, there was no contest. Even with all the ups and downs and the craziness and the shit and the maxed-out credit cards, the church never stood a chance. I chose you, Ruth. And I'm glad. There. That's what my so-called career was about. And that's what I should have said to you. And I'm sorry I didn't. I'm sorry, Ruth. I'm sorry."

He stays leaning against the wall, head down. Breathing through his mouth. Feeling the tears well and drop. Forcing himself to see her. To ask himself the questions.

Would she have heard the phone, if he had called back in time? Was she already out on the porch in that bitter cold, shivering under the quilt she had allowed herself, washing her pills down with the bottle of cabernet she had selected from their wine rack? And even if he had called and she had heard, would she have been capable of getting back inside the house?

Or did she sit and wait on the couch? The quilt folded beside her, the bottle and pills resting on it? Feeling, as the darkness deepened and the stars got sharp in the sky, his tacit permission sinking into her bones?

What was it about this woman? He had to take charge here. He was starting to feel ridiculously close to tears again.

"How about I start by touching base with you, Kelly? What brings you through the door of this place every Sunday?"

She had every right to remind him that she wasn't the one being interviewed. But she stopped writing and sat very still, her eyes on his desk blotter.

"It keeps me real."

He wanted to prompt her—*real in what way*—but sensed that the answer was coming.

"I mean, I work with a lot of people who are a lot younger than me, okay? And they've all got their gadgets—their cell phones and their iPads and whatever everybody's just got to have this week. And that's what they talk about. Gadgets and clothes and TV. Even when I'm on the bus, I hear all the phones going off, and all the people flipping them open and saying, *Hi. I'm on the bus.* And I just get scared. And I'm not even sure what I'm scared of."

She was silent. He waited, watching her mouth.

"It's just so easy to—I mean, I worshipped my ex. I did. He was everything. And then he left me for somebody else. And I felt like Alice for a while—you know? Falling and falling and never touching bottom? And you want to touch bottom. But at the same time you're scared of what bottom might be?"

Simon nodded. "Getting back to your word, real," he said. "Are you saying that coming here saves you from worshipping false gods? I'm sorry. I shouldn't be putting words in—"

But she was nodding. "No, you've got it. I mean, I don't know if All Saints is the be-all and the end-all. But it's about something. And whatever that is, it's not going to be obsolete next week. And it's never going to dump me."

Simon is back at his desk. The window behind him is turning pale. He sits and faces the sweater. Searches his memory for the end of the penitential rite.

"Blessed are they whose transgressions are forgiven;"

"And whose sin is put away."

"The Lord has put away all your sins."

He hesitates, then says, "Thanks be to God."

"Go in peace, and pray for me a sinner."

He smiles, imagining Kelly's embarrassment, the way she would wrinkle her nose over having to say that final line.

Kelly.

He gets up, goes around to the front of his desk and lifts the sweater off the back of the chair. Shakes it gently and folds it. Stands looking down at it in the growing light. It's as soft as ever in his hands. He raises it to his face. And still that hint of Ivory soap.

What They Have

THEY HAVE TWO FORKS, TWO KNIVES, two spoons. She sneaked each utensil out of the residence cafeteria last term. "You're not stealing, Babe," he told her. "You're taking back."

It felt like stealing to her. She would sit alone, pretending to read. She would finish her soup, put her spoon down, then quickly drag it off the edge of the table and into her pocket. The next day, she would have a salad and do the same thing with the fork. Keeping her head down, letting her hair hide her face. Secretly proud of her new skill.

They have no plates or mugs or glasses yet. They've just been using whatever they find in communal kitchens. But now, she's thinking as she follows him to their latest address, they should get some of their own things. Mugs and plates, at least. Maybe a pot or two. A set of bowls.

They have her student loan. His part-time job at the music store. They'll manage.

They have a mattress, almost new, which a friend with a car has already delivered to the house. Both their pillows are his, from a former relationship. The first time she saw them, she thought of pillows in cartoons—grey-and-black striped, with bits of feather sticking out. She quickly covered them with the white-on-white embroidered pillowslips she had brought from home.

"There'll be sheets in the residence," she had said when her mother showed her the set.

"They'll be like burlap. Here. Take these. Percale. Feel."

They have his Hudson's Bay blanket, half an inch thick, with the trademark stripes. "All we'll need, Mama," he'd told her, winking. He was right. She was used to Ontario winters. Here in Vancouver she hardly needs her coat.

They have their books, mostly hers, and their records, mostly his. Her unfinished poems and stories in a three-ring-binder. His harmonica, which he calls a harp. He plays it alongside his favourite blues albums, jerking his mouth back and forth, making a sound that reminds her of train whistles far off in the night.

He is seven years older than she is—old enough to have been a hippie, one of the originals living on Fourth Avenue. She saw hippies once, the summer she was fifteen, in Yorkville. Her mother insisted on keeping the car windows rolled up as they drove through on their way back to Willowdale because of the threat of hepatitis. A young man who looked like Jesus tucked a flower under their windshield wiper. A young girl in a long dress smiled at them and made the peace sign. Emily looked down into her lap, aware of her mother's eyes on her in the rearview. Her hand was making the peace sign back.

Now in bed she sometimes fingers the scar on his temple that he tells her he got from a police baton. His knuckles are scarred, too, from old fights. He still carries a knife. His features are sharp and fox-like, his voice light but flinty. The look in his eyes, except when they're resting on hers, is furtive.

Whenever she asks about his family, he says, "Babe, we gave up on each other years ago." But he likes to hear about hers. The smallest detail tickles him. The Christmas hand towels her mother puts in the bathroom every December, red with white satin poinsettias edged in gold thread. They hang there for a month, never absorbing a single drop of water, then get put away dry until next year. Nothing is ever said, but everybody understands that you do not touch the Christmas hand towels.

"I'd touch 'em, Babe." Pretending to dry his armpits and groin.

When she asks him, he tells her about being on the street, collecting pop bottles and turning them in for money for food. Posing for art students. Doing a little dealing. Anything to survive. "End of nineteen sixty-eight, I weighed a hundred and twenty pounds." That was just five years ago, but it gives him the air of a different generation, like someone who fought in a war she has only read about in textbooks.

Three times since they've been living together, she has wakened in the early morning while he was still asleep, has placed her hands on his shoulders and has thought, *Come here.* Three times—she has counted them—he has come to her in his sleep and has curled up small in her embrace, his beard pricking her breasts. Each time, the weight in her arms, the warmth of his head under her chin, has made a space hollow out under her breastbone. She has rocked him, yearning after his hungry younger self, wanting to feed him, willing him to sleep on and on, willing the morning to take its time.

This will be the third house they've lived in so far. Also the cheapest. As soon as they turn onto the street in East Van, Emily knows which one it is. She keeps hoping, as they walk up the dirt path through the weeds, that she's wrong, that Dave will stop, consult the piece of paper he scribbled the address on and shake his head. But she's right. This is the house. With the room in it that they're going to rent for twenty-five dollars a month. Which is half what they were paying in the last place. They're going through her student loan faster than she thought they would.

Stub. That's the first word that comes into her mind. It's half the size of the surrounding houses and set far back from the sidewalk, as if withdrawing from the street. *Stump.* It isn't just small. It's chopped-off, mean-looking. Grey stucco that might have once been white. No shutters. No awnings. Porch steps made of cinder blocks that rock. "Careful, Mama," Dave says, holding a hand out to her. There's no railing. *Runt.* Yes. That's the word for it, the one that sticks in her mind. The one she will write down in her three-ring binder. *The runt house.*

For the rest of her life, she will have a recurring dream about the runt house. She will dream that she and Dave are back together, or maybe never apart in the first place. They're broke again, with no place to go. They find their way back to the runt house, but Rick is still there and won't let them in. So they wait till dark, then break in and creep down the basement steps to their old room. The basement is flooded again. This time, the water is up to their waists.

The dream will always leave her with an emotional hangover—a mix of relief and regret. *It's in the past,* she will remind herself. *You were only there for two months, for God's sake. Two months.*

"This is Em," Dave says to Rick once they're inside. Em is what he calls her when he isn't calling her Mama or Babe. She's not used to it yet. She's always been Emily. She likes the sound of *David and Emily,* but he insists on Dave. Dave and Em, then. Em sounds older and tougher than Emily. Em would have laughed when she first saw this house. Or shrugged.

Rick smiles down at her, takes her offered hand, then looks back at Dave and repeats, "Em," as if fixing the name in his memory. Twice in the first week, he will call her Liz by mistake. The name of the former relationship. The one the pillows came from.

"And I'm Cass," says a woman who has just come out of the kitchen. Rick's old lady, as Dave described her when he was telling Emily about their new living arrangements. "I'll be down in a minute to help you move in." She jerks her head at the men. "Let these two get caught up." Cass wears big swaying hoop earrings and glass bangles that clack up and down her forearms and a pendant in the shape of a cowbell that dings. Emily feels quiet and plain beside her, like a Quaker. When she extends her hand, Cass giggles, takes it and pulls her into an awkward hug. Her hair and clothes give off a sharp, sweet scent. Patchouli oil, Dave will explain later when they're alone.

"How old are your friends?" Emily will ask carefully.

"Same age as me. Give or take. Why?"

Twenty-seven just got closer to thirty. Rick has a bit of a paunch, and his hairline is receding. The hair he does have is shoulder-length like Dave's, but he's clean-shaven. Not even long sideburns. She always thinks that makes a man look odd. Almost womanish. And Cass has one of those prematurely old faces—hook-nosed and small-eyed. Her hair is dyed a bright red, with grey roots. It looks like it might take off from her head without the green paisley bandana tying it down.

She's being judgemental again. Getting hung up on the age difference between her and Dave. It shouldn't matter. Her father's five years older than her mother. And her mother was nineteen—a whole year younger than she is now—when she got engaged to him. Not that she and Dave are engaged, or anything like that.

"Whatever you do, don't fall in love with him." Cass says this out of the side of her mouth, with one eyebrow cocked. Emily suspects it's how she says most things. "I mean, Dave's a hell of a lot of fun. So yeah, have a good time. But don't even think about a cottage small by a waterfall, or anything like that."

Emily makes herself smile. Goes on folding socks and underwear and putting them in the top drawer of the dresser. *I don't remember asking for your advice.* That's one thing she could say. Another is, *Don't believe everything Rick tells you about him and Dave in the old hippie days.* But she says nothing.

Cass is helping her get settled in the basement room while Rick and Dave have a beer together in the kitchen. Every now and then there's a burst of hard laughter from above. She's never heard Dave laugh quite that way before.

She has just gotten off the phone with her mother. She wanted to call from the house, but Rick said no. No long-distance calls. Suppose the bill comes weeks later, he said, and whoever made the call has moved out or gone broke? Who's going to pay for it? She turned to Dave, who shrugged. Rick was their landlord. Sort of. So she lugged a fistful of coins to a payphone down the street.

"Don't call," was all her mother said, once she had heard about the house and about Dave. "Just don't call again. Not while you're—living the way you are."

Cass is jangling coat hangers in the closet at the end of the room. "Tell you what," she says, fingering the sleeve of one of Emily's nylon blouses. "I'm really into fabrics. I can show you where you can get stuff that's a little more—you know—funky?" Crinkling her nose over the word and grinning.

Emily takes a deep breath. *Careful. Don't burn your bridges.* She closes the top drawer of the dresser and opens the next one down. No mouse droppings in here either. Well. That's something. There were baited mousetraps in the hall upstairs. *Beggars can't be choosers.* She makes herself smile again. Says, "Let's go shopping some time."

When Cass is finally gone, she spreads the Hudson's Bay blanket out on the mattress and plumps both of Liz's pillows inside the percale pillowslips that her mother gave her. Then she sits down on the bed, draws her knees up and buries her face in her arms. Upstairs, she hears the two men laughing again.

She could have said no when Dave came up to her at the end of that Survey of World Literature 110 class and asked if she wanted to go someplace for a coffee. And before that, she could have given in to her mother's wails—*There are schools that aren't thousands of miles away, you know!* Stayed home and gone to U of T. Ridden the bus back and forth every day. Eaten supper every night at her old place at the table between her parents. Gone on sleeping in her childhood bed.

But she didn't. And this is her bed now. *The bed you've made for yourself,* as her mother would say. All her mother's favourite sayings have been going round and round in her head since the phone call.

The thing to do, the thing *Em* would do, is treat this as an adventure. Something to write about. Something to laugh about one day with Dave—*Remember the runt house?*

The room Dave and Em are renting is built on top of a wooden platform. This puzzles Em until the basement floods for the first time. It floods three times in the two months they live there. Each time, they have to stop near the bottom of the basement stairs, take off their shoes and socks and wade through instep-deep water to their room. Em hangs one of their towels on a nail just inside the door so they can dry their feet.

The walls of their room are painted green. Em supposes that if the lighting was better, she might be able to name the shade of green. But the first time she pulls the string that's knotted to the chain that jerks on the bare forty-watt bulb in the ceiling, she just stands there staring. It's sort of a military green, she tells herself finally. Whether it's closer to the green of camouflage or of heavy artillery, she can never decide.

Their room is tiny, with no window. They have the choice of crawling across their mattress or inching sideways around the edges of it to get to the closet at one end and the dresser at the other. The closet door is constructed of open slats, like a fence, and is held shut with a hooked latch. They bunch their clothes together in the middle to keep them from touching the walls, which are always damp. During floods, the dresser drawers swell up and screech whenever they're opened or shut.

Rick and Cass's bedroom is on the main floor. The kitchen, bathroom and living room are theoretically communal. But because Rick has arranged this fantastic deal for them and rooms are scarce and he could be charging them a lot more than he is, the shared spaces are, by unspoken agreement, just a little bit more his and Cass's. Which is why he and Cass can hang their towels in the bathroom, but Em and Dave have to carry theirs back and forth from the basement. And why Rick and Cass can jam-pack the freezer and take up most of the fridge with their food. And why they can leave dirty dishes in the sink, but if Em and Dave do the same thing, they hear, "Hey. Guys? Like, I don't want to come on heavy, but … "

Rick and Cass's bedroom is right off the living room. When Em and Dave are watching the late show on TV they hear Cass sucking in rhythmic gulps of air—*ah ah ah AH!* Usually about twelve. Their own room is right underneath Rick and Cass's. Em is secretly pleased that she can go on longer and louder than Cass.

There is one last room in the runt house that Em only sees twice. It's at the end of a little hall off the kitchen. From the outside, the house doesn't look big enough to contain the rooms they all use, let alone this extra one whose door is kept shut.

The first time Em sees into it is the day they move in and Rick gives them the tour. He opens the door for just a moment, telling them that this is the old guy's room. The old guy who was buddies with his father in the war and who owns the house and who's paying Rick to look after it while he's in the hospital. And even though he's probably never going to come home again, his room's still off limits.

The name Rick gives to the old guy sounds like Marbles. A few days later, Em is sorting through the mail, bracing herself for yet another Priority Post from her mother begging her to come home and be decent and normal again. Most of the envelopes are addressed to a Mr. Marples. Mr. Garth Marples.

In the instant that Garth Marples' bedroom door is held open, she catches a whiff of old man—a mix of cigarettes and unwashed clothes and neglected flesh. She sees dingy floral wallpaper, a high narrow bed with a white-painted metal frame and a night stand with a drinking glass and a photograph on it. The photograph is turned to face the bed.

What They Have

The second and last time Em sees inside that room is just before she and Dave move out. On that day, she opens the door, locks it behind her, climbs onto the bed, pulls her coat up over her head, and stays that way, ignoring the knocking and the calling of her name.

But until she opens it herself, the closed door of the off-limits room keeps catching her eye. Who is in that photograph on the night stand, she wonders. Who ever slept in that narrow bed with Garth Marples? Did Garth Marples build the sad little windowless room on its platform in the basement? Did he put the screeching chest of drawers down there and hang the slatted closet door and then paint it all that hideous green?

Why? Who for?

Em never does go shopping with Cass for funky clothes. She never goes to the laundromat around the corner with Cass either, or helps her prepare a communal meal. Cass works evenings in a fabric and sewing supplies outlet and Em attends classes by day, so they hardly see each other. When they do, they keep things light. Small talk. They happen to be living together because they happen to be sleeping with two guys who happen to be old buddies.

Em is learning what *old buddies* means. It has a subtle, layered meaning, kind of like *married couple.* "Still going to do something with your music someday?" Rick will say loudly if Dave's harp playing has gone on too long. Dave once started a degree in music, but only went to half the classes, then dropped out completely because they couldn't teach him anything. "Get thrown out of any city council meetings lately?" Dave will shoot back at Rick just before putting his harp away. Rick did two years of a political science degree because he planned to change the system from within. Then he got himself banned from City Hall by crashing meetings stoned and yelling about power to the people.

"Rick, you are such a pig," Dave will state rhetorically when he finds a knife glued to the kitchen counter with marmalade in which a fly is drowning. "You wanna light a match in there next time?" Rick will bark after Dave as he's leaving the bathroom.

"You guys don't seem to like each other very much," Em ventures to say one time when each is accusing the other of having thrown out the TV Guide. As one, they stop and look at her. Look back at each other. Grin. "Whaddya mean?" Rick says. "Yeah, what're you talking about?" says Dave. "We're old buddies." Then, as if to prove it, they start swapping stories about the communal house on Cambie Street where they met. The toilet that leaked into the pantry. The pothead who masturbated into the peanut butter.

There are other old buddy stories that Dave will only tell Em when they're alone together in bed. About him and Rick spending an afternoon going down on a pair of chicks, trading them back and forth. Being late on their way to meet up with two other chicks, because they were driving around looking for a gas station where they could go into the men's and wash their faces.

"You were *horrible!*" Em whisper-shrieks after one of these stories, punching him on the chest and trying not to laugh.

"I still am, Mama," he says, catching her fist and sliding his other hand up under her nightie.

Emily will always keep track of Dave, one way or another. Over dinner with a mutual friend, she will say with studied casualness, "So how is my erstwhile ex?" Through the years she will learn that he has divorced again, married again, is buying a house, is thinking about retiring.

Every couple of years or so they will encounter each other. Once he tries to sit down beside her on the subway, so she gets up and moves away, her face hard, her skin feeling as if it is lifting up off her flesh. Then there is the time on the street corner when she is waiting for the light to change and hears him whistling behind her. That cool shaft of sound she will recognize forever, coming through lips she can still taste. She forces herself not to turn around, feeling him watching her all the way across the street. And, once, she catches sight of him and what must be his latest wife on the fourth floor of the Bay. Housewares and Appliances. She is shopping for a new coffee maker, and they are looking at an ironing board together. She hides behind a pillar of boxed food processors and watches them. An ironing board? Why would you ever need a new ironing board? She still has the one she and Dave packed and brought with them from Vancouver thirty years ago.

When she gets home she does an inventory of the things she still has from her time with Dave. There isn't much besides the ironing board. A couple of prints. An old breadboard. That piece of driftwood from Spanish Banks. Amazing, considering all the stuff they acquired and used up and discarded together.

She begins to picture the trail of cast-off possessions she and Dave left behind them as they moved from one place to another. Each place bigger and more expensive than the last. Each place one they simply had to have, once they had seen it. Once they knew it was there.

They always shed some of their old things—threw them away or gave them away to the Sally Ann—in anticipation of the better and more expensive things they were going to get to fill their new place. Those old pillows Dave took from Liz. They would have been one of the first things to go when they left the runt house. What would they consist of now? Shreds of rotting cloth under tons of landfill? Fragments of feather?

The first place they moved to was on Alma Street in Kitsilano. A two-room suite in a converted old house that had a shared bathroom on each floor. They still had to carry their towels back and forth, but at least they had their own kitchen, where they ate off a card table they found at a garage sale.

Dave took Emily shopping on Fourth Avenue, where India print bedspreads were cheap. She put one on the bed and split another in half for curtains. He took her downtown to the Army and Navy store, where she picked out a square wooden breadboard and thick white china plates and stainless steel pots and cutlery.

Their bed, which now doubled as a couch, took up most of the adjoining bed-sitting room. But there was space enough left over for the perfectly good armchair they found on the street and carried home one garbage day, and a corner for the tiny tree they decorated at Christmas.

Dave got taken on full-time at the music store while they were living on Alma Street. Emily finished her second year at university, started her third and began thinking about maybe grad school. Or maybe not. Sometimes in the middle of a class she would picture their two little rooms in her mind and have to stop herself from gathering up her books and leaving and going home to them.

She liked to imagine showing her mother around the place. The two of them were talking on the phone again, but if Dave took the call all he would hear was, "May I please speak to my daughter?" Emily was sure that if she could show her mother their kitchen, her face would soften at the sight and she would start telling stories about the things she had managed to make do with when she and Emily's father were just starting out.

The brightness of that first small kitchen, its fresh yellow paint and dark red floor tiles, stirred something in Emily every time she turned the key and opened the door. She cleaned it and cleaned it like a cat, never allowing a drop of coffee to dry on the counter or a cup to sit unwashed in the sink.

Their rent is due. Their rent is overdue. Twenty-five dollars. Twenty-five dollars they don't have. Her student loan is all used up and she won't get the grant portion till next term and it's four days till Dave gets paid. He's had to go to Rick and ask him to let them off for this month. And maybe next month too. They have just enough food to last till payday. If they run out of milk or bread, Em will have to go to Cass and ask if they can share.

"Something'll turn up, Babe," Dave says. "Just stop worrying and try to relax."

She can't stop worrying. She can't relax. And she can't understand how he can. How he can go on playing his harp and bickering with Rick and whistling while he's tying shoe-laces that have broken and been knotted and then broken again.

Her worries follow her. Surround her. Fill her up. She's late for class because she has to hitchhike up to the campus because the bus is twenty-five cents. She worries all through the lecture, her pen stalled at the top of a blank page. She can barely smile when Dave clowns for her, trying to make her laugh. In bed she lies under him unmoving and unmoved, mentally adding up dollars that are forever short of what they need.

Over the Christmas holidays, when Rick and Cass both leave to visit their families, Em and Dave get into the habit of staying up half the night watching TV, then sleeping in the next day till one or two in the afternoon. They wake to a grey day that fades to a deeper dusk then blackens into night. For hours until they go to bed, the TV screen is their only light. They watch old movies together, imagining themselves as Fred Astaire and Ginger Rogers, or Nick and Nora Charles. Inexplicably rich. Ridiculously carefree.

On Christmas Day, Em takes the coins she has saved up one by one and plinks them one by one into the slot of a pay-phone. She listens just long enough to hear her mother say, "Hello? Hello? *Hello!*" before hanging up. That night in front of the TV she falls asleep beside Dave on the couch in the middle of the movie. She wakes to find herself being walked tenderly down the basement stairs to their room. Dave murmuring in her ear about how he'll take off her clothes and put her to bed and cover her warm.

"I want a bedroom I don't have to entertain my guests in. I want a dining room. With a real dining-room table in it. And I want to take a crap in my own bathroom without my neighbours banging on the door."

Dave had been talking this way for months, slapping his palm down on the card table in the kitchen. Emily loved his mock outrage, his easy rhetoric. Loved being able to afford it.

She couldn't get used to having enough money. A little more than enough.

She and Dave were going for long walks together on the weekends, exploring neighbourhoods, taking down phone numbers from FOR RENT signs. Stopping somewhere in the middle of the afternoon to compare notes over coffee and a croissant. Emily always lingered over hers, moistening a finger and picking up crumbs from her plate. Looking forward to the sight of Dave casually flipping open his wallet to settle the bill and leave a tip.

"We're not students any more. So why are we living like students? Look at us. We don't even look like students."

Emily's hair was newly cut in a 1920s bob. She had started painting her fingernails a dark red and wearing eye shadow and foundation and blush. She had finished her degree, decided against grad school and taken a part-time job in a library that left her mornings free for writing. She had completed four poems and two short stories, and had started sending them out to magazines.

Dave had shortened his own hair to jaw length and trimmed his beard into a neat goatee. His sales had gone up. He was becoming known to their friends as a sound-system expert, advising them about upgrades and inviting them to come down to the store so he could cut them a deal.

One Friday afternoon, he phoned Emily at the library to tell her he had been promoted to assistant manager. That weekend while they were out walking, they found a real apartment in a real apartment building on a tree-lined avenue off Granville.

If there was ever a Golden Age of Emily and Dave, Emily will decide, it would have to be when they were living in that place off Granville. Bluebirds used to nest in the trees outside their bedroom window, for God's sake. And remember the way the venetian blinds sliced the afternoon sun into bright stripes along the living-room floor? And the way the handles of their two umbrellas, in that white ceramic stand by the door, used to lean away from each other to form a heart?

They started subscribing to *The New Yorker* while they were there, trading the latest issue back and forth and posting their favourite cartoons on the refrigerator door. They developed a taste for Art Deco and did the whole place over in black and white—a black and white striped couch, a white dining-room table, black chairs, black frames for the old movie posters on the white walls. They taught each other about gourmet foods and fancy drinks. Together, they cooked expensive, complicated meals full of ingredients their mothers had never heard of and served them to their friends.

Friends. They discovered they had a talent for friendship. They made friends with everybody. Their workmates. Their neighbours. People who waited on them in stores. "I met somebody today I think you'll like..." became a dinnertime mantra.

Whenever they were giving a dinner party, there would come a moment after everybody was sitting down and eating and the clatter of cutlery and the clamor of talk was starting to rise. Emily would catch Dave's eye, or he would catch hers, and they would silently toast each other. *Look at us. All grown up.*

Rick has started going out while Cass is at work, then arriving back at the runt house minutes before she's due to walk through the door. Not looking at Em, he tells Dave about this chick he's just been with—this absolutely gorgeous, fantastic chick. Then, winking, he says, "Hey. Not a word about this to Cass, right?"

Later that night, they hear Cass taking in her twelve orgasmic gulps of air. "Don't worry about it, Babe," Dave says, seeing the look on Em's face. "Rick's always been an asshole when it comes to women."

Then how can you be his friend? Em wants to say, but doesn't. She should be asking Cass that question, except it's none of her business.

Don't fall in love. Does Cass take her own advice? Does she just get whatever she can get out of Rick—a good time with no strings attached? But how do you do that? How do you open yourself to a man night after night, take him inside, feel your skin dissolving into his, wake up every morning smelling of him, and still stay cool and apart and able to walk away any time?

Sometimes at night Em hears Rick and Cass laughing together behind their closed bedroom door. She wonders if Rick is telling Cass the same old stories that she hears from Dave. She wonders if Cass does the same thing she does with them afterwards. First forgive them, then file them in a place called *Then*. A place that has nothing to do with *Now*.

What is it about Thursday? Emily was working fast, flashing her automatic smile at each borrower. *The whole world decides it just has to come to the library on Thursday.* She was sliding the next stack of books toward the humming checkout machine when she noticed they were all about clothing design and fabric painting and decorative bead work. *Don't glance up*, she warned herself, just before glancing up.

"Hi." Cass looked nervous. "I didn't know you worked here. And then when I saw it was you, I wasn't sure if I should—"

"It's okay," Emily said evenly. And it was. Well, it should be. It had been almost three years. She had wondered what it would be like to run into Rick or Cass. If she had seen Rick, she would have ducked behind something. But she had never had anything against Cass. Not really.

"I'm off in half an hour," she said, checking out Cass's books. "We could go for tea, if you like."

Over tea, Cass told her that she had quit the fabric outlet ages ago. Now she was teamed up with two other women, and they were starting a business together. They were going to make and sell one-of-a-kind outfits geared to women just like them—under forty, fashion-savvy, feminist. They were looking at a property in Gastown. Sure, the rent was steep, but that was where their target clientele went to shop.

Emily assumed that what Cass was wearing was the kind of thing she would sell. Flared jeans, a Laura Ashley print smock and a denim vest decked with sequins and feathers and swatches of velvet and brocade. The bangles were gone from her wrists, but the big hoops still swayed from her ears. She had let her hair go grey, and had that frizzy fin-de-siècle perm that everybody was getting. Everybody except Emily, who kept the 20s bob because it was easy and it suited her. She had on her pink-striped cotton blouse that day, and her navy skirt. The library insisted on skirts and dresses for its female staff. But at least her blouse wasn't nylon. None of her blouses were. Not any more. She considered telling Cass this, then almost blushed at the thought of how feeble it would sound.

"So," Cass said carefully, shaking her spoon over her cup and putting it into the saucer. "You and Dave are—"

"Still together. Getting married, as a matter of fact."

"You're kidding! When?"

"We haven't set a date. It'll be after we move east. There's a new store going up in Toronto. They want him to manage it. And maybe a couple of others too. In time."

Cass was shaking her head and grinning. "Wow. You guys. I used to give you six weeks, max. What with Dave's track record. Oh. Sorry. That was a bit—"

"It's all right," Emily said, then made herself smile. Same old Cass.

So were they going to buy a house? Have kids? Cass asked all the right questions, but Emily could tell it was a polite act. She knew her plans were as unfashionable as her clothes. The papers and magazines were full of angry articles by angry women referring to marriage as prostitution and women like herself as Uncle Toms.

"I'm really glad to hear you guys are okay," Cass was saying. "Especially after—" She looked at Emily. "I was worried about you."

"We're fine now," Emily said quickly, looking away.

And they were. And she was proud of Dave, damn it. Proud of how far he had come. How great he looked setting off for work each day in his designer jeans and Oxford-cloth shirt and tie. ("Gotta be able to sell to either generation, Mama. Oops. Emily.") She loved lying in bed in the mornings half-awake, sleepily aware of him standing and looking down at her, doing up his cuffs. He was collecting vintage cuff links that he found in antique stores. She was always at her desk by the time he was ready to leave. He pointed at her, raised an eyebrow and said, "Write me a Pulitzer."

"But I'm still glad we ran into each other," Cass was going on. "Because you just kind of disappeared. And I always wanted to talk to you. Tell you how sorry I was. About—That I didn't do anything for you, I mean. That day."

"There's nothing you could have done." Emily did not want to discuss this. Anybody else would have picked up on that. But not Cass.

"It was just so weird. Like, I thought I knew Liz. I never thought she'd—And I never knew Dave was—If I had, I'd have told you. Promise. But all of a sudden Liz just barges in the door and pushes past me and goes charging down the basement stairs and then I hear yelling and what sounds like a fight and I just stand there thinking, What do I do? Do I go down there and try to break it up? Rick had just stepped out, or else he could have—"

"How is Rick?" Emily couldn't believe she was asking. But she had to change the subject.

"Rick?" Cass blew through her lips. "I don't even know where Rick is, and I don't care. You know what happened? A week after you two left? Marples came back from the dead."

"Marples? Garth Marples?" The man Emily had never seen, but whose smell she could conjure up in an instant, having spent an hour with her face buried in his pillow.

"The one and only. Fresh from the morgue. With his hospital bracelet still on his wrist. Hollering at us, calling us Goddamned hippies and giving us half an hour to get out of his house before he called the cops. First thing in the morning. I'm in my nightie. And in thirty minutes I'm going to be out on the street with no place to go. Hell of a way to start the day."

"But Rick said—"

"Rick was full of shit. As usual. This was another one of his dumb-assed schemes. He wasn't supposed to live in that house. And he sure as hell wasn't supposed to let his friends move in. All he was supposed to do was keep an eye on the place and cut the grass. And he couldn't even do that."

Emily nodded, remembering the field of weeds in front of the runt house. "So what happened?"

"What happened to me was, I got taken in by the two friends I'm starting the business with. And I have to tell you. Getting thrown out of that house was my click. You know about click, don't you? When you're picking up some guy's dirty socks and something goes click in your brain and you think, Hey. I'm just as smart as he is. And I work just as hard as he does. So how come I'm picking up his dirty socks? Well, that's what happened to me when Marples came back and threw us out and it turned out that Rick had been lying to me. Again."

"So you just walked away from Rick?"

It was so strange to be saying that name. Asking about him. Rick was a taboo subject between her and Dave. She herself had declared it taboo, that day in the runt house when she listed her conditions. Some of them were easy, like him calling her Emily instead of Em or Mama or Babe. Others were harder, like him having nothing to do with Rick, ever again.

All this time, whenever she had allowed herself to think about Rick, she had pictured him still living in the runt house with Cass. Which would have made Garth Marples either dead or in the hospital, dying. Now that picture had just been ripped into a million tiny pieces. Like the photograph the old soldier rips up. In those fragments of—what? A poem? A play? Fragments she wrote down just after she and Dave moved out of the runt house. They never grew into anything, those strange scribbled bits. But she kept them.

"No," Cass was saying. "I didn't just walk away from Rick." She looked down at her tea. "He walked away from me." She looked back up at Emily. "We'd been making love, right? That morning. That's what Marples walked in on. So I'm still wet from Rick when we're standing out on the sidewalk with our stuff in garbage bags. And I'm crying and asking him what we're going to do now. Well Cass, he says. We both knew it wasn't going to last, didn't we? And I don't get it. I'm going, What? That what wasn't going to last? Living here, you mean? So that's when he tells me. There's somebody else. There's been somebody else for weeks. Some chick he's been balling the whole time. Right under my nose. While we were all in that house together. And now he's going to go stay with her. So I'm on my own. And then he picks up the bags that have his stuff in them and he walks away from me. And I just stand there on the sidewalk. Watching him—Shit. Oh, shit."

Emily searched her purse for a Kleenex. Cass's tears shocked her. But so did the way they made her feel oddly vindicated.

"Sorry," Cass said, wiping her eyes. "That fucker doesn't deserve this."

Emily arranged her face into a mask of concern. Hoped what she was really thinking didn't show. *Score one for Uncle Tom. And so much for click.*

"I just want to know one thing." Cass's nose is red, her face splotchy and old. *Won't be able to sell to the under-forties for long*, Emily could imagine Dave saying. "What I want to know is, did you and Dave know? About Rick cheating on me, I mean. When we all lived together. Did you know? You can tell me. I won't be mad. Just tell me."

Emily hesitated. What good would it do to tell Cass the truth now, after all this time? Besides. Garth Marples was alive. And so were those fragments on those yellowing sheets of paper in her three-ring binder. She wanted to end this conversation. Get home. Get writing.

"No," she said at last, looking down into her cup. "We didn't know. She wished her hair was still long. She could feel the blood rising in her cheeks. She hoped Cass would think it was just the hot tea.

As soon as she got home that day, Emily would start writing a story called *Barney*. It would be about a man building a room in his basement. Building it up on a platform for the damp, and painting it military green as a joke. A joke between him and his old war buddy. Who has no place to go. Who's living at the God damned Y. With a roommate who smells. And all because his wife threw him out. *Wives. Jesus. His own is up in the kitchen. Cooking her mad into his supper. He can smell it. He'll taste it soon. Well, he's got his own mad. And he can hammer it, he can. Loud. Nail by nail. Barney is his friend. Friend. Can't the woman get that into her head?*

The story would grow into a novel that would become a bestseller and win several prizes. Dave would read about the first of them in the paper and call to congratulate her. She would hang up when she heard his voice. Then she would cry.

The pillow is grey. *This is how grey smells,* Em thinks inside the cave she has made out of her coat. Grey smells of sweat. Hair oil. Dust. Old cloth. Feathers from long-dead chickens. Maybe all possible smells go into making up the smell of grey, the way all possible colours go into making up the colour grey. The voices on the other side of the door are grey too.

"Cass, what's she doing in there? She's not supposed to be—"

"Rick, just leave her alone. Just—"

"Em? Look, I'm sorry you're upset, but you're going to have to—"

"Rick! Bugger off!"

Her mind has become a wandering thing. Like that dog she walked. All that summer. Up at the lake. When they rented that cottage. When she was—what? Eight? Nine. Black cocker spaniel. Barney. Long fluffy ears hanging down.

"Em? It's just Cass out here. Rick won't bother you again. And Dave is—he'll be back soon. Are you okay? Do you want me to come in? I could make some tea. Em?"

Barney. Shiny-eyed, pink-tongued Barney. Every morning. As early as her mother would let her, she would knock on the neighbours' cottage door. *Now, you make him go where you want to go,* the lady would say, snapping Barney's leash to his collar and handing the end to her. *Don't just follow along behind. Or he'll get spoiled.*

She wasn't spoiling him. Wherever Barney wanted to go was exactly where she wanted to go. She wanted to zig-zag through the dust of the road leading up to the highway. She wanted to sniff under leaves as big as plates and woof at seagulls screaming overhead and spend a long moment with a flattened frog. She didn't know that she wanted to do any of those things until Barney led her to them. But once she got there, yes. Of course. She was Barney, and Barney was her, all that long summer. The leash tingled like a nerve in her palm.

"Em? It's me. Cass and Rick are gone. So is—you know. She won't be back. Ever. I promise. And Cass says she and Rick are going to stay away all day. Give you and me time to work this thing out."

Em sighs. Lifts her face from Garth Marples' pillow. Pushes her coat down so she can breathe. The old-fashioned springs of Garth Marples' bed squeak and jangle beneath her as she turns over on her back.

"Em? Will you open the door? Will you let me come in? Please?"

The ceiling of Garth Marples' room is plaster, done in big swirls with a little nippled flourish in the middle of each one. There would have been an art to that. A learned gesture, practiced over and over. Something to take pride in. She can imagine the master plasterer atop his ladder, demonstrating to the apprentices craning their necks below.

"Em? Will you just let me know if you're okay?"

Okay. Is she okay? She feels one spot on her scalp that's especially tender. Did Liz actually get any hair? There's a mirror on Garth Marples' dresser. She could go and look.

"Em, please open up and let me in. I need to see you. I need—"

She takes off a shoe and throws it *clunk* at the door. Dave stops talking. She turns on her side. *Jangle. Squeak.* Garth Marples' night table is inches from her nose, with the empty water glass and the picture frame. Did he ever wash the glass, she wonders. There's a cloudy high tide mark halfway up. Maybe when he went into the hospital he just left the last of his water to evaporate.

The picture frame is empty too. Strange. For weeks, she's been wondering about a photograph that isn't even there. Just a rectangle of brown cardboard under glass, surrounded by cheap black-painted wood. But there must have once been something in the frame. Nobody puts an empty picture frame beside their bed.

"Okay, Em. You don't want to look at me. I can't blame you. But will you listen? Please? Will you just listen?"

Where could that photograph be? Did he take it with him to the hospital? Was it that precious?

"You remember a couple of weeks ago? When Rick and I went out drinking and came back real late? Well, Rick had invited Liz along. He always liked Liz. He got a kick out of her. He always thought we shouldn't have broken up. Babe, what can I say? I had a few. I went back to her place. I was a stupid asshole. And I'm sorry. I'm sorry."

Or did he hide it? Was Garth Marples afraid of anybody finding out whose picture he kept beside his bed? Maybe he got rid of it, then. Yes. That would make more sense. Because when you die, people go through your things. Your effects. Paw through them. Show them to each other. Talk. Better get rid of it, then. Get good and liquored up, fumble it out of its frame, rip it into smaller and smaller pieces. Pause to swipe furiously at the wet on your cheeks, the slick on your lip. Then flush the pieces. Press the lever with ceremony. Snap to swaying, drunken attention. Salute. Goodbye. Goodbye who?

"I was never going to see Liz again. I swear, Babe. And I thought she understood that. I thought she knew it was a one-shot deal. Just for old time's sake. But she must have got Rick to tell her where we were living. Wouldn't surprise me if Rick engineered this whole thing."

Barney. Yes. That's the name. That's who. Goodbye, Barney. See you soon.

The smallest place they ever had was the bedroom they occupied for two days and three nights on the train going east. It had a bathroom the size of a phone booth with a sink no bigger than a soup bowl. When Emily filled the sink to wash her hair, the water sloshed back and forth with the rocking of the train, slapping her face and invading her nose.

There was a table the size of a chessboard that folded down under the window. While Dave passed the time traveling through the cars talking to people, Emily sat at the table looking out the window and writing in a lurching scrawl in her journal. Every time the train pulled into a station, she rushed out and bought postcards to send to her parents from Calgary, Saskatoon, Winnipeg.

She had insisted they visit Dave's parents once before they left. "You can't just disappear. You have to let them know that you're going." *And that I exist.*

His parents lived in a robin's-egg-blue bungalow in Burnaby. They were little and English and old. Dave's mother began to cry as soon as she saw him, her eyes big and frightened, as if her son was back from the dead. His father, bent and balding above a curiously mask-like face, looked at him and growled, "Been a while."

The living room, which Dave's mother called the sitting room, was flocked with doilies and peopled with knickknacks. "It keeps me busy, the dusting," she whispered from behind a Kleenex when Emily looked around and said something polite.

Emily could see that Dave's father was one of those men who is never at home in his own house, who is forever being reminded to wipe his feet and knock his ash and use his handkerchief and not leave fingermarks. She wondered if he had a shed or something out back where he could go to fart and swear and spit. While Dave's mother sniffled and Emily chattered absurdly about the upcoming trip and their plans, he sat silent, sliding hooded eyes now and then toward his son, then quickly sliding them back. Emily had the sudden strange notion that she was seeing Garth Marples. She knew that whenever she worked on her story after that, she would imagine the Garth Marples character looking exactly like Dave's father.

Dave said almost nothing during the two-hour visit he had agreed to. He sat hunched, in unconscious imitation of his father, checking his watch and sliding his eyes now and then toward Emily, his expression unreadable. ("I don't want to talk about it," was all he would say on the way home. And so they never did. It was a trade-off. Emily had gotten her introduction. In return, she never asked him to go back there again.)

"I could show you his room," Dave's mother whispered, tapping Emily's forearm with a damp hand. "Where he used to sleep." They went and stood together in the doorway of the most feminine room Emily had ever seen—flowered chintz wallpaper, billowing ruffled curtains, a rose-patterned sofa bed choked with those little shaped cushions that men pull out from behind themselves and throw on the floor.

"I did it over. It's the guest room now. I tried to keep it— you know—just the way. For the longest time. In case. But then—"

A bark sounded from the living room, followed by a growl. Then another bark. "Oh no," Dave's mother whimpered. "Oh no no no." She darted away, first turning to Emily and hissing, "I *knew* this would happen!"

Emily stayed where she was, looking into the guest room, trying to strip away the ruffles and chintz, trying to picture Dave in it somewhere. "Stop it stop it stop it now!" she heard Dave's mother yelping. "I'll not have it! I'll not have it in this house, and both of you know that!" Then silence.

Back in the living room, she found a tableau. The two men squared off and stiff, their teeth bared. The woman tiny and hunched between them, but defiant. "I'm sorry," Emily said. And they all turned and looked at her, silently accepting her apology.

Through the train window, whenever Emily glimpsed a CN truck on the highway running parallel to the tracks, she imagined it was the one that was carrying their things. All their clothes, books, records, dishes, towels, sheets, address books, tax files, photo albums, toiletries, framed posters, appliances, planters, shoes. Everything they had spent days wrapping in newspaper and wedging into boxes. Everything that would greet them at the end of their journey. Give them a sense of a shared past. Of continuity.

There had been a moment when Dave had looked at the still-empty boxes and the newspaper still in stacks and had suggested seriously that they just get rid of everything. Start over clean in the new place.

The *No!* that had come out of her had been visceral. Wounded. The train tickets were bought. The hotel, where they were going to stay at the company's expense until they found a place, was booked. Their pre-wedding tasks were written down in a list. Her mother, who was finally talking to Dave on the phone and starting to call him Son, was ticking a copy of that list off at her end, item by item. It was all of a piece. It was their life. It was what they had. Couldn't he see that?

"Hey," he had said to her stricken face. "It was just a suggestion." Then he had shaken out the first sheet of newspaper. "C'mon. Let's do this." Gradually, the crackling of the newspaper and the strangely satisfying discipline of wedging as many anonymous shapes as possible into each box had settled her down.

Each night on the train they dressed for dinner and went to the bar car for a cocktail. A porter in a starched shirt and black bow tie poured martinis for both of them out of tiny chilled bottles. Each night, they clinked glasses and toasted a future that was hurtling toward them while they ate, while they slept, while the wheels clacked and the whistle moaned and the landscape out their window changed by the second, whether they were watching it or not.

Em gets up off Garth Marples' bed. Walks slowly toward the locked door. Stands looking at it.

She can sense Dave on the other side. Waiting. Listening to her breath, the way she is listening to his. If it wasn't for the door, they would be looking into each other's eyes.

They can look forever into each other's eyes, their faces inches away on the pillow. Not speaking. Not needing to. She can't imagine looking for so long into anyone else's eyes. But in bed, they can study each other's faces for hours. Breathing each other's breath. Smelling each other's smell.

Do other couples do that? Do Cass and Rick? Did Dave do it with Liz? And with the others before Liz? She doesn't know. All she knows is him.

"*Babe?*" Just a whisper. Hardly more than a breath.

She opens her mouth. Closes it. Opens it again. "My name is Emily."

They were married in All Saints church, where her parents had wed. He slid the ring onto the wrong finger of her hand, then had to fumble it off and try again. They bumped noses during the kiss.

"You're us now," her mother said afterwards, hugging him tearfully.

"Welcome," her father said, shaking his hand. Then he added, "Son." Emily could tell her mother had coached him.

The reception was at her parents' house. All her uncles and aunts and cousins were there, and the neighbours who had watched her grow up and the old high-school friends she had almost forgotten but now greeted with a scream. Each and every guest got introduced to Dave, whose smile looked like it was making his face ache and whose voice, when he got a chance to talk, sounded sticky and dry.

His parents had sent a card with a cheque in it. The card sat in a little space that had been cleared for it among the gifts— all the appliances and linens and flatware and stemware and stoneware that had been crammed into the sunroom for display. "My God," Dave had breathed when he had been taken to see it all. He had sounded dismayed, as if he was looking at some huge, impossible task he was expected to do.

They do it on Garth Marples' bed. She is dry, and doesn't come. He is serious for once, almost humble. The only sounds are the jangling squeak of the bed springs. The empty picture frame stands like a mute witness.

Afterwards they lie side by side, staring up at the plastered ceiling. She knows it is up to her to speak, to break the silence, to bring things back down to some safe and ordinary place. She takes a breath. He turns his face to her.

"So much for this room being off limits," she says.

They had just gotten it all together. They had just started to come into their own.

Their place—their final resting place, as they were calling it as a joke—was exactly the way they wanted it. Lemon-yellow walls with dove-grey accents. Narrow grey shelves at intervals, filled with her books, his records. A painted Scandinavian hutch stacked with her grandmother's wedding china. A linen closet stuffed with sheets and towels and comforters and shams. A kitchen gleaming with chrome and copper and the latest gadgets. A state-of-the-art sound system. A big colour TV. Two bedroom closets tight with clothes.

She had just gotten her hair cut almost as short as his, and was helping herself to his tube of gel. He had just shaved clean except for a tiny triangular patch on his chin. She was just starting to reassure him that he wasn't fat, while secretly keeping an eye on the little bulge above his belt. He had just conceded that maybe she did need to wear a bra. Only with certain outfits.

In bed, they had found what worked. They would begin with this, continue with that, then finish with the other thing. If it wasn't as adventurous as it used to be, it was comfortable. It was satisfying. It happened three times a week.

She had just published her first book, a collection of stories dedicated to him. She was just starting to take another look at one of those stories—*Barney*—and to wonder if there was a novel in it. He had just been named regional manager, with six stores under him. He was just starting to decide whether to convert his record collection to tape, or wait for the new compact discs to come down in price.

She had just fallen in love with him all over again. With his face that had softened and started to settle into folds. With his talk, that was rarer and less animated. With his politics, that were more considered, less radical. With the reading glasses he needed now for the paper and the phone book.

She had just started to caution herself, half-jokingly, not to rely on him quite so much. Not to feel quite so relieved by the chime of his keys in the lock at the end of the day. Take quite so much comfort in the sight of his thinning hair poking up above the back of his chair while their dinner was turning slowly in the microwave.

His guilt. Her anger. That's what they have now. That's what they carry around. Damned fool things to hang onto. Why don't they just put them down?

Emily will ask herself this question one day while she's saw-ing a baguette into bite-sized chunks on the breadboard she and Dave bought at the Army and Navy Store in Vancouver thirty years ago.

She buys baguettes and other special breads at a bakery two subway stops south. That morning, just as she was getting off the train, she spotted Dave at the back of the crowd pushing to get into the same car.

Did she just happen to be looking in his direction, she wonders now while she saws the baguette. Or did something— the set of his shoulders—something familiar and known, even expected—pull her eyes his way?

And what about him? Because he was looking back at her. And he said her name. And her own lips formed the word *hello*. No sound, just a shape. Her lips held the final syllable a beat longer than necessary. All he would have seen was her mouth forming an O. Maybe, she thinks, he's still trying to decide whether she said *hello* or *no*. Maybe he's thinking about her right now, while she cuts up a baguette on their old breadboard.

"Is she younger than me? Do her tits still stick straight out? Is that it?" She hated what she was saying, hated the sound of her own voice. Shrill. Shrewish. She had become a walking cliché. "Have there been others? Oh God. All the years. How many others have there been?"

"None. Not since we've been married."

"Before, then. What about before? Liz. You told me Liz was the only one."

"Look. All I can say is that I'm sorry. I did not plan this. I did not go looking for it. But it has happened. So can we please just do what we have to do? The Chinese porcelain lamps. Can I have one of them?"

Today they were dividing up their things. Yesterday they had met with the lawyers. Tomorrow they were going to the bank to close their joint accounts. Their shared life consisted of get-togethers whose purpose was to score them as a couple neatly down the middle and rip them apart.

"Who else knows? About you and her? Besides me? Do all our friends know?" This is how it must have been for Cass. Needing to ask. Hating to find out. Knowing that nobody will tell you, because nobody wants to admit they knew and didn't tell you.

"We've been discreet. Can I have one of the Chinese lamps, please? Yes or no?"

"It's blow jobs, isn't it? She gives you more blow jobs. Or she does them better. Okay. Okay. I'll do anything. Any way you want. Just tell me. Tell me what you want."

"Emily. I am going to box the lamp. If you don't want me to have it, just take it out of the box when I'm gone. I'll have all this stuff out of here by tomorrow. Promise."

"I could put it out on the street. I could. Every one of these boxes. For anybody to take. The second you're out of here. I could do that."

They both knew she wouldn't.

"What about when things break around here?" All the stupid things she couldn't help saying. *Is it my writing? You don't want a writer wife? Okay. Okay. I'll stop. I will. If I feel a story coming on, I'll pull it out like a weed.* "Who's going to fix things for me when they break?"

"I'll leave you the tools."

"The tools? The *tools*? You'll leave me the fucking *toools*?"

He came and enfolded her and pushed her face into his chest and she bit him hard through his shirt and he said "Ow!" so comically that they both laughed and he got a hard-on and she unzipped him and knelt and sucked him off. Then she stayed on her hands and knees, wailing, while he boxed the lamp and left. Then she crawled to the couch where he had sat and lay face down. Sniffing. Sniffing.

It feels strange to have to ask him to sit down.

"Martini?" She doesn't even know if he still drinks them.

"Sure. Thanks."

In the kitchen she remembers to run the lemon twist around the rims of the glasses. She hasn't had a martini in years. He made the first one she ever had, and she managed to get it down. She had her second because she wanted to be sophisticated. By her third, she was starting to like them.

She can't put her finger on what's different about him. Besides more lines and less hair. She expected that much. He seems smaller. Narrower through the shoulders. Or maybe it's the same with people as it is with places you haven't seen in years.

She puts the glasses on a tray and carries it clinking back into the living room. He stands up when she enters.

"Mind if I—" He gestures toward the bathroom that used to be his.

"No. Go ahead." She puts the tray on the coffee table and sits and waits for him, watching condensation gather on the glasses. Smiling at the sound of the bathroom door being locked.

He came to the launch of her latest book. She spotted him immediately in the audience and stayed aware of him, just off to her left, all through the reading. She knew exactly where he was at any given moment in the long line-up during the signing afterwards. When it was finally his turn to slide a copy in front of her, she did not look up. Just wrote, *I'm still in the same place* above her signature on the title page.

"I've got all your books. They're really good. They're—"
"Thanks."

They ask the requisite questions. Find out that all four of their parents are dead. That he and his third wife are going to sell the house and go into a condo. That no, she never remarried. "Fooled around some though," she says over the rim of her glass, and he grins.

They fall silent. He puts his empty glass on the coffee table. Glances at his watch.

She has thought about what she will say to him. Has written it down and practiced it: *Dave, whatever we had is sealed up in a room. Once I was inside that room and couldn't see out. Now I'm outside it and can't see in. I wish there could be a window, or a door ajar. I don't want to go back inside. I just want to be able to look.* It seemed brilliant at the time. But now she knows it would sound written and rehearsed.

The gin is humming in her throat. She stands up. Walks around the coffee table and stands over him. He does not look up. She puts her hands on his shoulders. Thinks, *Come here.*

It's different. The top of his head looks like a baby's might. That hollow feeling she used to get under her breastbone doesn't happen.

Remember the runt house? She wonders if she should say it aloud. If she needs to.

Magnificat

Julia takes pride in still not needing a cane. Her feet might be soaked in sweat and one of her toes starting to blister, but she will not allow herself to limp. Nor will she pluck at her hip where she can feel her underwear riding up under her skirt, or pull her blouse away from where it sticks to her skin. She will not so much as swipe with a finger at the moisture beading her upper lip.

This summer, as always, she has resolved to face the hot, empty weeks head-on, making no concession for them. Yes, her book club has disbanded until September. But that is no excuse not to read. Yes, her theatre and concert series rang down their curtains in the spring and will not raise them again until well into fall. But there is radio and television and the occasional film with which to pass the time.

This Sunday evening, though, the time would not pass. Dinner—a salad and a roll—took a few minutes to prepare and fewer to eat. Washing, drying and putting away her plate, water glass, knife and fork, took almost no time at all. She was left with long hours before bed, during which the sun would hang high in the sky, as if daring her to be the first to retire.

She opened her book. Closed it. Turned on the television. Turned it off again. Ran through her mind the names of friends she might call to suggest an early film. In each case, just as she was reaching for the phone, she remembered them telling her about a visit from their grandchildren that weekend, or a trip to the cottage.

She felt the start of an old melancholy—one that afflicts her most often in the summer. She dreads it more than the humidity touching her everywhere like small sticky hands, more than the odour coming from her discarded clothing at the end of the day despite its having been freshly laundered and herself freshly bathed that morning. It can come over her at any time. She will be making up a grocery list. Writing the word *milk* on a slip of paper. All at once she will be convinced that when she has bought the milk and brought the milk home and poured the last of the milk over her cereal in the morning or into her tea in the evening, there will be nothing. Nothing for her to do. No means of passing the time. She breathes deeply during such moments and tells herself sternly, *It will be all right, Julia! It will be all right.*

There was a moment, toward the end of her youth, when she realized that none of the expected things were going to happen to her. She had had a fragile, morning glory prettiness, but it had closed in on itself before anyone noticed. Now, no one was going to look up and suddenly see her. Find her remarkable. Think twice about her. Her mind had recoiled from the long, shapeless span she imagined her life might become.

But that had not happened. She had not allowed it to happen. She taught herself to give shape to time, to let not a moment go by without marking it for some purpose and eking from it some use. It was her only talent. She became a woman who volunteers, who lends support, who is always there. She adopted a slogan—*I did not take unto me a husband.* She liked to think the phrase *take unto me* gave her an ironic edge, and *did not* made her solitary state look like a choice. Almost a religious vocation.

Religion. Church. Yes. That was how she would make the time pass this evening. She pulled on fresh stockings, stepped into her better shoes, and, though she had attended matins that morning, went back to All Saints for evensong.

The priest's face glowed like candle wax in the dim chancel light. He skipped the homily and went straight to the *Lord, now lettest thou thy servant depart in peace,* as if afraid he might melt under his robes if he didn't speed things up. Still, Julia managed to derive some satisfaction from the service. She is fond of evensong, largely because modern liturgists have yet to tamper with it. In recent years, she has been disturbed by mention of sex and the Internet creeping into church services. She prefers her religion distant and monumental, like the language of *The Book of Common Prayer. We have left undone those things which we ought to have done; And we have done those things which we ought not to have done; And there is no health in us.*

As a young woman, Julia might have listed the things she had either or neglected to do, thereby compromising her spiritual health. She might have questioned whether the entreaties, *O God make speed to save us; O Lord, make haste to help us* were indeed cries from her heart, the prescribed kneeling a sincere gesture of humility, the getting to her feet at the mention of the Trinity a true show of respect. She may even have entertained some doubts as to the very existence of the Trinity, of a God who hears and answers prayer, of much that she continues to sing and chant and murmur in the church she has attended all her life. She never voiced those doubts and barely remembers them now. What she has come to believe in is the singing and the chanting and the murmuring. Religion itself. Its habits and rituals. Habits and rituals are what give shape and structure to the otherwise characterless day. What she fears, as others might fear God, is the immense shapelessness of time. *As it was in the beginning, is now, and ever shall be, world without end.*

Her blister breaks. The sear of pain makes her draw in her breath and miss a step. She puts the wounded foot firmly back down on the pavement. Soon, she reminds herself, she will be home. It is just a matter of taking one step at a time.

Cathy looks at her watch. Gabe will wait for her. Sure he will. She's never been late before. She hates taking the stairs. She'll give the elevator another chance.

Looks like it's stuck on seven. Owen's floor. It would be just her luck if Owen was stepping into it right now, and the thing finally started to move with her still standing here. *Cathy!* His eyes going from dull to bright in a blink. *What a surprise! Are you perhaps feeling better?* She can't even remember what she told him, to get out of going to that—what was it? A poetry reading. Headache? Upset stomach? Why did she say yes in the first place?

The number seven is still lit up.

Owen. No matter where she goes, there's an Owen. The one at the party nobody's talking to. The office screw-up. She smiles at them or covers for them exactly once, and then they're hers forever. Why doesn't she just blow them off, the way everybody else does? Why does she get stuck the way she did on the street last week—smiling until her face ached while Owen told her all about the bundle of library books under his arm. Which one he had enjoyed the most. And why. Which one he had enjoyed the least. And why.

The elevator still isn't moving. Maybe it's a sign. Maybe—

No. She's being silly. She always feels afraid after Gabe calls to dictate his latest address. Even while she's fumbling for a pencil because she knows he won't repeat himself, she is hoping deep down that something will keep them from getting together.

They met in a ticket line-up. He was ahead of her. She can't remember now what the tickets were for—a movie, a play. He turned and looked at her as if he had known all along she was there, knew where she had been before that, and before that. Then he said something to her that no one else ever had. Then she was gripping the headboard of a bed, grunting out deep, guttural screams while he slammed into her from behind. He kept one hand crooked under her so he could tickle her where she was wet and aching. He tickled her the whole time, his touch lighter and more delicate than she knew a man's fingers could be. It went on for what felt like hours, and she couldn't stand it and she wanted it never to end.

Time you got what's coming to you.

Did he really say that to her when he turned and looked at her? She had never heard those words. But it was as if she had been waiting to hear them all her life. Whenever she tries to think back on that moment, it's like trying to remember a dream. She can see his mouth moving, can hear words coming toward her distorted and muffled, as if spoken under water. *Time yougot whatscoming toyou.*

She goes back to him whenever he summons her. Last time, she faked a family crisis to get off work because he had phoned in the middle of the day. And tonight she lied to Owen.

Fuck the elevator. She'll take the stairs.

On the fourth floor landing, a crouching human shape in the corner makes her jump. It's only a garbage bag, full and slumped over. People do sometimes creep into the building, though. Last winter she found a smelly nest in the laundry room—a ragged sleeping bag made of pink shiny material, with plastic bags and empty yogurt containers around it.

Third floor landing. She's convinced a woman made that nest—maybe because the sleeping bag was pink. It scared her when she saw it. She actually turned and ran back up the stairs with her laundry basket, afraid to look behind her. For days she kept thinking about the nest. Imagining herself in it. What if she lost her job? How long would it take for her to end up on the street? Only when she was all out of clean socks and underwear did she creep back down to the laundry room. She peeked around the door to where the sleeping bag had been. It was gone. The patch of floor it had covered was shiny from disinfectant.

Second floor landing. Once, before she knew better, she asked Gabe if it bothered him to have no permanent home, to never know from one month to the next where he would be sleeping. He was silent for a long time. She was used to men like Owen—the kind who are just dying for her to ask them something—anything—so they can go on and on about themselves. But Gabe said nothing. Was he angry? How would he punish her? Sometimes he pinched her nipples hard and pulled on them like reins when he made her ride him. Or he jammed fingers into her before she was ready and kept them there until she was. This time, all he did was push her flat, knee her legs apart and stop her mouth with his tongue.

Ground floor. Please don't let Owen be in the lobby. If he is, she'll have to come up with some reason for going out when she's supposed to be sick. She could say she needs Kleenex or stomach medicine. But then he'll probably offer to get it for her and bring it to her apartment. Then she'll have to think of some way to persuade him not to, and that will make her really late for Gabe. And Gabe might not—

The lobby is empty. She stands still, wasting time, looking around as if she expects Owen to materialize out of thin air.

Stupid. She hurries out the door, down the steps onto the street. *Half an hour*. That's what Gabe said before hanging up. But he'll wait for her. Sure he will. She's never been late for him before. That should count for something.

Julia looks at her watch. Eight-thirty. The sun is still showing no sign of setting. Even on the shaded side of the street it is oppressively warm. The trees are motionless, their branches hanging as if weighted as she steps along beneath them, still refusing to limp. To judge from the stabbing hurt of each step she takes, a blister must have formed and broken on the toe of the other foot now. Well. She will not look at her watch again. Constantly checking the time merely serves to slow it down.

To distract herself, she focuses on a man and woman who have just turned into the street a block away and are now walking toward her. The woman trots along beside the man, taking two steps for each of his strides, tilting her face to his profile, offering up little gifts of words that he shows no sign of having heard. The sight stirs a memory in Julia that it takes her a moment to place. Her mother. The way she used to chatter to her father while he chewed his supper in silence. Julia would watch the two of them and wonder what had drawn them to each other. What kept them together. They never touched in her presence, or used endearments. Nor did she ever hear any sounds from their bedroom in the night. Not that she listened.

Something has happened. The man has stopped walking. He's standing looking down a flight of stone steps that lead to the park. Julia slows her pace, allowing herself to take note of the man's dark curly hair, his bare muscled arms. The woman says something—Julia can tell it is a question, though she cannot make out the words. When the man doesn't answer, the woman asks what sounds like the same question. She seems confused, turning her head back and forth between the path they had been taking and this new direction. She wears a blue tunic over a white, low-cut T-shirt. Her long hair manages to look flyaway, even in this unmoving air.

Now the man has started down the stone steps, leaving the woman alone on the sidewalk. Julia stops walking altogether and stands, watching. The woman calls something after the man's back. He barks a reply without turning, his tone at once dismissive and threatening.

Julia sidesteps into the shade of a tree. It would look perfectly reasonable, she tells herself, to anyone observing her. As if she is simply resting in some shade before continuing her own journey. Not as if she is actually watching the couple. Curious about them.

The man's head is sinking lower with each step he takes. The woman appears to be sinking too. She bends her neck, watching the man. Her shoulders are slumping and she is sagging a little at the knees. Just when Julia thinks she might actually crumple to the sidewalk, she hurries after the man down the stone steps into the park.

If you know what's good for you…

Is that what Gabe said? Maybe she didn't hear him right. Maybe—

That's what he said.

Cathy's toes are inches from the edge of the top step. She watches the back of his head getting lower and lower.

When he called and told her to meet him outside on the street for once, she wondered if he was in trouble. If a house he was counting on had fallen through, leaving him really homeless for once. That's all she knows about him—that he's a professional house-sitter. That he never knows more than a month ahead where he'll be living.

He knows everything about her. She told him all about herself in that first still, sweaty time after he had finished with her, when her heart was just starting to slow down. About her job. Her apartment. Her niece and nephew. She thinks she even told him about Owen. He listened, or appeared to, lying on his back, blinking lazily and smiling that faintly amused smile with which he had sized her up in the ticket line.

No one had ever looked at her the way he had at that moment. It was like being seen—really seen—for the first time. And nothing she could tell him about herself—she knew this even as she chattered on and on—could matter at all. Because he knew the one thing about her that did. Knew what had happened to her. Knew what she was.

"Hand!"

Which one do you offer first?

"Hand!"

Your right. Because you are right-handed and you always put your right hand out for things. Even this. Which cannot possibly be happening. You are the good girl. The teacher's pet. You do not get sent to the office.

When you got up from your desk and walked toward the door on shaking legs you could hear the incredulous whispers—Cathy! Cathy?—behind you. Some of them sounding glad. Because you were finally getting what was coming to you.

Your hand as you put it out is pale and small. The strap rises in a perfect arc. Comes down. Nothing, for a second. Then pain that makes your mind go white. Then something else. Far from your mind. Down where you don't think and mustn't touch. An opening and a closing. A throb.

"Other hand!"

The strap arcs down. Nothing. Then white pain. Then again that throb you've never felt and want to feel. Again and again.

But there is no more. It is over. You are being shown mercy because it's your first time and you're the good girl.

You don't want mercy. You don't want to be good. You want to get what's coming to you.

The place I'm in doesn't have air conditioning. That was all Gabe said until they got to the entrance to the park. Then, *It'll be cool down here.* Then, when she hesitated, *If you know what's good for you...*

In a second, he'll turn a corner and be out of sight. He could disappear. She might never see him again—his green eyes tilting up in that vaguely oriental way, his curly black hair spilling down the back of his neck. She might never kneel again to unbuckle his belt, never see his cock springing free, bumping her cheek. Never feel his fist bunching her hair, holding her head in place. Never taste his salt at the back of her throat.

She might never be afraid again, either. She's afraid all the time now. When he doesn't call. When he does. He never says *hello* when she snatches up the phone, or even *It's Gabe*—just dictates his latest address and hangs up. And that makes her afraid all over again—that she'll find out the address doesn't exist. Or that it does, but Gabe isn't there. Or that he is there, but won't fuck her, even when she begs. Or that he'll have another woman with him. Or another man. Or that he'll want to do more and more things that hurt. And that she'll let him. Because it's time she got what was coming to her.

If you know what's good for you....

Gabe has disappeared around a corner. Cathy starts down the stone steps, hurrying to catch up.

You are *not* merely curious, Julia tells herself firmly. There is something not quite right about this situation. That young woman looked distinctly troubled. Frightened, even. And if that is the case, then it is your duty to be of assistance. Offer your home as a temporary refuge. The use of your telephone. A cup of tea.

Still, she hesitates at the top of the stone steps. They lead down to a park which is the first in a chain of parks, stretching for miles, each one less well-groomed, more deserted, more wild. Even the terraced rose garden close to the street has dark corners and walls of sculpted hedge. Beyond that is an unlit stretch of grass. And beyond that, trees. Not a safe place once the sun sets, as it is finally beginning to do.

She moves carefully from step to step, trying for quiet. *Be not afraid.* Strange. Those words haven't gone through her mind for—well, not since she was a girl.

She stands still for a moment on the stone landing where the steps veer to the side. If she continues, if she turns the corner, she will be able to see down into the park. And very likely, she will see nothing. A stretch of dark grass, just now abandoned by a perfectly ordinary couple who were having a perfectly ordinary quarrel about something that does not concern her.

Be not afraid. She remembers lying in bed, imagining herself the Virgin Mary. Imagining the eyes of the angel on her. And his next words, the ones that would change her life forever, giving her cause to sing the Magnificat. *My soul doth magnify the Lord…*

She is afraid. In a queer, thirsting way. She slips out of her shoes. Picks them up and carries them. The stone through her stockings is cool to her blistered feet. She takes the next step down. Turns the corner.

Turn your head to the side.

Owen is here. Owen has found her. That is his voice, telling her what to do to save herself.

If someone's forearm is pressing on your windpipe, turn your head so you are facing into the crook of his elbow. That will give you a bit of space to breathe in.

Cathy turns her head. Gabe's arm immediately tightens, pressing now into the side of her neck. With every thrust from behind, he shoves her up against his arm. She can feel her pulse beating feebly against his muscle.

Gimme your clothes, he said. Then, when she was naked, *Turn around.*

The grass is chafing her knees. Her fingers dig into the dirt. Her head feels empty and light, as if there is no blood in it.

But she is surrounded by angels. Gabe. And Owen. And now this lady who is watching her. Has she always been there? She is in a blue robe and a kind of white headdress, like a nun's. Her feet are bare. She is wearing shoes on her hands.

As Cathy watches, trying to breathe, fighting the darkness that is moving in from the edges of her vision, the woman opens her mouth and starts to sing to her. Wonderful words. So wonderful she can't hear them.

Yes, Lady. Give me your song. I will do this. For you. And you will give me your song.

Julia is crouching, clutching at herself. Slowly, she straightens. Her whole body aches. All she can think about are her clothes. Are they still—

Is she still—

Yes. There is the hem of her skirt, decently level with her knees. The zipper still closed, the fastener fastened. Her blouse still tucked in, each button still buttoned. Her handbag still over her arm and her shoes—

She is holding her shoes in her hands. The toes of her stockings are torn and spotted with blood.

When she saw the blue tunic come off, she pressed her palms flat to her heart. Prayed through dry lips, *Make speed to save us, Make haste to help us.* Then when the white T-shirt and the flesh-coloured bra were shed, she wrapped her arms around herself to stop the swaying of freed breasts. *Have mercy upon us. Lighten our darkness, we beseech thee, And by thy great mercy defend us from all perils and dangers of this night.*

The man took each piece of clothing and knotted it—once, twice. Then he swung it around above his head. Released it. It snagged in the branches of the overhanging trees.

And the whole time, he was looking at her. Seeing her. Telling her with his eyes to be not afraid.

Now she limps to a stone bench and collapses on it, gripping its edge. In time her heartbeat slows and her breathing steadies. She realizes she is shivering. It is getting dark, and the air is finally starting to cool.

Out of habit, she looks at her watch. She can barely see the hands, and in any case cannot remember what time it was the last time she looked. No way of knowing how long she has been in the park, then. How long *it* took. The thing that happened. The thing that was done to her.

Yes. Something was done. And it was done to *her*. She begins to cry. And she was terribly frightened by it. She has suffered something dreadful, she whimpers to herself. Something that ought not to have been done.

That is enough, Julia! Stop this minute.

But she can't stop. She sees herself as if from high above. A tiny figure sitting alone on a park bench on a summer night. On one side of her is a garden and a lamp-lit street. On the other, seen in glimpses through the dark trees, is a winged man-shape skimming the ground. And behind him a loping naked woman, head thrown back, mouth open in a howl.

My soul doth magnify the Lord.

Is she actually singing? Her mouth is so dry.

And my spirit hath rejoiced in God my Saviour
Because he hath regarded the humility of his handmaiden.

She hugs her handbag to her. Opens it and looks inside at keys and a comb and a change purse and a packet of tissues. She knows these things are hers. But she cannot yet lay claim to them.

Because he that is mighty
hath done great things to me.

The words of the Magnificat are coming back to her from girlhood. She's not sure she remembers them correctly or is singing them in the right order.

He hath shewed might in his arm:
he hath scattered the proud in the conceit of their heart.

She looks again into her handbag. Manages to take out a tissue and dry her cheeks. Blow her nose.

He hath put down the mighty from their seat,
and hath exalted the humble.

She is bone-weary. Shivering again. She must get up and go home. At home, she can discard her shredded stockings and soak her wounded feet in a comforting bath. But first she must get there. So she must move. Now. But she cannot move. Not until—

What is the next part? *He hath filled the hungry with good things; and the rich he hath sent empty away.*

Is that all? Has she sung the whole Magnificat? Was she singing at all? She sits very still, hardly breathing. Listening to crickets nearby and traffic sounds in the distance.

My soul doth magnify the Lord…

The words are new in her mouth. An unfamiliar taste. An unrecognizable shape.

She whispers them over and over, and each time they become stranger, further separated from any meaning they might have had.

Mysoul dothmagnify theLord

Her mouth is working independently, as if it knows it must repeat those words that the rest of her no longer understands, repeat them a specified number of times. And only then will she be free to go.

ECCE COR MEUM

POLYP.

Funny little word. Sounds botanical. A bed of flowering polyps. Gather ye polyps while ye may.

Kelly takes another swallow of coffee. She's sitting in a Starbucks across from her doctor's office, having a wedge of apple cake for breakfast and watching through the window while the street wakes up. It's just after nine. Usually by this time she's had two big mugs full of coffee, but this morning she had to fast for her physical. She can feel the caffeine—

Simon? Is that him? Across the street? She leans forward, trying to see. No. Not Simon. Just a guy with his hair. The set of his shoulders. She sits back in her chair. Spears the lone chunk of glazed apple in her cake with her plastic fork and eats it.

She went and dreamed about him last night. A silly teenager's dream. They were dancing. He was breathing into her hair, his mouth close to her ear. He said, *I think I'm falling in love with you.* Even in her sleep, she knew the dream was hokey.

She drains her coffee, looks at her watch. Her bone density test isn't till ten. She takes her empty cup and goes and fills it back up with Columbian Dark. Wonders what they'll charge her for a refill; if that's the word. Maybe it's rerun or redo. These places have their own language, and she doesn't come into one often enough to pick it up.

I don't belong in the world. She made Simon laugh with that. She'd just handed his Blackberry back to him after examining it. It's true. At some point, it all just started to elude her. Starbucks and Blackberries and iPods and iPads and YouTube. And young female celebrities who all look the same and all seem to be leading the same disastrous life. It all just makes her feel old. At fifty-seven. Meera, the young Hindu woman she works with, asked her the other day if her church forbids cell phones. She couldn't get over the fact that Kelly still doesn't have one. "Anglicans don't really forbid anything," Kelly said. "We just decide we're above it."

Her refill turns out to be a dollar. She smiles while she tops it up with one percent milk. Simon would get a kick out of that. *We just decide we're above it.* She stops smiling. She wasn't going to do that anymore. Tuck away tidbits to share with Simon.

Back at her table, she looks around and wonders if she's in somebody else's usual spot. It's prime real estate, right by the window. The man at the next table has regular written all over him. He's staked out the other two chairs with his coat and satchel, and settled in for the morning with his newspaper. And didn't he give her a sharp look when she first sat down?

Give yourself a break, Kelly. Simon's voice. Lighter and more musical than most men's. *You're a paying customer.* His pale blue eyes, their expression a little exasperated. *You don't think enough of yourself.* His hand, reaching for hers across—

Shit.

She puts her cup down. Straightens her back. Places her feet flat on the floor. Closes her eyes. Takes in a deep, deliberate breath. *Create in me a clean heart.* Breathes out, focusing on the air leaving her lungs. *And renew a right spirit within me.* Does it again. Following the breath. Repeating her mantra. Which she suspects is too wordy.

She took a meditation course last winter in the basement of All Saints. Their teacher was a Buddhist nun with a shaved head—a woman originally from Savannah, Georgia, whose accent kept making Kelly smile. *Fallow the bray-eth. Ee-yin. Owt.*

The nun suggested some one-word mantras (*may-an-truhs*) for them to try. But the psalm refrain from Sunday's service was still going round in Kelly's head.

Breathe in. *Create in me a clean heart.*

"Loo lah-bee?" A toddler at a table behind her is asking the same question over and over.

Breathe out. *And renew a right spirit within me.*

"Loo lah-bee?" Each time, the mother answers, "When Grandma comes."

Breathe in. *Create in me—*

"Loo lah-bee?"

"When Grandma comes."

Kelly sighs. She opens her eyes and takes another forkful of apple cake. One night the Buddhist nun brought in a small loaf of bread and had them each take a bit and eat it very slowly. She tries savouring her cake now the way they savoured the bread that night, concentrating first on texture. Crumbly, dry. Now flavours. Sugar, cinnamon, artificial apple.

Meditative eating was the only thing in the whole course that she did half decently. She came to dread the actual meditation sessions, which grew over the four Tuesday nights from ten minutes to thirty. Two minutes in, and all kinds of itches would be blooming between her shoulder blades, on the ball of her foot, at the backs of her knees. Five minutes in, and her thigh muscles would be jumping.

"Trah stay-anding up," the Buddhist nun advised her one week. And then the next, "Trah lying daown on the floah." No good. Others in the class would talk afterwards about how they floated away during the long silence or lost all track of time or recovered some precious memory from their childhood. "Ay-and what abowt yoo?" the nun would ask Kelly each week, looking more and more worried.

Polyp.

There it is again. Like a dripping tap. Funny how she can forget all about it for long stretches, then—*polyp*. Well. She can't see it. Or feel it. And anyway, Susan said it was probably nothing.

Kelly shrugs off her jean jacket and sits for a minute in the short-sleeved black turtleneck she chose that morning with her blood test in mind. The place is filling up. Getting warm. People at the other tables are unwinding scarves, peeling off sweatshirts. It's a damp February day—a degree or two above freezing, enough to keep the slush soft underfoot, but with a raw wind that chills through.

She can't remember Ash Wednesday ever being this early. She arranged to take a PD so she could go to the noon service at All Saints without having to rush right back to work. Other years, she's designated the time as Religious Observance, but last December an e-mail from Human Resources said that Religious Observance would hereafter be covered by Personal Days, so employees taking time off for RO should identify it as PD on the time sheets.

It shouldn't have made a difference, but it did. Besides Meera the Hindu, Kelly works with a feminist Muslim and a non-observant Jew and a lapsed Catholic and a part-timer in high school—a girl with facial piercings—who's sort of Wiccan. She missed the bit of interest she's stirred up other years by putting RO on the time sheet. ("Does the priest dump the ashes on your head?") She missed getting teased by Bev, the lapsed Catholic who once wanted to be a nun, then got pregnant instead. ("You Protestants are toast.") She could have just told them, but it's hard to work Ash Wednesday into the lunchroom talk. And since it was a plain PD, she felt obliged to book a couple of medical appointments she was due for into the morning. Now she's thinking she could clean the oven after the service. Wash the bathroom walls.

"I can't just sit and stare into space. I have to do something with every minute. It's the way I was brought up."

The things she's told Simon about herself. Little silly nothing things.

"There was this poem about time that my mother clipped out of a magazine and framed and hung in the kitchen. Breakfast, lunch and supper—there it was. I'll never forget it."

Did he ask her to recite it? She hopes so. Because she did.

> See the little day star moving.
> Life and time are worth improving.
> Seize the moments while they stay.
> Seize and use them,
> lest you lose them,
> and lament the wasted day.

She loves the way he laughs—his freckled, planar face opening up in that sudden way it does. His mouth—

Fuck. She's grinning down into her coffee like a fool. She straightens up. Drops her lips. Breathes in. *Create in me a clean heart.* Breathes out. *And renew a right spirit within me.*

It really is too wordy for a mantra. And you're not supposed to use meditation as a quick fix for a specific problem. The Buddhist nun said the benefits were things like enhanced concentration and lowered stress levels, and that you would only start to notice them over time. But she's got to do something. She's driving herself nuts.

She's been divorced for twenty years. Hasn't had a lover in almost five. "You're getting a little dry," Susan told her during last year's physical. "And you're dropping a bit. But that's natural for your time of life." *Dropping and drying.* It didn't sound natural. It didn't sound like anything that should be happening to her.

Then one Sunday last fall she was sitting in church waiting for the service to start when Simon came hurrying down the side aisle toward the vestry, looking distracted. The morning sun caught the traces of red in his greying hair as he headed through the arch. She found herself enjoying the way his robe accentuated the spread of his shoulders, the narrowing at his hips.

She said a quiet, "Oh!" to herself.

Kelly has been coming to All Saints for more than fifteen years. ("Everybody else was having a midlife crisis. Me, I went back to church.") When she first started, she would feel an odd little thrill each week as Sunday approached, almost as if she was going to meet a lover. The church of her childhood would have disapproved of All Saints and what goes on there. ("My vestigial Presbyterian lets me kneel, but won't let me cross myself.") But the strangeness of the service, with its incense and chanting, aroused a hunger in her.

She can hardly remember feeling that way now. She sits in the same pew every week. Chats with the same people. Edits the newsletter, *Saints Alive*, and jokes about being a church lady. On Sunday mornings she sits, stands or kneels on cue with that seasoned Anglican casualness that used to shock her when she had to watch others to see what to do. And she stopped trying to take every word of the service to heart years ago. Especially the Prayers of the People, when a member of the congregation goes up to the lectern and asks God for everything from peace in the Middle East to healing for so-and-so who's recently broken their collar bone. In the moment of silence for personal petitions, she'll sometimes mouth the name of a friend or workmate who's sick or upset about something. She figures it might help, and anyway can't hurt. But she never asks for anything for herself.

That Sunday morning last fall, she did. As she knelt, she breathed into her knuckles, "Would You consider letting me have Simon?" Then she added, "Please?"

He walked into her library the next day. Her heart came up like a glob in her throat and she almost ducked down behind the front counter. He did a double take when he saw her and came right over. "So this is where you work. When do you get lunch?"

It was a coincidence. Of course it was. Like when your horoscope comes true. She told herself not to read anything into it. But after that first lunch, if she was doing some chore like getting groceries or folding laundry, she would start to imagine Simon there, helping her. He came to inhabit one room of her apartment after the other that way, sitting across from her in the dining nook, rinsing and stacking the dishes with her in the kitchen. In bed, she *was* getting dry, damn it. But it didn't really matter, because what she imagined was mostly about before and after. Especially after. The drowsy warmth. The drifting together into sleep.

People told her she was looking younger. Asked her what her secret was. Something warned her not to tell. But it was like carrying around a little unopened gift. So she told Bev at work, who promised not to tell. Not that it mattered, because soon after she told the rest of the staff, even the teenaged Wiccan. Then she told a couple of old friends she sees for dinner once a month. Then the rest of her friends. ("You won't believe what I've gone and done.") And they would congratulate her, cheer her on, as if falling in love was an achievement.

Maybe that's what spoiled it. Even just putting it into words for herself—*I've fallen in love.* Because it has gone bad. No doubt about it. She's always on the lookout for Simon now. If she sees him, or just thinks she does, something in her clenches hard. If he's talking or laughing with another woman on Sunday morning, she hurries out the door without saying hello. Or worse, she sidles over and lingers on the edge of the conversation, hating the desperate, let-me-in smile cracking her face.

Her daydreams have turned into booby traps. She comes to from them abruptly and cruelly, reminding herself that none of it is real and likely never will be. The Buddhist nun told them to treat stray thoughts and daydreams as if they were birds chattering in the trees, or leaves blowing along the ground. She said they should acknowledge them, but not follow them or dwell on them. Just let them go. Kelly's tried to let hers go, and she can't. It's more that they won't let *her* go.

She wishes she could travel back in time, to just before that Sunday morning last fall. Her life was all right. It was fine. She had her job. Her friends. Her church. Her RRSP. She felt safe. She was even used to being alone. Took a grim pride in it, on those rare days when she woke up with a hollow ache under her breastbone. Imagined carrying a leper's bell,

silently pealing, *See my pain! See my loneliness and stay away!*
Told herself to grow up and get real. To quit feeling sorry for
herself and get busy with something. Because this too would
pass. And it always did. Soon she would be back to feeling safe
in her life again.

Then came that Sunday morning last fall when she asked
God for Simon. Now all the stuff that used to make her feel
safe—her job, her friends, her church, her RRSP—has started
to scare her. She feels afraid. All the time. Afraid of her own
life.

Nine-fifteen. By this time at work she's on the front
counter, doing intake, topping up copier cards, keeping an
eye on Dwayne in the corner with his cat and dog magazines,
hoping he isn't going to have one of his days.

Polyp.

She pictures a tiny mushroom, poking palely into the dark.
A little round head on a skinny neck of stem. There. That's
what she should be afraid of. But she can't even keep it in
mind. Can't quite believe in it.

"You have a small polyp growing on one side of your
cervix."

They were sitting in Susan's office again, once Kelly had her
clothes back on. Susan's tone was light, almost casual, and she
kept her eyes down while she went through Kelly's file. "It's
probably nothing to worry about. But I'll make an appointment for you to have it frozen and taken out and tested. That
way we'll be sure." She looked up then and smiled.

She would have found it during the internal. Kelly sips her
cooling coffee, thinking back over that part of the physical.
Trying to remember a hesitation, a change in tone.

"Do you know how we learn this procedure when we're
in school?" Susan had her back turned. She was keeping the
speculum out of sight, holding it under the warm water tap
for a minute before inserting it between Kelly's trying-to-relax
thighs. "There. Too cold? Too hot?"

Kelly said, "Just right," reminding herself of Goldilocks.
"No. How do you learn to do this?" She was staring at the

ceiling, breathing in, breathing out, willing her mind to be as white as the tiles. *Create in me—*

"We hire prostitutes and practice on them."

"You're kidding."—*a clean heart.*

"Nope. That's what we do. And it's good, because they don't mind us fumbling around, and they're off their feet, and they know they're in a safe environment for once. Okay. You'll hear a clicking noise. And you'll feel some pressure. There. All done." No indication that she had seen anything out of line. Just the distracting chatter.

Kelly needs her jacket again. It's going to be that kind of day—jacket on, jacket off. Just before she puts her left arm into the sleeve, she peels back the Band-Aid in the crook of her elbow and takes a look at the tiny puncture. It's already formed a scab. And on the ball of cotton, there's a twin dot of blood.

Why does she always dread the yearly blood test more than the internal? Maybe because she's never seen the speculum, but there's nothing stopping her from watching every step of the blood work—the cold alcohol swab, the nurse's fingers tapping to raise a vein, then the point of the needle denting her skin. This morning she tried to keep her eyes straight ahead, focused on a box of latex gloves. But she looked back in time to see the ampoules clicking around like the carriage of a six-shooter, filling up in turn. Every year, she's surprised by how much is being taken out of her, and the darkness of her own blood.

She puts the Band-Aid back in place, noticing how the skin of her forearm is starting to crepe. The first brown spots are blooming on the backs of her hands too, and the veins there are getting wormy. Susan routinely asks about hot flashes now. And this morning, for the first time, she said, "How's your libido?"

It's nine-thirty. Her apple cake is gone, and she shouldn't have any more coffee. The bone densitometry office is in the medical building she left an hour ago, right above her doctor's. There's a little card shop beside it across the street. A minute ago the CLOSED sign in its window got turned around to OPEN. She could browse in there until her bone test.

Outside, she has to S-curve around lakes of slush to get across the street. She pushes open the card shop door, breathing in perfumed warmth. The whole place is done up in reds and pinks. Heart-shaped helium balloons and cardboard cupids float at eye level. Little round tables are covered with white lace cloths and crowded with Valentine's Day trinkets. Kelly can almost taste the sweetness in the air from scented candles and potpourri.

She goes over to a rack of cards and starts opening them, reading the messages inside and putting them back. She picks up one that says *For My Good Friend on Valentine's Day*. Inside it's blank.

"I could talk to you all day."

He did say that to her the last time he phoned about an article for *Saints Alive* and they ended up chatting for more than an hour.

You could talk to me all day and all night, if you like.

What if she had said that into the phone? She was so close. Sometimes she imagines herself very old, thinking back on all the things she could have said throughout her life, but didn't. Because she didn't want to make a fool of herself. Or didn't want to make a scene. Or rock the boat. Or find out the truth. Which could be that he meant nothing by the little things he said. That he was just being nice.

No. There had to be more to it than that. What about the time he was late and she waited for him in the restaurant? Ten minutes, fifteen, twenty. He finally came through the door, flustered and apologetic. An angry parishioner had buttonholed him just as he was leaving the church, and wouldn't let him go, even when he told her—

"Everybody assumes I'm there for them and them alone," he said, snapping open his napkin, his face flushed. "They never stop to consider that I've got a whole congregation to look after. They just think I'm their personal Rock of Gibraltar."

I don't think of you that way.

"It never occurs to them that I'm just one human being. That I've got my limitations. My boundaries. Maybe even a lunch date."

It occurs to me all the time. He called what they were doing a date. And he was confiding in her. Even though he had apologized for dumping.

"Dump away," she had said lightly. She says most things to him lightly. Breezily. He would never guess how she cherishes his every word, holds it in memory the way she would carry in her pocket some beautiful stone she had found.

For My Good Friend On Valentine's Day. What if she did send this one to him? With some casual, breezy little message inside, aimed at keeping things light?

She puts the card back. Picks up another one that says *To My Secret Valentine.* Also blank inside. She could send this one unsigned. Get Bev to address the envelope for her so he wouldn't recognize the handwriting.

For God's sake, Kelly. You're not in high school.

Why did she have to go and say she'd fallen in love when Susan asked about her libido? She can't keep on telling people. It's too small a world. Six degrees of separation. Last week she told the woman she talks to every Saturday morning in the laundry room of her apartment building, and it turned out this woman knows somebody who goes to All Saints. She promised not to tell, but ever since a cold panic has started up in Kelly whenever she imagines her laundry room friend telling her All Saints friend, who tells somebody else, who tells somebody else, until the story works its way up to Simon. She knows it's far-fetched, but—

Anyway, it's pathetic to tell people. It's just bragging. *Look what I've managed to do! At fifty-seven! So much for dropping and drying!*

Nine-forty. Still too early to go back to the medical building. She wanders around the card shop, hugging her purse close to keep it from swiping china cupids off tables. Every now and then a hanging cardboard heart gives the top of her head a spidery caress.

There was a labelled diagram of a heart on the wall of Susan's examining room. Kelly studied it while she stripped to the waist for her electrocardiogram, wondering how anybody could look at a real heart and come up with something as smooth and symmetrical as a valentine. She lay down on the padded table and the nurse put cold sticky disks on her skin—a few in a rough circle around her left breast, a couple on each arm. Then she attached wires to the disks and started up a machine that hummed and clunked and extruded a printout, inch by inch.

Later, as Kelly was putting on her coat in the waiting room, looking forward to coffee, Susan walked by, waving the printout at her. "This looks good." Then she winked and said, "Let me know how things work out!"

She got all excited about Kelly being in love. "I'm a matchmaker," she said. "And I'm brilliant. I got my brother and sister-in-law together. I've found partners for three of my friends. So. You say you're friends with this guy? You have interests in common? You go for lunch? And now your feelings for him have changed? But you're afraid to tell him because it might screw up the friendship? Is that it? Have I got it right?"

Kelly kept nodding, even though that wasn't quite it. She has imagined telling him. Blurting it out, with sudden tears. Or planning it ahead of time. Making reservations at a restaurant. Or making an appointment to see him in his office at the church. Even asking him to lunch at her place. She always has a speech prepared which she has rehearsed so she can do it without either tearing up or sounding cold and crafty.

No matter where she sets the scene, she can only ever imagine one response from him. She sees first surprise in his expression, even shock. Then embarrassment. Then worry. And when he speaks, it is so gently. He chooses his words with such care, ever the professional counsellor. *Very fond. Greatly admire. Cherish our friendship. But.*

The scene always ends in her apartment, with him sitting on the couch and her in the armchair facing him. She has stopped hearing his voice, is reading all she needs to know from his face and hands and the slow drawing back of his body. They talk for a little while. She makes it easy for him. Makes a show of being okay.

Then she is closing her door against the sight of him waiting in the hall for the elevator. There's the click of her chain lock sliding into place. She turns to face her empty apartment. The ghastly sunlight streaming through the blinds.

"Kelly? Hello? Lost you there for a minute. Okay. I was saying, so don't tell him. Show him. How's the casual touch situation? You hug, right? And maybe there's a friendly little kiss every now and then?"

Kelly smiles. Once a week she kneels in front of Simon and cups her hands to receive a round disc of bread marked with a cross. His fingertips brush the ball of her thumb as he presses the bread into her palm and says, "The Body of Christ. The Bread of Heaven." She looks up and meets his eyes. He smiles. Sometimes he winks.

"We ... hug."

And they do. Whenever they're saying goodbye after one of their lunches, they embrace, briefly and awkwardly. Kelly always initiates it, reaching up, and Simon bends from the waist, preserving a space between their pelvises.

"Okay. You hug. This is good. So, next time, you prolong the hug. Just a bit. Then look into his eyes. Maintain eye contact whenever you can. And find reasons to touch him. Just little touches. On the arm, say. Trust me. It all sends a message."

She wouldn't be talking that way if she was really worried about the polyp, Kelly thinks now, sniffing a lavender-scented sachet. *Would she?*

Nine fifty-five. Time to start back to the medical building.

There are two other people in the waiting room of the bone densitometry office, an old couple sitting together and talking in what sounds like Russian. Their voices are gentle, hesitant, pitched as if to comfort each other. Kelly wonders which of them has the appointment, and which is just there for support. Or there because they're there. In the same bed for decades, breathing the other's breath. Their clothes rubbing up against the other's in the closet. Their shoes lined up beside the other's on the closet floor.

In a far corner of her mind, Kelly still feels married to her ex. She still sometimes runs scenes through her mind of the two of them in old age. Herself peeking at Phil from around corners, watching his chest for the rising and falling before going back to her ironing. Phil reminding her every morning to take her medication, then running water in the bathroom to cover the sound of opening the medicine cabinet to count her pills.

The last time she saw him was three years ago in a subway station. She was going up the up escalator and a man who looked strangely familiar was coming down the down. By the time she recognized him, he was past her. He didn't look in her direction and she didn't call his name. Not long after that, she started scanning the obituary page in the paper every morning for Phil's name. She's not sure what she'll do if she ever finds it. Go to the service? Sit at the back and slip out without signing the guest book? She just wants to know. That's all. She doubts she'll feel any grief. But it troubles her to think of him gone without her knowing.

The receptionist calls her name.

In the examination room, a thin dark young man in a white coat takes her hand for a second without shaking it and murmurs that his name is Unni. "Hello, Unni," Kelly says. She would rather call him Doctor something, even though his surname takes up a line and a half on his ID badge. She's funny about names. She thinks there should be just a little ceremony involved. It took her four internal exams to get from *Doctor Fisher* to *Susan*. And she refuses to wear a name tag in church. "We look like a cult," she said to Simon once over lunch. "As if everybody's been baptized HI MY NAME IS."

Unni asks her to sit down. He opens a file. Studies it for a moment. Sighs. Closes it. Very gently, as if breaking some shocking news to her, he informs her that she is menopausal. And because she is menopausal, he confides even more gently, bone density will start to become an issue. Particularly in her spine. And pelvis. He looks away when he says pelvis.

Kelly is leaning forward, eyes wide and encouraging, the posture she adopts when she's interviewing someone for *Saints Alive*. "So," she coaxes, "we're going to do a bone density test?"

This seems to strike Unni as an excellent suggestion. He cheers up and asks her to remove her boots, belt and jacket, then lie down on the padded table under the scanner. "Put your bum here," he says, pointing to a piece of yellow tape, "then swing your legs up." He was so shy about saying pelvis that it takes Kelly a minute to realize he has actually said bum. Well, she thinks as she sits and swings her legs up, it's probably important to get the pelvis into the exact right spot. And what was he supposed to say—put your *gluteus maximus* here?

Once she's on her back on the table, Unni grasps her ankles and stretches her legs out straight. He asks her to unzip her jeans and spread the flaps. Looks away while she does it. Then he puts a bolster under her knees and asks her to be as still as possible, so as not to blur the images of her bones.

The scanner hangs over Kelly's groin like the arm of a scaffold. When Unni flips a switch, it starts making a noise like *wheenga! wheenga!* and advances, jerk by jerk, toward her face. She can see a panel on its underside, and a glowing light moving back and forth like a shifting alien eye.

Kelly used to be afraid of bones when she was a little kid. She used to have nightmares about human skulls. Lately in the shower she's started running her fingers over her soap-slippery face, exploring the angles of her jaw, the shield of her forehead, the round balls of her cheeks. She has never broken a bone. She's never even had a cut deep enough to reveal the bone beneath the skin. What's that from, she wonders now—*the bone beneath the skin?*

Wheenga! wheenga!

"This is nice," she says encouragingly to Unni. "As tests go. Just lying here."

"Please." He puts a finger to his lips. "Even a little bit of talking makes movement." She mouths *Sorry* and is still.

It's hard to be still. *Create in me a clean heart.* Breathe in. *And renew a right spirit within me.* Breathe out.

What is a clean heart and a right spirit, anyway? She's been going to church for years now and she still hasn't a clue what it's all about. She's not even sure why she goes. Why she's going today.

"You're afraid of death," Bev said one day at work, shrugging. "That's what any religion's about. They promise you a lot of crap about heaven, just so you'll follow their rules."

Bev can piss Kelly off sometimes with her cynicism. It's not her fault that the nuns laid such a guilt trip on her that she gets a migraine every Good Friday. "I'm *not* afraid of death," she said, trying to keep it down because they were both on front counter and the borrowers shouldn't see library staff arguing. "I'm no more afraid of it than anybody else. And I don't believe in heaven. I mean, I have no idea what's going to happen. After. And I'm not even sure I care."

"Please to be still," Unni says. He must have noticed her tensing up.

Don't think, Kelly, she thinks. *Relax your brain. Just be.*

Wheenga! wheenga!

"We don't believe in our own death…"

Simon. He's been going on about death in his sermons for a couple of weeks now. Prepping them all for Lent.

"…We know, of course, that we are going to die. But unless we have come close to death, have been touched somehow by the nearness and reality of death, whether our own or a loved one's…"

His wife died a year and a half before he was appointed rector of All Saints. "My life changed," Kelly remembers him saying simply when she interviewed him early on for *Saints Alive.* "And sometimes one change can lead to another."

Wheenga! wheenga!

"…even then, death can remain an abstraction. Not something we believe in and know. In our bones. In our blood."

Has he ever said anything about heaven? Where does he think his dead wife is? Does he expect to meet up with her again when he dies?

She would never ask him. Unless. Her eyes are closing. Unless they were closer. Much closer. Than they are. Now.

Wheenga! wheenga!

They're in a car. Simon's car. He's driving. She sees his hands on the wheel. The cuffs of his shirt. Flannel shirt. Red plaid.

Wheenga! wheenga!

They are going somewhere. His place. His place in the country. A cabin or a farmhouse. They're going to have a lovely time. As long as. Because there's something. Something between them on the car seat. She has to take care of it. It's very important.

Wheenga! wheenga!

The scent of him. Smoky. Woodsy. Coming off his red flannel shirt. Filling the car. He's keeping his eyes on the road. Talking about his place. That he's so eager to show her.

Wheenga! wheenga!

She keeps her eyes on him. His hands on the wheel. His moving mouth. It all depends on her. She has to keep it quiet and still. What's between them.

Wheenga! wheenga!

It's asleep. Under a blanket. She reaches and touches it softly and feels his skin sliding over hers. She presses down gently on the warm blanket and feels his breath on her neck. The shape of him inside her.

Wheenga! wheenga!

She mustn't touch it any more. His red plaid shirt, his happy talk, the lovely time they're going to have at his new place, they all depend on her. She has to take care of them. She puts her hand back in her lap.

Wheenga! whee—Chirp!

The scaffold arm judders to a stop just south of her chin. Kelly opens her eyes. Blinks. Rolls her head back and forth. Her neck cracks.

"You may be sitting up now," Unni says, swinging the apparatus to the side. "And you may..." He gestures at the spread flaps of her jeans, looking away.

She doesn't want to sit up. She wants to lie there and stay inside her dream. It was so real. The wood smoke coming off that red plaid shirt. And the feel of that delicate sleeping bundle.

She sits up slowly and carefully. Swings her legs down. Zips and buttons herself. Stands. She's light-headed. Part of her is still inside the dream. It's like one of those early morning dreams you can go back into by shutting your eyes. But every time you do, it's a little more faded, a little less enveloping.

She barely hears what Unni is saying while she puts on her boots. Something about analyzing the results of her scan, then conferring with Susan, who might recommend a calcium supplement. She nods absently, thinking of all the widows' humps she sees in church.

Outside, she steps around the edge of a deep puddle on her way to the subway. It's ten past eleven. All Saints is just two stops north. She would walk it, if it wasn't so cold and slushy.

Polyp.

This is turning out to be an interesting day, she thinks as she goes through the subway turnstile. *First I find out I have a growth that might or might not kill me. Then I fall asleep under a bone scanner and have an erotic dream. Now I'm off to church to get a dab of soot on my forehead and be reminded that I'm nothing but dust.*

"Jesus, I used to hate that," Bev told her once. "They'd take us out of school and herd us into church just so some old man in a dress could tell us we were going to die. Child abuse. That's what it was."

Kelly thought it best not to tell her that she likes receiving ashes every year. Except, *likes* isn't the right word. There's something big and dark and solemn about the moment that appeals to her. She's very aware afterwards of the mark on her forehead, even though her bangs hide the smudge. And she always feels a small pang of regret when, at some point later in the day, she forgets and pushes her hair back with her fingers and rubs it off.

The subway car is almost empty and the ride takes less time than she thought it would. It's barely eleven-thirty when she mounts the stone steps of All Saints and pulls on the brass door handle. Inside it's quiet and dark. She hangs her coat on a hook in the narthex.

There's a little table in the nave with a sign propped up on it—THE ASH WEDNESDAY SERVICE WILL TAKE PLACE IN THE CHOIR LOFT. She walks in her damp boots up the centre aisle toward the chancel, trying to muffle her footfalls in the hush. In the choir loft she slides into a middle pew. The old wood creaks as she sits down.

She's never been up here before. They've always sat out in the regular pews for Ash Wednesday. She can remember when fifty or sixty people would show up for the noon service. But in the last few years they've dwindled to a dozen or less, so it makes sense to cluster in the choir loft. The attendance on Sunday has been getting steadily sparser too.

To pass the time, she studies the stained glass windows— the three above the organ that she hardly ever sees. There's one of Jesus on a donkey, entering Jerusalem while the crowd waves palms. The middle one is the Garden of Gethsemane, where he's praying not to have to go through with the crucifixion. The third one shows him risen from the dead, greeting Mary Magdalene outside the empty tomb. Nothing about the actual death. Odd. There is the plain wooden cross hanging above the altar. But no hint, anywhere in the church, of what happened on it—no nails, no thorns, no blood. She's never noticed that before. She should ask Simon about it.

He's probably in his office right now. Or maybe in the vestry, putting on his robes. It's eleven forty-five and she's still the only one. What if it ends up being just her and Simon? Will they go through with the service together, the two of them? The thought embarrasses her, after that dream. She wants, and does not want, such a thing to happen.

Just then an old woman in a green wool hat comes in through the east transept door. Kelly recognizes her from Sunday mornings. Thinks her name might be Julia. The woman spots Kelly and asks her in a chilled English voice if *this* is where the Ash Wednesday service is going to be held.

When Kelly nods, the woman looks sceptical, then sighs, mounts the stairs to the choir loft and sits down in a pew on the opposite side. She takes off her coat but keeps her hat on. If she recognizes Kelly, she makes no sign of it. *Classic cradle Anglican,* Kelly thinks. *Probably considers me an interloper. And sitting up here a desecration.*

She looks to be seventy, maybe even eighty. What would it be like to have that much behind you, Kelly wonders. That little ahead? But she should talk. She'll be sixty in just three years. She can't get used to that. It surprises her, every time she remembers it. She doesn't care what the magazines say about sixty being the new forty. Sixty is sixty. You can't call yourself middle-aged any more, once you've hit sixty. Sixty is the start of old.

Just then the woman in the green hat looks at her, and catches her staring. Kelly averts her eyes. *Please make more people come*, she prays silently. Doing the service with just Simon would be one thing. But she hates the thought of having to share it with this third party. *That must be my Christian sentiment for the day.* She smiles down at her lap, wondering if the woman across the aisle is thinking the same thing about her.

And then more people do arrive. There's an old man—another Sunday morning fixture. Lloyd somebody? He seems to know Julia, if that's her name. Sits down beside her and says something that gets a smile out of her. Then young Melanie, who lights the candles on Sunday and directs communion traffic. She comes in with a man who looks like he could be her father. They both nod to Kelly and sit on her side of the choir loft. Five of them, then.

The vestry door opens. Simon emerges, robed in purple and carrying a white linen cloth and a brass bowl. He puts the bowl down beside the lectern, folds the cloth over the altar rail, checks his watch and smiles around at the little group. "We'll give it a minute," he says, then turns and heads back into the vestry.

The brass bowl is full to the brim with black ash. Far more than the five of them will need. Kelly wonders where it came from. Years ago, when All Saints still had a Sunday School, the kids used to save their Palm Sunday palms then bring them back just before Ash Wednesday to be burnt. The priest would add oil to the ash to blacken it, dab it on their foreheads at a special morning service, then send them off to school with signed certificates to prove they hadn't been playing hooky. *Those certificates will soon be collectors' items*, Kelly thinks.

Poor old All Saints. So bustling and smug when she first started coming. It's sad to see Simon's purple robe, the fresh white linen and polished brass, all for just the five of them. What happens to churches that get emptier and emptier until nobody comes at all? There was one downtown that was gutted then filled back up with condominiums. But that was a huge building, and All Saints is small. Maybe it could be reborn as some kind of funky boutique or café. More likely it will be knocked down so another Starbucks can spring up in the empty lot.

She's just imagining a wrecking ball sailing through the stained glass above the altar when three more people arrive—a pregnant woman, a man in a suit and tie and a teenaged boy. She's never seen any of them. While they're settling into their pews, Simon enters again, walking more slowly. He goes to the lectern and opens a prayer book. "Our service begins on page two hundred forty-seven of the prayer book," he says. "That's the green-coloured one." He waits while they pull their copies out of the troughs in the backs of the pews and turn to the right place.

"The Lord be with you," he begins.

Together they respond, "And also with you."

"Let us pray."

They lower the kneelers and slump into position.

"Almighty and everlasting God," he reads from the prayer book, "you despise nothing you have made ... "

Polyp.

" ... Create and make in us new and contrite hearts, that we, worthily lamenting our sins and acknowledging our brokenness ... "

It's there. Inside her. Growing. Right now.

"...may obtain of you, the God of all mercy, perfect remission..."

She feels a thin cold stab of fear low in her belly.

"...we are but dust. Our days are like the grass..."

She could be dying. Right this minute. She may have been dying for weeks. Months.

"...we flourish like a flower of the field; when the wind goes over it, it is gone, and its place shall know it no more."

She's going to disappear. She's going to be nothing.

"...But the merciful goodness of the Lord endures forever on those who fear him..."

Will it be quick? Or will she have treatment after treatment, drop flesh and lose hair, go around with a hat pulled down to her ears to hide her naked head? In the obits almost every morning there's a notice about a woman her age or younger. *After a courageous battle...* Kelly's throat thickens. She isn't courageous. She doesn't want to battle anything.

Simon closes the prayer book. They all slide off their knees and sit back in the pews. *Simon,* Kelly thinks, not looking at him. *I'm scared.*

He opens a Bible. "The reading is taken from the Book of Joel, chapter two, verses one and two, then twelve to seventeen."

Kelly pulls a Bible out of the pew trough and opens it, pretending to read along. But she just wants to keep her face down. The words on the page are a blur.

"Let all the inhabitants of the land tremble, for the day of the Lord is coming, a day of darkness and gloom is at hand, a day of cloud and dense fog..."

A tear runs down the side of her nose. Her nostrils start to itch and fill.

"Yet even now, says the Lord, turn back to me wholeheartedly with fasting, weeping, and mourning. Rend your hearts and not your garments..."

There's Kleenex in her purse, but she doesn't want to make noise fumbling and rummaging. She breathes shallowly through her mouth, willing her nose to dry up and the tears to recede. *Simon.*

" ... turn back to the Lord your God, for he is gracious and compassionate, long-suffering and ever constant, ready always to relent when he threatens disaster ... "

Kelly tries to sniff quietly. Her snot rattles and another tear blisters the page of her Bible. *Look at me, Simon. See me. Just you.*

"The word of the Lord," Simon finishes up.

Wetly, she mouths the response along with the rest, "Thanks be to God."

"Well that was cheerful, wasn't it?" Simon grins around at them. Kelly quickly swipes the back of her hand down her cheeks and under her nose. Catches green-hatted Julia giving her an appalled look. Thinks, *Fuck you, lady. And the horse you rode in on.*

"Ash Wednesday is a tough one," Simon goes on. "We get told not to make an empty show of things, to rend our hearts instead of our garments. And in the gospel reading for today, Matthew says that only hypocrites stain their faces with dirt to show how pious they are. So what are we doing here? Is it a good thing to receive ashes on our foreheads or isn't it?"

His eyes meet Kelly's for a second. She knows she must look like hell. Her eyes are still smarting and her nose feels big. He quickly looks away from her.

"When I was going over the readings last night, I was struck by all the references to hearts. Given that Valentine's Day is right around the corner, it got a little spooky." He grins again. "And then I remembered a concert I took in late last year—a performance of the oratorio *Ecce Cor Meum,* by Sir Paul McCartney. *Ecce cor meum* means *behold my heart,* and according to the program notes, McCartney took the title from an inscription he found in a church, beneath a depiction of the crucifixion."

You're so good at this, Simon. You charm your way through a service. Just the right balance of light and serious. The way you charm your way through a phone call. A lunch.

"In the first movement of the oratorio, McCartney invokes what he calls *Spiritus*, and asks it to teach us to love. And in the final movement there is a magnificent outpouring, over and over, of *Ecce cor meum, behold my heart,* in which he makes his central statement, namely, that to hear his music is to know what is in his heart—indeed, that his music *is* his heart."

So what's your heart, Simon? She remembers him in her dream, chattering away in his red plaid shirt.

"The part of the oratorio that touched me most deeply, however, was not the climax I've just described. Between the second and third movements there's an interlude which, though voiced by the choir, is wordless. Just a kind of humming, and *ah*-ing. It's very slow. Very sad. Elegiac. And indeed, it is a lament for Paul McCartney's wife Linda, who as you know died of cancer several years ago."

He pauses. Kelly wonders if he's thinking of his own dead wife.

"So, as I was trying to pull all this together last night, it occurred to me that just as the resurrection would have been impossible without the crucifixion, so too that joyful musical climax—that *Ecce cor meum, behold my heart,* may not have been written, or at least, may not have been written with such beauty and power, were it not for the heartbreak that preceded it."

Well, that's pretty goddamned convenient. And what do you know about heartbreak, Simon? Oh all right, maybe you know something. Maybe you know plenty. But what has it taught you?

"And I think that's why Joel tells us to rend our hearts rather than our garments, and why Matthew warns against disfiguring our faces. It's not that these gestures are intrinsically wrong. But in order to be something other than vain show, they must be done wholeheartedly."

Who do you think you are, telling me you could talk to me all day? Saying things like that to me? I'm not some dog for you to pat on the head. And I'm all by myself. And in three years I'll be sixty. If I live that long.

"So we can certainly begin Lent by receiving ashes as a reminder that our lifespan is limited. But we shouldn't stop there. We need to go on to acknowledge the thing in our life that most frightens us, most pains us. The thing we are most reluctant to face. It doesn't have to be death, though it can be. It can be the need to confront someone and say, 'You have hurt me.' Which is the first step on the road to forgiveness. Or it can be the need to tell someone that we love them. Whatever it is, I suggest you enter this season of Lent with the intention of saying, in effect, *Ecce cor meum*. Behold my heart."

He goes to the altar rail and picks up the brass bowl. He turns back to them and recites, "We begin our journey to Easter with the sign of ashes, an ancient sign, speaking of the frailty and uncertainty of human life." Then he gestures them forward.

When Kelly's turn comes she keeps her eyes down. Does not give him a chance to smile at her. Or wink. His fingertip feels gritty and dry on her forehead. "Kelly, remember you are dust and to dust you will return."

Once they're all back in their pews, Simon wipes his sooty hands on the linen cloth. Then he steps forward and says, "Go in peace to love and serve the Lord."

They respond, "Thanks be to God."

He walks down the chancel steps through the church to the narthex. They wait until he's out of sight to start buttoning coats and gathering up purses and scarves. Then they make their own way out. Simon will be waiting for them at the entrance to shake hands and say hello.

Kelly stays in her pew. That's the tradition. If you need to talk to the priest, you stay in your pew after the service. He won't be long, with only seven people to greet.

Polyp.

Her eyes fill again. Spill over. It's not dying that she's most afraid of. What she's most afraid of is picking out a valentine with a safe nothing of a message inside. Then deciding not even to send that.

She wipes the wet off her cheeks, then pushes her bangs back off her forehead. Too late, she remembers the ash. Now her fingertips are black. She stares at them.

She can hear the last murmurs of greeting. He'll be pulling the door shut now. Coming back through the narthex. Soon he'll turn and enter the church.

She raises her hand to her face. Draws her sooty fingertips down one cheek. Then the other.

And there are his steps, coming up the centre aisle toward the chancel. They pause. Resume more slowly. She does not turn to face him. Not yet. Her heart is thumping against her breastbone. She takes in a deep breath. *Ecce cor meum.* Lets it out. *Behold my heart.* Breathes in. *Ecce cor meum.* Out. *Behold my heart.*

KIM'S GAME

No. surely not.

He takes a second look round, turning in a circle as if doing a slow dance. The light has thickened from yellow to gold. The shadows of the trees have grown together in a tangle. And in the minute or two since he stopped to get his bearings he has started to shiver.

He turns in a circle again, jerkily this time, peering hard through his glasses from each point of an imaginary compass. Trying to ignore the sudden sick clenching in his stomach.

There is no undergrowth. He should have registered that when he set out from the cottage. He does remember being a bit disappointed that the trees were mostly conifers. He would have liked a bit more autumn colour. A crunch of leaves underfoot. Something that might give him the first line of a poem.

Now an old geography lesson from school comes back to him. How pine needles form a layer on the forest floor that turns the rain into acid, making the topsoil infertile. That's why no undergrowth. And no path.

No path. All this time, first on his way into the woods, then doubling back the way he came—or so he thought—he has merely been walking in the spaces between the trees. And now, wherever he turns, such spaces beckon like the paths they resemble. A dozen mock paths. A hundred. Leading out in all directions from his thin-soled shoes.

"No. Surely not."

He shouldn't have spoken aloud. It was a concession of defeat to send his voice out into the darkening quiet. He will not do it again. Instead, he will think. Conserve warmth and think.

He wishes he had brought his gloves. His bare fists are icy in the pockets of his windbreaker. He crosses his arms over his chest, shoves his hands up under his armpits and does a mental inventory. He has no matches. No flashlight. No water. No blanket. No compass. So much for his old scouting motto—*Be prepared*. All he has with him are his wallet and the keys to his apartment. Which is hours away. South of here. Wherever *here* might be. He's sure Cathy must have mentioned what town the cottage was near. But he never remembers such things. Not that it would help him now.

Just north of Toronto, he had said vaguely when someone at work finally asked him where this cottage was. He had made a point of saying he was spending the weekend in a cottage with friends. He had said it more than once. He doesn't often have something to say as Friday rolls round and everyone starts talking about what they're going to be doing.

He chafes his hands and blows into them. Wonders why people do that. All it does is wet the hands and make them colder. Wallet and keys. Christ. *Going to rub them together, Owen? Start a fire?* He recalls picking them up off the green-painted dresser in the little room that was his for the weekend. Thinking about leaving a note—*Just going for a walk. Back soon.* Then deciding not to. Any note from him, however breezy in tone, would at this point seem precious. He had, as the younger people say, blown it.

Do you want to come, Owen? One of them—one of the women—Sue? Jen?—said this over her shoulder as they were all heading for the door. It was an afterthought on her part, he could tell, one of those little half-hearted kindnesses that come his way. And he knew how to respond to it, as surely as he knew, when the subject of the excursion first came up—a trip to town to pick up wine and food for that evening's dinner—that he was not expected to come. It is a lore he acquired early, knowing when to step aside.

"No, no, no," he chuckled, making a shooing motion. Trying for avuncular again. "You all just go along. I'll be fine. Might take a nap." Then he barked a laugh, as if this was the funniest thing in the world.

He was just as glad to be left out. He had not wanted to cram again into a car, packed thigh-to-thigh with people who were all two decades younger than he was, and whose names he was still trying to memorize. The trip up last night had been bad enough.

The worst part was the stop halfway for dinner. The talk was not of writing or even of books, as he might have hoped, but of television shows he does not watch and movies he would never think of spending money to see. The one time he spoke up was to ask if anyone else's food was as cold as his had been. He hadn't meant to put a damper on things. But they had all gone silent and startled looking. *No, no, mine was fine. Mike? Was yours cold? Nope. Sue? How about you?* Then when the waitress came to ask how everything was, they all said it was fine. But he felt he owed it to himself to point out, politely but firmly, that his food had been cold. So of course the waitress said that he should have told her, that she would have taken it back to the kitchen to have it heated up. Which obliged him to remind her that she had chosen to absent herself from their table until they were all but finished eating, and when people are paying inflated restaurant prices—

Just then one of the group interrupted to say they still had a ways to go, so they'd better hit the road.

He hadn't meant to cause any unpleasantness. Be the complainer. While he was getting ready for the trip, shopping for his windbreaker and his pair of blue jeans and all the miniature travel toiletries he was going to put into his new leather case, he had thought up things he might say, little jokes he might tell. He was starting to look forward to the weekend. With Cathy. So when the idea of Kim's Game came to him, it had seemed nothing less than inspiration.

He doubted any of the rest would even have heard of Kim's Game. But that would be good, for once. After all, the writers' meeting they were going to have on the Saturday night wouldn't last forever, thank God. There would be a long stretch afterwards by the fire. They'd be glad of a game to play.

He imagined himself gathering objects from each of them—a watch, a set of keys, a comb, a pencil—then explaining the rules, the way his scout master used to. Maybe throwing in a charming anecdote or two about this scout master, who had been so kind to him. Always sitting beside him at the annual Father and Son banquet because his own father wasn't living—the phrase his mother had always preferred he use. So much more tactful than the word dead.

Perhaps he wouldn't mention the scout master after all. No. He'd just stick to the game. He'd arrange the objects on a card table—every cottage has a card table—then cover them with a sheet or tablecloth. Once the group had gathered round, he would whip the covering off and give them exactly three minutes—he would time them by his watch—to memorize what was on the table. After that, he would replace the covering and give them another three minutes—no more—to write down from memory everything they had seen. Longest list would win.

It's all about observation, he imagined himself saying while they listened raptly and Cathy's eyes glowed with pride for him. *It's the way spies used to be trained. I believe soldiers are still given it as a test. And police. Furthermore, there is a more complicated form of the game. If I may.* He would instruct one person in the group to wait until he had his back turned, then remove one object from the table and nudge the other objects together to close the gap. When he turned back around, he would amaze them all by guessing the missing object almost immediately. *It's harder than it looks*, he would caution them while they all clamoured to be the next to try. *Seeing what isn't there. Out of sight out of mind, you know.*

He knew he would emerge the victor, just as he used to all those years ago in scouts. He was never very good at the practical side of things. He didn't like eating outside and was nervous around water and always managed to come home with a cold. But he was the undisputed Kim's Game champ. The secret, which he had never divulged but thought he might just share with Cathy, was to take particular note of the most ordinary, least interesting objects. Anybody could remember the jewelled brooch or the unusual keychain. But the plain book of matches? The worn and smudged eraser? It was his peculiar talent to notice such things and, more crucially, to remark their absence.

Yes. The game would be his contribution. He had reminded himself of that when they stopped for dinner on the trip up, and it had lifted his spirits after the cramped ride. Even without Cathy the weekend might turn out to be not so bad after all. Bit of an adventure. He had even toyed with the idea of springing for a round of beers. Once they all sat down, he had almost said, *Let me spring for a round of beers.* The older fellow, jolly and avuncular. Yes. That's who he could be. Who he always used to be at work. Sort of a built-in mentor for anybody who was new. Something of a grand old man, as time went on. Until the damned computers came in, and turned him into—

If Cathy had been there, he wouldn't have hesitated to suggest a round of beers. But Cathy wasn't there. So he missed his cue. Started to worry that his generosity might look patronizing. Wasn't even sure, come to think of it, if that was the way you said it these days—*spring for a round of beers.* And then the baffling conversation about television and movies had started up, and after that the business of his food being cold.

At breakfast this morning—brunch he supposed it was, at ten-thirty when he had already been awake for hours without so much as a cup of coffee—he had thought he might redeem himself through his spice loaf. He had baked it, after all. From scratch, as they say. Using his mother's recipe, transcribed in her lovely handwriting on one of the yellowing index cards he had asked her to fill out for him when he left home. He had imagined smiling modestly at the compliments the loaf would garner, murmuring something about *an old family recipe*, finally giving in when they all but begged him for it, reciting the ingredients and directions he had made a point of memorizing, for just such a moment.

But the moment never came. He sat and watched his spice loaf disappearing slice by slice into the chattering mouths. God, they all looked alike. No wonder he couldn't keep them straight, what with their generic names. A Jen and a Jan. A Mike and a Mick. Two Chrises—a male who looked female and a female who could be anything. He suddenly missed Cathy so fiercely that tears started into his eyes. Cathy was as young as the rest, yes, but she seemed older somehow. More mature. Ageless. Classic. Eternal.

Still, he had tried, at breakfast. Brunch. "That's an excellent fruit salad," he had said pointedly to the woman who had just swallowed the last of his spice loaf. "It's fresh fruit, isn't it? Not canned?"

Now, really. What had been so funny about that? Maybe if they'd been born in England while the war was still on and knew what it was like to grow up seeing exactly one orange a year, on Christmas morning, and not even that until he was fully eight years old, they might not turn up their noses at the notion of canned fruit.

"Did you sleep well, Owen?" one of them asked, probably seeing the look on his face and feeling a twinge of guilt. Kind of thing you ask an elderly aunt. And no, he had not. The bed in his tiny room had been lumpy and the sheets damp. But he knew by then not to complain. "Very well, thank you. And you?"

He was just as glad to see the back of them when they all left for town. Besides. There was another reason—secret and a bit shameful—that he needed to be alone.

He hadn't been able to move his bowels that morning. The restaurant food of the night before, the strange bed, but above all the exposed pipes of the old cottage through which rang the sound of every opening of a tap, every flushing of the upstairs toilet, had blocked him. Plus, there was no air freshener that he could find, not even a scented candle the like of which he had at home in his own bathroom. The thought of executing a potentially thunderous and malodorous movement for an audience gathered in the living room directly beneath was simply—well, unthinkable.

So the second they all got into the cars and left, he grabbed the box of matches he had spotted on the fireplace mantle, got his book of Larkin's collected poems from the dusty wicker lamp table beside his bed and headed for the bathroom.

Nothing. He felt solid inside, as if he was made of fudge. *Fudge that won't budge*, he thought desperately while he sat and strained, listening for the sound of the cars returning. He had no idea how far away this town was. Well, maybe he should write a poem about constipation. Read it aloud at the meeting tonight after dinner. *My latest excretion.* Rub their noses in it.

Oh, come on, Owen. They're not such a bad bunch. Give them a chance.

He could imagine Cathy saying those words to him. Dear, kind, thoughtful Cathy. Who had invited him to join the writing group. Had sat beside him at the two meetings he had so far attended. Had persuaded him to come along on the weekend away. Had offered to give him a lift up in her Volkswagen that would have been just big enough for the two of them and their bags. Then had gotten bronchitis and begged off at the last minute.

"*No, Owen, you have to go,*" she had croaked over the phone. "*Please. I've arranged for Greg to pick you up. He's taking Mick and Mike and Chris and Chris, but he's got an SUV, so there'll be room. And he's probably on his way right now. Please go, Owen. For me. I'll be very disappointed if you don't.*"

So he had picked up his bags and gone outside and waited glumly on the sidewalk for—Greg? Or had she said Brad? Not that it made any difference. Yes, he would do this. For Cathy. The unsuspecting lady to his superannuated knight.

A walk. Just the thing, he decided, getting up from the toilet. A walk would loosen him up. And it was a gorgeous October day. A little cool for October, actually, but still lovely. Yes. A walk in the woods. Perhaps a poem might come to him.

The scent of leave-taking—
The aroma of elegy—

He had replaced the box of matches, put on his windbreaker, decided against wearing his gloves or leaving a note and, last thing, made sure he had his wallet and his keys.

Be able to identify my body, at least. Enter my apartment and dispose of my effects.

No. None of that. He must not waste time with that kind of nonsense. He must keep his head and think. What does he have to work with? The light. Going fast, but not gone yet. And where was the light when he set out? On his left? Yes. The light was on his left when he stepped into the woods. And where was it when he turned and doubled back? Did he think to keep it on his right?

He doesn't know. He can't be sure. He thought he was walking a path, damn it. And now he's cold. And thirsty. And it's getting dark. And—

Stop it. Stop it. Use your head, man. What did you learn in scouts about being—his mind flinches from the cliché—*lost in the woods? Well, you learned not to get lost in the first place, didn't you? Always carry a bloody compass. All right. What do you know about being lost already? What do people do when they're lost? They walk in circles. Yes. They waste time and energy going nowhere. So the best thing is to stay in one place and wait to be found.*

There. A solid, sensible decision. Something to give him focus and purpose. He will stay right here and wait to be found. For he will be found. Of course he will. He didn't come up here alone, after all. He's part of a group. They will be back from town and beginning to wonder about him by now, surely. Getting a bit worried, perhaps. Standing on the porch, peering into the woods. Maybe even starting out after him. Fanning out in all directions. Calling his name.

He listens. Hard.

Well, they may not have started out yet. They could be still standing on the porch. And if he has indeed been walking in circles, then he can't be that far from the cottage. So it would make sense for him to call to them. Yes. He would be justified in raising his voice. Under the circumstances.

He clears his throat. "Hello?" His voice sounds very small. He takes a deep breath and tries again. "Hello!" No answer. No footsteps. But at least he has made a decision. To stay in one place and call. Until he is found. "Hello? Anyone there? Owen here. Owen James. I'm over by the—" He almost laughs. "Tree."

Owen James. James Owen. He used to think that if he ever started to publish, he would do so as James Owen. Yes. The poet James Owen. *The Collected Works of James Owen.*

He has never particularly cared for his given name. But it was his father's name, and it didn't lend itself to shortening. After all, what were the possibilities? Owe? Wen? Then when he went away to university, his first year roommate—a nastily clever type who said everything in a tone of such dripping irony that Owen could not object to any of it without appearing petulant—nicknamed him Ovoid.

"Enter the Ovoid!" greeted him whenever he returned to their residence room, which this roommate never seemed to leave. Though he was fairly sure of its meaning, he looked the word up, hoping he was wrong. He was not wrong. *Ovoid.* The aptness of it, the cruel accuracy, took his breath away. He was already thickest in the middle, the way his father had been, to judge from photographs. And his hairline was starting to recede in much the same way. His father had lost his life in the war at the age of twenty-two—*Don't say he was killed, Owen, say he lost his life.*—so Owen had no idea how much hair he himself was likely to lose. Whether it would stop at some point, leaving him tonsured, or whether he would end up bald as an—

"Ovoid!"

"Tell you what," he said early on to his tormentor, trying to be reasonable, "If you want to call me something, why don't you just call me O?"

"As in, *The Story Of*?" the roommate snickered.

Owen endured till the end of the semester, then moved off-campus on his own. Best to be on one's own.

"Hellooooo!" I'm here! Please!"

He doesn't know when he started adding the *please*. At least he hasn't said *help*. And he will not say it. Even though every *helloo* threatens to become a *help*.

His mouth is dry. The light is almost gone. The clenching in his stomach has become an unmistakeable heaviness. *Devil's in the timing*. Soon he will have to drop his pants and squat. But not until absolutely necessary. He will not allow it until the only alternative would be to soil himself.

He keeps his shuddering back pressed up against the trunk of the tree that he will not leave. He is aware of a deep childish desire to turn around and embrace it, his tree, press his face to its bark. But he will not allow himself to do that either.

Cathy. He'll think of Cathy. Play the man for her.

"Helloooo!"

Cathy. Could he really have been so irritated by her the first time he saw her? People do tend to irritate him. The too-large family that stops his elevator one floor from ground and crams in, buggy, dog and all, forcing him into a corner. The stranger ahead of him in the cashier line-up who feels moved to turn and engage him in a conversation about how long they've been waiting.

All Cathy did, that day in the laundry room, was take his clothes out of the dryer in order to put her own in. She was even folding them neatly when he caught her at it. "It's just that there are never enough machines," she said when he protested, "and some people leave their stuff inside for hours."

"Well, I'm not one of them!"

Really, he was only five minutes past the time. He wouldn't even have been that late, had not the phone rung just as he was starting for the door—a telemarketer who had to be told in no uncertain terms to remove his name from her list. So it was not fair of this young woman to empty his dryer. And it embarrassed him to see her handling his clothing.

"No, I can see you're not one of them." She grinned as she spoke and gave the shirt she had just folded a friendly pat. Afterwards, he ran their brief conversation through his mind several times, searching for a hint, a trace of irony in her tone. Finding none.

The next time he saw her was on a Saturday morning just outside their apartment building. She was coming toward him carrying bags of groceries and he wished there was something he could duck behind before she caught sight of him. But she gave him that grin again and called out, "Hi! How are you?" Then she actually stopped and put her bags down. Which obliged him to stop too.

He has never liked small talk. Never seen the point of it. Even the briefest exchange makes him feel as if he is lumbering along in a dance whose steps he will never master. "I'm very well, thank you. And yourself?"

She turned out to be one of those people who take such a token inquiry as a request for information. Nevertheless, while she was going on about her recent promotion, how scary it had been at first but how she was finally hitting her stride, and how much she was looking forward to Sunday, when she would be taking her niece and nephew to see the latest Harry Potter, he found himself, to his surprise, to be actually listening. With some pleasure.

"I'm Cathy Grant, by the way," she said, sticking out her hand.

"Owen James." He took her hand, which was small and dry. "I'm very pleased to meet you. Cathy." And he was, oddly enough.

"You've lived in the building for quite a while, haven't you, Owen?"

Probably since you were in diapers. He was glad afterwards that he did not say that. "Oh, decades." Then, because he felt he should make at least a little effort, he added, "It's an excellent location."

"Is it ever!" Then she started telling him about her previous apartment and how inconvenient it had been, how she had had to take two buses to work, and—

"I'm sorry," he interrupted gently, "but I have to be going. It was very nice to speak to you. Cathy." He was normally not good with names.

Thank goodness she didn't ask where he was headed. Not that there was anything wrong with going down to Harbourfront to take in an International Festival of Breads. It had looked intriguing when he read about it that morning in the paper. But for some reason he did not want this Cathy Grant to know that that was what he was going to do with his Saturday.

Still, as he stepped along toward the subway, he felt relieved by their brief exchange. Redeemed, even. His testiness that day in the laundry room, bordering as it had on rudeness, must have troubled him more than he realized.

Later, when he got back from the International Festival of Breads, which had been less absorbing than he had hoped, he did something he had not done in years. He sat down at his desk. It was actually his mother's old writing desk, with pigeon holes where she used to file receipts and letters from England. He drew a piece of paper toward him. Picked up a pen.

~~Her fresh face a flower upturning to~~
~~Like a sun-drenched flower, her face upturned to~~
~~Her face a~~

He had almost stopped wondering what ever happened to the poet James Owen. To *The Collected Works of James Owen.* He would have been grateful by now to be plain old Owen James, who'd published a few poems. A very few would do. One. Just so he could tell himself there was more to him than—

"Seem to need a bit of help here. Gotten into something. Can't seem to get out of it."

His flushed face poking over some young thing's cubicle wall. Then, a disgracefully few minutes later, "Owen's done it again." Chuckling desperately. "Think you can help him out?"

There had been a time in the office when he was Mister James. A time when a file was something he could hold in his hand and put in its place. When others came to him for help. *Mister James? Where would I find*—And he always knew. He was—what do the younger people say? The go-to guy.

Now, a file is something he cannot even touch, let alone find and open. *Where did you put it this time, Owen?* The question he dreads most from these children he will have to work with for God knows how many more years while the gap between the cost of living and the amount his pension would be if he retired grows wider and wider.

"Well, I believe I may have put it—" Pointing a shaking finger at the screen. "But it doesn't seem to be there now."

None of them knows about his poetry. He would never tell them. Years ago, he used to have the sort of colleagues who cracked good-humoured jokes about the company's poet laureate. Some of them were actually aware that T.S. Eliot had supported himself with an ordinary job. But those people had all moved on. The ones he works with now have likely never even heard of T.S. Eliot.

I feel her smile upturning
At the corners of my own

"Help! Help me please! I'm lost! Please come for me! Help!"

He is weeping, bawling into the dark. He wipes at his face, careful to use only the backs of his hands. His glasses are gone. He tried to hook them off his nose, using just the tip of his baby finger, which he thought might still be clean. But they fell to the ground, and now in the dark he'll never find them.

He couldn't help it. He couldn't wait any longer. And then while he was squatting, he felt something—a cobweb? A bat's wing? Something brushed near his mouth and he jerked back and fell on his naked backside in his own mess. He tried to wipe it off, then had to wipe his hands in the pine needles, which stuck to his palms. So he wiped his palms on the knees of his brand new jeans, the only pants he has with him, and now they're shit-smeared, inside and out. He can smell himself with every breath. And he is so very cold. And his teeth might break from chattering.

Where are they? Why don't they come for him? Where is—

"Cathy! Catheeee!"

It was such a mystery. The last thing he would have expected. For a long time, he refused to believe such a thing was even possible. For a person like him. At his age. He felt so foolish. And at the same time so glad.

When did it happen? And how? He hardly knew her. True, ever since that first conversation in the street, they had been stopping to chat whenever they met in the elevator or the laundry room or the vestibule where they picked up their mail. But that didn't really explain it. *Friends*, he told himself tentatively at first. *We are becoming friends. Well. Nothing so strange about that, surely.*

Then one morning as he was hurrying to the subway to get to work, he caught sight of her just ahead of him on the pavement. He slowed and watched her. She had a bouncy walk that made her ponytail flop back and forth across her shoulders. It must have been annoying her, because she reached back and pulled off whatever was holding it, and her hair—

He wouldn't call her pretty, exactly. Her teeth were a little buckish, and her eyes on the small side and her ordinary brown hair too often pulled back into that careless ponytail. But there was her smile and her warmth and her dear little hand inserting her mail key. Apartment 502, he couldn't help noticing. Two down and one over from his own.

That night in bed he imagined her pulling on her nightdress, folding back her bedclothes, and felt a stirring he hadn't felt in years. *It's all right*, he told himself afterwards, wiping his hand on a Kleenex. *Perfectly natural. Normal. And these young single women. These days. She wouldn't be still—No. Surely not.*

He himself was not completely inexperienced, after all. There had been Fran, years ago. Decades ago. He didn't like to think about Fran. Her bullying, teasing manner that he had always had to be a good sport about. Long after it had stopped being a tease. (*"Jesus, Owen, you are such a stick!"*) He had no idea where Fran was now, or even if she was still alive. And why should he care? She couldn't hold a candle to Cathy.

You have strong features, he assured his mirrored reflection the next morning while arranging his hair over his scalp. *And wasn't Larkin a rather—well, a man one wouldn't necessarily notice? With an ordinary job? And yet he had a lady friend. A relationship.*

Was it really so impossible? He guessed Cathy to be forty at the most. That hardly made him old enough to be her father. Well, it did actually, but what of that? What did chronological age matter? He sensed something old-fashioned in her. Something that might appreciate a man who still believed in courtesy and ritual and reserve. A courtly man. A gentleman.

Cathy, would you like to come for tea?

He would put out his mother's bone china cups and cake platter. Except perhaps he shouldn't ask her to his apartment. Not the first time.

Cathy, do you think we could go to lunch some time? My treat.

A nice local restaurant. Nothing too fancy. Except perhaps he shouldn't offer to treat. These younger women can take offense at such things. Though he doubts Cathy would. But still.

Then Cathy herself, in all innocence, took the proverbial bull by the horns. In the laundry room, of all places.

There was a bulletin board on the wall where people posted ads for furniture and appliances they were hoping to sell. This particular day, he found Cathy looking at a flyer for some kind of creative writing workshop someone named Emily would be teaching in the basement of All Saints, just down the street. By then he was feeling nervous and excited around her, so he started in rather pompously about how writing surely couldn't be taught, that you either had it or you didn't, or at least that had been his experience, furthermore—

"Do you write too, Owen? You do? You're kidding! Oh, this is so amazing."

So of course she wanted to know all about it, and queried and coaxed until, blushing, he actually recited one of his shorter poems, the one about the scent wafting out of the cedar chest his mother had brought with her when they came over from England, and which he still had in his bedroom. His blush grew fiery when he said *bedroom*, but she didn't seem to notice. At least, he hoped she hadn't.

Then she told him about a short story she kept trying to write about her grandparents, and how they met during the war. "My group thinks it's kind of boring," she said wistfully.

"What group?"

The woods are lovely, dark and deep—

Part of him can still do that, can come up with things like that, can think and remember and observe and make note of irony. The other part thrashes and pants in the dark, stumbling over deadfall and bumping face-first into tree trunks. His nose is bleeding. He can taste the blood on his upper lip. He knows it isn't snot. Not any more. He stopped crying when he started to move.

He could not stay by his tree any more, bawling for help into the growing darkness, pleading, smelling his own shit. When the dark finally fell, as swiftly and silently as a curtain of black silk, he heard a voice. *You are going to die,* it said. A calm, matter-of-fact voice inside his head. *No one is going to find you. Soon you will be dead of exposure. Insects will crawl into your nostrils and into your anus and lay their eggs. Small animals will sink their fangs into your face and peel it from the bone.*

But then, from out his bone, from out his flesh, a different voice howled *No! No! Nononononononono!* And he set out into the dark, his hands outstretched like a blind man's.

He was such a bloody fool. Mooning over a young woman. Thinking he could ingratiate himself with her by befriending her friends.

"They're nice, aren't they, Owen?" she said in the car after the first meeting he attended with her. "We met in one of those All Saints writing courses, and we clicked, so we decided to keep getting together once the course was over."

No. They were not nice. But he couldn't tell her that. The group reminded him of the people he worked with. There was a sharpness to them, and a shallowness that made him want to run back out the door. Cathy either didn't see it or didn't mind it. He suspected the former. It was that innocence of hers again. It kept her from knowing how casually cruel most people were. Kept her from seeing the flash of incredulity in her friends' eyes when she introduced him. The looks they exchanged whenever he ventured a comment on something one of them had written: *If I may, I would like to suggest…*

For her sake, he agreed to go to a second meeting. This time, though he polished his wing tips and selected a good white shirt, he left his tie off. And he tried for that jocular, avuncular tone he suspected was the key, the thing that would get him in.

"Greg!" Pumping the startled young man's hand. "Got your hair cut! Good man! How are you?"

"Fine. Um—I'm Brad."

"Of course you are! I knew that! I was testing you!"

And into the silence, Cathy's small, helpful laugh.

Cathy. It was for her sake alone that he agreed to spend a weekend with these people he did not like and who did not like him. In a cottage. In the woods.

He trips. Falls. His hands skid in the dirt. Dirt. Not pine needles. He raises his head. Squints around. Is the darkness somehow less dense? He pushes himself up onto his knees and reaches out, waving his arms like feelers.

Bite! Something bites his hand. Won't let go. He pulls back and the piercing turns to flame. He reaches with the other hand. Tries to feel, to know what's—

Wire. Wire leading to the pinioned hand. A barb. Yes. A horrid little knot of sharpened ends. Barbed wire. He has found a barbed wire fence. He pulls himself up carefully, climbing the sagging wires. His uninjured hand comes down on another barb and he jerks it away, then flails frantically in the dark to find the fence again. He must not lose his fence.

Once on his feet, he works his way along, using the top wire as a guide, trying to avoid the barbs but getting stuck more often than not. Soon his shit-smeared hands are slimed with blood. He'll have to get a tetanus shot. The thought of it makes him laugh and cry—a strange *Hoo hoo hoo* sound. A tetanus shot!

The barbed wire ends in a wooden post. And then there is an opening. Onto a road. He can just make out the edges of the road. He can feel its gravel surface through his shoes. He begins to walk. With every step, he stands straighter. Wipes blood and snot from under his nose. Breathes hard, smelling his smell. His shit. His blood. He steps hard, tramping the road, almost marching. Into the light. For there is more light. With every step he takes.

A clearing. The clearing around the cottage. He has found his way back. The light is coming from inside, through the floor-to-ceiling window of the front room where the big dining table is. He stops and stands at the bottom of the porch steps, just outside the lit circle, where he can see in without being seen.

They're all there. Sitting around the table. Eating their dinner. Laughing. Talking. Passing bowls of food. Topping up each others' wine. Without his glasses, their faces look even more alike than ever. He squints, trying to see. Is there a space left for him? An empty chair? An extra place set at table?

Just then one of them says something and the rest burst out laughing. The laughter comes to him muted through the glass of the tall window, as if through water.

He hears that voice again. Calm, matter-of-fact. *Here is what you are going to do, Owen,* it says. *You are going to open the door and go inside. You are going to smile sheepishly and keep your distance, because you know how you smell. You are going to pretend not to notice their guilty, startled looks when they see you. Pretend to believe their lies about thinking you were in your room the whole time. Taking a nap. The way you said you might. You are going to chuckle, 'No, no, all my fault. Got into a spot of bother out there. Bit of silliness, really. Should have known better.' Then you are going to creep up the stairs to your room and pull off your shitty pants and wrap yourself in a sheet and sneak to the bathroom and soak your clothes in the tub and wash yourself all over and wonder all the time what you're going to wear while your clothes dry and—*

Another burst of laughter from behind the bright glass.

Out of sight.

Out of mind.

He puts his hands over his face. Breathes in. *Out of sight.* Smells shit. *Out of mind.* Blood. Breathes out in a low growl. Starts to sway rhythmically back and forth. Growling.

Out of sight
Shit and blood
Out of mind

More laughter. Owen stamps his feet. *Out of sight!* Claps his hands. *Out of mind!* Stamps his feet.

Shit and blood!
Out of sight, out of mind
Shit and blood! The Shitblood Man!

Stamping and growling, he moves into the circle of light. They could see him. If they looked. *Out of sight!* He unzips his windbreaker and drops it on the ground. *Out of mind!* Pulls off his shirt. Shoes. Socks. Jeans. *Shit and blood!* Takes down his underpants. Dances out of them, hopping and yanking. *The Shitblood Man! The Shitblood Man!* Puts his underpants on his head. Pulls them down over his face like a mask. Hopping, growling. *Shit and blood! The Shitblood Man!* Picks up his shoes. Curls a fist inside each one.

The diners still don't see him. Their faces, serious for once, are turned toward the one sitting at the head of the table, who appears to be telling a story.

Outside, glaring through the leg-holes of his underpants, Owen knocks his shoe-clubbed hands together over his head, stamping in a circle, thrusting his belly, flapping his penis, chanting, *The Shitblood Man! The Shitblood Man!* Faster and faster. Starting to run. Finally rounding on the cottage.

Just then one of the women turns and looks out through the window. Is the first to see what none of them will ever stop seeing, as Owen James, head down and arms out, charges straight for the glass.

Return

THE HORSE IS STANDING THERE when she wakes up. The floor is cold under her back. She keeps looking up and around at walls. Pictures. Doorways. Where is she? She doesn't know this place.

The horse takes one step forward, lowers its head and nudges her slippered foot with its nose. She only has the one slipper on. The other is lying on the hardwood a few feet away from her bare foot. She keeps looking from the empty slipper to the horse.

She knows this horse. From somewhere. She is familiar with the way it dips its head and shakes its mane and blows through its lips. She recognizes every ripple in its white hide, every gradation of pale blue and yellow and grey where its muscles dip and swell.

You're here for me, aren't you? As if in answer, the horse nudges her foot again.

Some of the horse's familiarity begins to seep into her surroundings. This is her apartment. She is on the floor in the hall. Between the bedroom and the bathroom. It is morning. She had just gotten up. Was just heading toward the kitchen to make the coffee. Now she's on the floor.

The horse. It's standing in a field. Shouldn't that be remarkable? That a field seems to have sprouted in her apartment?

Not every part of it, just the part where the horse is. When she rolls her head to face the other way, she sees baseboard and area rug. But when she rolls her head back, there is grass and wildflowers.

And the horse. Watching her with eyes like globes of night.

"That's terrific, Emily! Keep going! Step! Step!" The horse keeps pace with her, its eyes white-rimmed, its nostrils flaring.

EMILY WALKED FOR THE FIRST TIME TODAY! Whenever she sees that cheery note tacked to the bulletin board beside her hospital bed, she wants to cross out WALKED and write in LURCHED. How could anyone call what she did that day walking? Her left leg in a brace, a member of her rehab team supporting her under each arm, her right leg waving like a feeler, making tentative taps on the ground. "Good, Emily! Take your weight on your right. Now lean. Now use your back muscles to swing your left hip. Stabilize. And ... step!"

The horse is calmer now, getting used to her daily walks, which are getting longer. It's been—what? Two months? There's a calendar on the bulletin board, courtesy of Della. Baby animals. Just the kind of thing Della would pick out. When Emily first came here, the baby of the month was a giraffe. Now it's tiger cubs. She's walking with a wheeled walker now, and only needs one member of the team helping—lurch-slide, lurch-slide. The horse steps along slowly beside her, up and down the halls.

You're here for me.

She decides it's like having a new lover. You wonder what they're doing there, what they want from you, how long they'll stay, what state you'd be in if they left. You tell yourself to live in the moment. You remind yourself that too much analysis could jinx things.

There is still that maddening familiarity. She can't ground the horse in any specific time or place, and senses that she shouldn't try. But she does try sometimes, in a forbidden corner of her mind. It's like overhearing your own name in a snatch of conversation. You know you shouldn't listen in, that whatever you hear might throw up a distorted, funhouse mirror version of yourself more true than any you have ever chosen to see.

Whenever she starts wondering where the horse came from or worrying that she might wake up in her hospital bed one morning and see nothing but hospital walls, she repeats *You're here for me* in her mind like a mantra. The horse always hears and responds, taking a step toward her, gazing at her with its large black eyes.

"Use your neck muscles to keep yourself stable, Emily."
My neck muscles?
Every other day she has to lie spread-eagled on a big drum. Two members of the team rock it—first gently, then almost violently. The first time, the horse flung its head up and nickered in alarm.

But it seems to be working. Not only does her neck somehow keep her from sliding off the drum, but it's getting stronger. Thicker. She can feel as much, with her right hand.

Her left arm, her afflicted arm as they call it, is kept strapped in a plastic brace.

Twice a day, they take the brace off and work the arm—pumping it, stretching it. "Do you feel any return, Emily? A tingling? An itch? Let us know the minute you feel the slightest bit of anything that might be return."

Return, she thinks. *As if my arm is going to come back from somewhere. Or maybe the spirit of my arm? Which is off wandering, having left its corporeal self behind?*

They work her afflicted left leg, too. They raise it straight up, while she lies on her back, then jackknife it practically to her chest.

"Does that hurt? Good. That pain is a very good sign."
For you, maybe.
The horse follows her on her rounds. She can hear it clip-clopping behind her wheelchair, over the squeak of the nurses' shoes. Wherever she ends up—hydrotherapy, OT,

cafeteria—she will glance out of the corner of her eye, and there it will be. It brings its own dimension of space with it, like a bubble. When it grazes, Emily can see a circle of grass at its feet. Sometimes it turns and trots off toward a stream she can see in the distance, under a cloud-dotted sky.

What would it be like to have no awareness of the passage of time? No expectations to live up to? She only works at her therapy to please the team. They get so excited whenever she manages to do anything at all that it's sad. To her, the exercises feel like studying for an exam in some subject she did not elect.

"Are you looking for someone, Emily? Is there something we can get for you?"

She always shakes her head. But then when she's alone she glances again toward the horse. *Secret,* she says to it in her mind, and it dips its head.

Now the calendar shows a baby hippo. Emily tries not to think about how much it looks like Della. Della, she reminds herself sternly, is a godsend. She tries once to tell her so, pointing and concentrating as hard as she can to get the words *god* and *send* out of her mouth.

"Squeak bustle?" Della's small eyes get smaller.

Oh shit. Now she thinks I'm making fun of her.

"Did you say squeak bustle?"

"No." Emily tries to sound soothing. Conciliatory. "No."

She can say *yes, no* and *oh my.* Those are the only words that make it out of her mouth without being stopped as if by border guards, who confiscate them and substitute other words she had no intention of saying.

Yes.

No.

Oh my.

She can't remember saying *oh my* before the stroke. She wasn't an *oh my* kind of person. But at least it has an emotional element. She's able to sound appreciative of yet another flowering plant—"Oh *my!*"—or box of cookies. She can sound sympathetic too—"*Oh* my!"—which is necessary with Della, who has to take three buses to come and see her.

Before she became her godsend, Della was one of Emily's perpetual beginners, or PBs. Emily has labels for certain types who sign up for her writing courses. Besides the PB, there is the HS, or hotshot, who has never actually written anything but is apparently possessed of brilliant ideas that will translate into bestsellers the instant Emily finds them an agent. Then there is the TT, or true talent, that she cultivates like a rare orchid—too little attention and it will wither, too much and it will drown. Finally, the perpetual beginner. No discernible ability, just alarmingly prolific and as impervious to criticism—everything from gentle hint to bald insult—as a turtle to rain.

At the start of every course, Emily resolves to sniff out the PB in the group, take them aside, give them back their money and send them away. But she never does. And so, as she did with all the other PBs, she became Della's protector. She scrounged for something positive to say about her memoir, which was being narrated in turn by all the cats she had ever owned, and looked daggers at anyone in the class who snorted into their hands.

No good deed goes unpunished, she thinks now whenever Della comes through the door with her shopping bags and baby hippo smile. Still, who else would notice that she was running low on toothpaste or deodorant? Who else would badger the nurses into washing her hair more than once a week? She can't see Dave doing it. And it wouldn't be right to ask Simon, even if she could get the words out. Simon has enough problems as it is.

The horse just grazes with its rump to Della when she arrives, then trots off in the direction of the stream.

Now the calendar is turned to fox cubs. Four months.

Sometimes, as if exploring a sore tooth with her tongue, ready to stop at the slightest twinge, Emily thinks about home. The small things of home. That strip of counter space in the kitchen that is just wide enough for her coffee maker and just close enough to the stove outlet. The blue mug on the shelf in the linen closet, full of loonies and quarters for the laundry. The rocking chair in the bedroom, so handy to pile the pillows and quilt on when she changes the sheets.

Home. She can see and hear the word in her mind. Feel it behind her closed lips. What would come out if she tried to say it? And why doesn't she long to get back there? Resume her old life? Shouldn't she be hurting? She's not. Remembering things the way they were before the stroke is like remembering a vacation—some pleasant but slightly improbable place she might or might not see again. Either way, it doesn't really matter.

Either way. Might or might not. I live in the subjunctive. Ambiguity is my element, and negative my capability.

She remembers another calendar—one with no baby animals. It hangs above her desk at home and is busy with her own jottings. The deadline for her next book. Dates for the next course she is contracted to teach. Readings she agreed to do. Obligations. Commitments. Responsibilities. They are still there. But they have become as remote and insubstantial as the clouds in the sky behind the horse.

Cards keep arriving, and flowers. The flowers come directly to the hospital, but most of the cards are handed to her by Della, who picks up her mail at the apartment. "Do you want me to open these?" Della asks gravely over each and every bundle. Emily makes herself nod, just as gravely. "I would never go ahead without your say-so," Della has assured her more than once, while Emily tries not to imagine her steaming open the envelopes, reading the contents, then gluing the flaps back down.

Not that the cards ever contain anything personal or disturbing. No one dares to write a plain letter—black ink on white paper—containing, God forbid, words like *afraid* or *angry* or *sad*. The cards fall into one of three categories— pretty, perky and funny. The senders invariably compliment her, cheer her on, assure her they have every possible faith in her. *Might as well be an Olympic athlete,* she thinks after reading the latest batch and watching Della shuffle them into place with all the others on the windowsill.

Besides cards and flowers, she receives visitors. Neighbours, students, colleagues. They come in groups, and stand bunched together as if for protection in the doorway of her room until she beckons to them to enter. Once in, they chatter and laugh non-stop, exclaiming over her cards, her flowers, the size of her room, the view out her window, the lovely grounds of the hospital, and above all herself—*You look fabulous, Emily!* They stay for exactly two hours, assuring her they won't tire her out, then leave with promises to come again soon.

Emily knows that it's all going to stop. One day she will wake to a silence, and emptiness. And when that happens, so will something else. Kind of like a bubble popping. She will fall, very suddenly, onto something very hard. And she may or may not be able to get back up.

You're here for me, aren't you? No matter how far away it has retreated, the horse raises its head to let her know that it has heard.

Dave comes on his own. The first time, he arrives laden with chocolates and brown-eyed susans, starts in gamely, "Hey there, old girl," then bursts into tears. "Aw fuck, Em," he manages to say at length. He keeps saying it—"Aw fuck, Em." It's all he can say. She can't even remind him that her name is Emily, and that she hates being called Em. No point, anyway. He could never remember when they were married, so how can she expect him to now?

My ex-husband is my best friend. Since the stroke, she's been saying that to herself. It's been true for years—just not something she could ever admit. After the divorce, she kept herself cold and hard, not returning Dave's calls on her birthday, walking briskly away if they encountered each other on the street. Then about ten years ago he came to one of her launches and stood in line to get her autograph. She watched herself take the book he had bought out of his hands, turn to the title page and write, *I'm still in the same place.*

They started seeing each other now and then for dinner. He helped her move into her present apartment. She listened to him talk himself out of his second marriage and into his third. There remains a tenderness at the centre of their relationship, a touch-me-not that is strangely sexual. Emily has sometimes wondered if going to bed together, just once for old time's sake, might absolve them. Technically, Dave is the guilty party, since he left her. But she needs a ritual too—some way to demonstrate her forgiveness. If that's what it is. It has gotten all mixed up in her mind, and seems silly to try to pinpoint who did what to whom all those years ago.

But even now, she wonders if they should do something. Make a gesture. Sometimes during Dave's visits she imagines him cranking the hospital bed flat, then either unfastening her arm and leg braces or managing to manoeuvre around them, and starts to laugh. The oddest things strike her funny now. Her wheelchair. The first time the team got her into it and took her for a ride, she giggled all the way, imagining a Chinese empress in a litter. Cleopatra on her barge. And her walker makes her into a six-legged creature. *Ladybug, Ladybug,* she thinks, as she lurches down the hall. She has to keep control of herself around Della. Della is deeply suspicious of all humour.

The only one of her visitors that the horse seems to like is Simon. When Dave cried that first time, it jerked its head up and cantered away toward the stream. Now it just ignores him, the way it does Della. But whenever Simon comes to help with her speech therapy, the horse takes a few steps toward him and stands, swishing its tail. Swivelling the downy tubes of its ears toward his voice.

"Okay, Emily, how about this?" Simon is pointing to a drawing of coins and dollar bills on her picture board. She doesn't like the picture board. It embarrasses her. But she likes Simon.

Money, she thinks. Then, very precisely, she says it aloud.

"Pillage? Hmm. Interesting. I think the word might be money, though."

That's what I said. She tries again. *Money.*

"Okay. Pillage it is. Now what about this?" He points to another drawing.

It's a church. She thinks the word. Hard. Then says it.

"Fools' refuge? Did you say fools' refuge?"

No, I said church.

"Because that's brilliant, Emily. I love it. Fools' refuge."

Simon found her one morning when she was in the rehab lounge, looking out the window. The horse raised its head and focused on something over her shoulder. She turned her wheelchair to look. Grey-streaked red hair. Clerical collar. She recognized him, but couldn't remember his name.

"Emily? It's Emily, right? Didn't you teach a couple of writing workshops in the basement of my church? All Saints? A few years ago?"

"Boatswain!"

"Uh, Simon, actually."

That's what I said. Simon.

"Okay. Boatswain it is. Kind of like the sound of that. Hey, listen—I've got some folks I have to visit in here, and a funeral to do this afternoon. But I'll be back tomorrow, and we'll have a chat."

He's been dropping in once a week ever since. He asks her questions—a welcome change from being told how fabulous she looks—then listens to her strange replies and tries to make sense of them.

"Felicitous intake. This is kind of like charades. Intake. Do you mean the food, by any chance? Okay. Score one for me. And felicitous. Are you telling me the food here isn't bad? Bingo."

"Focus on the can of pop, Emily."

The team have started putting sticky electrodes all over her left arm and running a low current through them. It feels like pinpricks and makes her muscles jump. The horse laced its ears back the first time they turned the machine on.

"Envision reaching for the can. Then grasping it. Then lifting it up."

It might help if I drank pop, she thinks. Which comes out as, "Disrupt consistency."

"What was that, Emily?"

Maybe if it was a martini? she tries again. "Overthrow anomaly?" *I'm just trying to be funny.* "Grovelling for satyrs."

"Just keep seeing yourself reaching for the can, Emily. Look at your arm. Imagine it moving." The rehab team is relentlessly optimistic. They herald each bit of progress like the parents of a newborn and set goals for her. Transfer from bed to walker. Walker to toilet. Toilet to walker. Walker to bed.

"Good, Emily! You made it!"

Just don't put it up on the damned bulletin board.

Sometimes, feeling a bit subversive, she lets herself think the word *never*. The team doesn't like that word. ("We're not going to say that you'll never get some return in that left arm, Emily ... ") She hasn't written *never* yet. She can see the word clearly enough in her mind, but that's no guarantee it will travel down the tube of her right arm to the hand that holds the pen. Still, her written vocabulary is pulling far ahead of her speech. The team has given her a black notebook to collect her words in. It is spiral-bound, and lies flat. She has already filled a third of it. Her handwriting looks the same as it always did.

Della keeps bringing her notebooks, too—trendy-coloured ones with stiff bindings. Emily can't think of a way to get her to stop spending her money. Even if she could form the necessary words in her mind, get them out of her mouth or down the tube and out onto the page, she knows something would get scrambled on its way to Della's comprehension.

"Oh honey, no! It's my pleasure! And you're going to fill those notebooks up, sweetie! I just know you are!"

Emily wishes Della would stop calling her pet names, but can't think of how to tell her that either. Besides. Della is her godsend. Remember?

It was Della who called the ambulance. She had arrived for her private mentoring session—the eighth such series that she had paid for, despite Emily's increasingly broad hints that writing was perhaps not the best activity for her to be pursuing. When Emily didn't answer the lobby buzzer, Della roused the super and got him to unlock the apartment door.

So far, she has brought six notebooks for Emily, none of which can be held open with one hand. They are lined up on the shelf under the bulletin board. Della dusts that shelf with Kleenex, and keeps shuffling the notebooks into different arrangements of colours. At the moment, their order is lemon yellow, peach, robin's egg blue, lime green, burgundy and violet. Emily has made a point, with each new acquisition, of deciding on the exact shade—pulling the word into memory, getting it down the tube and adding it to her list.

This month the baby animal is a white colt, just two hours old, according to the caption. It braces itself on its tall stick legs and twists its head up and under its mother's belly to nurse.

Is that how you looked when you were a baby?

The horse does not respond.

It doesn't like questions. Whenever she starts to wonder where it came from or why it appeared right after she had the stroke, it goes as far away from her as it can. She still worries that it might disappear—abandon her altogether. That would be worse than the cards and flowers drying up, the visits ceasing. But she can no longer keep questions from forming in her mind. She tries to do her wondering idly, fleetingly, so as not to alarm the horse. Even so, whenever she starts, it raises its head and seems to be listening.

She takes a mental inventory of horses she has known. She remembers those safe, tethered pony rides in parks. The last time—she must have been seven or so—the pony defecated hugely the minute she was lifted onto its back, causing her so much embarrassment that she couldn't enjoy her five times round the paddock for twenty-five cents. Was that pony white? Maybe. She can see herself picking out a white pony to ride. She only ever rode a full-grown horse once, when she was a teenager, and was so alarmed by the distance between her stirrup-clad foot and the ground that she couldn't wait to get down. She can't remember what colour that one was, either.

There were the white Lipizzaner Stallions she saw one year at the Royal Winter Fair—a kind of horse ballet. The audience was invited to visit the animals inside the stable after the performance. Emily stroked a few long hard noses. She did it tentatively, ready to snatch her hand back at the first show of teeth. She couldn't get over the size of the stallions. Even though they were locked up in their stalls, she was nervous of their weight, their power.

Pegasus? Could her horse be from mythology? Pegasus was white. And unicorns are usually depicted as white. Alexander the Great's horse—Bucephalus—was it white? What about Napoleon? That famous painting of him mounted on a rearing horse. She can't remember if it's white or not. She could Google things like that. She could ask Della to unplug her laptop and bring it to the hospital.

She wishes she could talk to Simon about the horse. Sometimes, when he is visiting her, she has the odd feeling that he can sense its presence. The horse remains interested in him, coming close to sniff with softly flaring nostrils at the picture board.

Simon has started telling her odd little things about his life, his church. The way the roof is leaking at All Saints, and the basement floor buckling from tree roots—he calls it Revenge of the Druids. And how funerals have been outnumbering baptisms for years. When he apologizes for dumping his problems on her, she puts out her right hand and says, "No. *No.*" She is hungry for news of other peoples' lives, any details at all. She learns that if she adopts a certain demeanour—very still and receptive—he will forget himself and open up.

"I've got two potential sources of revenue at All Saints, Emily. There's what the old guard actually put in the plates every Sunday on condition that the place stays the way it was when they were kids. And then there's what a developer would give for the land All Saints is sitting on. So unless a bunch of critical thinkers get their asses into the pews real soon, my choices are death by creeping irrelevance or death by wrecking ball."

I'd come, if I could.

"Advent obstacle? Now there's a good one. Advent. Do you mean … "

"You've made incredible progress, Emily. The left leg has gotten back some strength—enough to support you. But the walker will likely have to stay in the picture. We're really excited by what you're doing speech-wise. You're grabbing hold of more words every day and making them your own. So keep up that notebook. Now, about the left arm. There hasn't really been any return, has there? We'll continue the therapy as long as you're here, but it looks like you're going to need help with basic things once you leave—shopping, cooking, laundry, cleaning. Take a look at these brochures. Assisted Living is probably the best … "

"Listen, old girl. I'd take you in. You know that. If I was on my own. But … " Dave's not on his own. He's on his third wife. Valerie. Or is it Janet?

"Damn it, Emily, I should be running an old-time abbey—a place where people could come if they needed shelter. But the fact is, I'm running a museum. And I'm starting to wonder if I should just let it die, one way or another. Maybe trying to keep it alive is vanity on my part. Or fear. Maybe All Saints is just asking me to leave it alone. Let it be. Take it off life support."

"Of course I've been delivering your rent cheques, Emily." Della's eyes sharpen on the word *rent*, followed by a question mark, that Emily is pointing to on a page of her notebook. "But the super told me your lease is going to be up soon. So I think it's time we talked." Della stops. Sits. "Emily," she begins again. "I've been thinking." She takes a breath. "I want you to come and live with me." She starts to cry. "It's what I want. I do. And I could handle it. I could take care of you. I could."

Della cries on and on, while Emily pats her hand. She had a feeling this was coming. Della is one of those people who wait all their lives for a disaster. Wait to be one of those people who pull someone out from under earthquake rubble and nurse them back to health. Or just nurse them.

"I could do it, Emily. I know I could. And I'd be good at it. I would. It's something I'd be very, very good at." Emily hands Della the box of Kleenex she brought with her that morning.

At night she lies awake. She knows she should be weighing her options, two of which are sensible and two silly. She should be putting the silly ones out of her mind and deciding between Assisted Living and Della's offer.

Instead, she entertains herself—if that's the word—with fantasies of living with Dave again. Rolling her walker up to her end of the table three times a day. Making cheery, unintelligible small talk in the face of Valerie's (or Janet's) baffled fury.

Or she pictures herself as a sort of modern anchorite, holed up in a corner of Simon's church. Living on casseroles baked by aging church ladies who die off one by one until there is no one left, and nothing for her to eat. But until then, people come to her with their questions and worries and she sends them away pondering her strange, oracular responses.

Assisted Living. That's what she should be thinking about. But she hasn't even looked at the brochures the team brought her. She keeps picking them up, one by one, then setting them back down. They're too glossy. The mature models on the covers smile with an impossible gladness, delighted by just everything.

Della, then. Could that work? It's a two-bedroom apartment. Della's mother lived there until her death five years ago. The bathroom is big enough, apparently. She could help Della with the rent. Listen to each succeeding chapter of her memoir. Negotiate carefully, for all the years ahead, to keep Della from crossing that line between devotion and resentment.

Options.

Even in the dark she can see the faint shine of the horse's white hide. Hear it snuffle softly and shift its feet.

You're here for me. Aren't you?

Yes. It is. And it would follow her into Assisted Living. Follow her into Della's cat-smelling apartment. Be there for her. For the rest of her life. If she let it.

If I let it.

The horse doesn't like that thought. She can tell by the white of eye it flashes at her through the dark.

It's all right. You're here for me.

That settles it back down. She says the words a few times in her mind, soothingly. But underneath, there is the new thought. More like the thought of a thought.

And I'm here for you.

She has to do it.

She opens her black notebook. Clicks her pen. Begins to write. *I have been in possession of a horse that is not mine to keep. I have come to realize that it is now my responsibility to return this horse to its rightful time and place. And in doing so, I set out on a quest. Or I gird myself for battle. Or I begin the slow gnawing away of a trapped limb.*

"Particularity," she used to say to her students. No. *Does* say. *Will* say. "Quiddity. Thingy-ness. Whatever you want to call it. Don't write about 'the man' and 'the woman' in 'the city.' Call them Fred and Frieda and give them a bungalow in Etobicoke. Ground them in the stuff of living. Give them your Aunt Irene's teeth. Your Uncle Harvey's foot fetish. Stop worshiping them like stone idols and bring them to life. Ordinary life. Give them the possibility of stepping off a curb and being hit by a bus. Give them the gift of their own death."

Behind her, the horse does a little dance with its front hooves. Nickers in alarm. Turns and canters as far away as it can get.

I'm sorry, she calls to it. But she does not stop writing.

143

It came to her in the early morning. A memory? Or a dream? It doesn't matter. She just woke up knowing.

The horse, she writes, *is a draft horse. Not a slender, light-hoofed thing of myth. No, a heavy, thick-bodied worker with dirty yellow hair furring its feet. Glue runs from its eyes. It smells of sweat and straw and dung.*

But to me, because it is the only horse I have ever seen, it is beautiful.

I am perhaps four years old when this memory or story or dream is taking place. Young enough and old enough.

Young enough to believe things will never change. Old enough to know they do. Young enough to tune out the boring talk of adults. Old enough to cock an ear. Young enough to love unreservedly. Old enough—almost—to know better.

Hate.

She hates everything. The beige-painted steel of her hospital bed. Her walker with its stained handgrips. The smudges on the walls of her room. The stupid bulletin board with that stupid sign about walking. The same view, day after day, out her one window, of the lovely grounds. She hates the lovely grounds. She wants streets. Sidewalks. Stores. Noise. Dirt. Police sirens. She hates the menu card with its little boxes to tick. She wants a martini. In a bar. She wants to grocery shop. Pick six tomatoes from a big red pile. She wants to make a meal for herself. In her own kitchen.

She throws the menu card down on the floor. Throws her pen down after it. Bursts into tears again. Says she's sorry again.

"It's all right, Emily. Most people go through this right away after a stroke. You just took your time. But we knew you'd get around to it."

She hates their patience. Hates their understanding. They do *not* understand. How could they possibly understand?

"Just cry, Emily. It's all right."

"No! It! Not! It's! Not!"

Nothing is all right. The chemical smell of the place. The sight of her fellow rehab patients—pale as skinned potatoes, slack on one side like marionettes with half their strings cut. Does she look like that? She has to get out of here. She has to get home.

"I. I'm. Sorry. I'm sorry."

"Can you hear yourself, Emily? Your speech has taken a quantum leap. Practically over night. You're starting to say exactly what you mean."

She's not talking to them, damn it. She's talking to the horse. Look, just look, at what she has done to the horse. What she has had to do to it.

It stands in harness. A thick collar around its neck. Leather straps along its sides and back. Blinkers on its huge eyes. The field is gone, replaced by grey asphalt under its iron-shod feet. Whenever she tells it how sorry she is, it lowers its head and shakes its mane. The bit and bridle make a clinking sound.

I'm waiting on the sidewalk. I know without my mother telling me that this is ice day. I have seen how small the block is in the top of the ice box, and I have watched her unscrew the cap underneath to drain the melt water. Ours is the only house left on the street now that gets a visit from the ice wagon. I believe this makes us special. Better.

I hear the ice wagon before I see it. First there's the clopping sound, like wooden sticks knocking together. Then the creaking. And now here it is, coming round the end of the street.

His name is Billy. He's white, but not all white. The long hair on his neck is yellow and crinkly, like his tail. There's more crinkly hair below his knees, too, almost covering his feet. He bobs his head with every step he takes.

Billy wears black blinkers that look like dark glasses, and a black harness. The reins lie slack along his white back. The ice man never has to slap them or pull on them. He just calls Ooohhh for stop and Eee-up for go.

Billy's coming closer. Can he see me yet from between his blinkers? I can see the dark streaks of sweat on his white hide, and I can smell his smell—kind of like dust and kind of like poo.

Billy is going to come and live with me when he doesn't have to pull the ice wagon any more. He's going to stay in the backyard in summer and the garage in winter. He's going to eat grass and the carrots off my plate. And whenever I want him to, he's going to let me ride him around the block.

Billy knows he's my horse. He looks forward to seeing me every ice day. He turns his head around now the way he always does and gazes at me while the ice man gets down, goes to the back of the wagon and finds me a clean chunk of ice to lick.

She has completely filled the black spiral-bound notebook. The team have promised her a new one, but they've gone home for the night. She can't wait till tomorrow.

Standing on her right leg and bracing herself with her left, she reaches up to the shelf above the bulletin board. Winkles the robin's-egg blue notebook out from between the others. Sits back down.

The damned thing won't stay open. Impossible to write with one hand in a book that won't stay open. What was going through Della's head?

What was going through her own? How could she have entertained the idea of living with Della for a single second?

She lifts her inert left arm in its brace and tries to anchor it across the top of the open notebook. Too stiff. She pulls at the Velcro fastenings and slips the brace off. The skin underneath is damp and delicate. But thanks to all the therapy, the muscles haven't withered. It's like a perfect soft sculpture of an arm. A doll's arm.

She drapes it across the top of the open notebook. Arranges the hand in a curve. Clicks her pen. Writes.

I'm patting Billy's nose the way I always do. From the top of his head to the bottom of his nose is almost as tall as I am. The ice man is supposed to be lifting a block of ice in big black tongs like spiders' legs and carrying it into our house. But this time my mother has come outside, and is talking to him about something.

Whatever it is, it makes him put his tongs back down and take his cap off and run his hand through his hair.

Billy nudges my shoulder with his nose to remind me that he's there. He lowers his head to look at me with his big black eyes.

My mother is trying to give the ice man money now. He says he doesn't want it, but then he takes it from her anyway.

"You're just about my last," I hear him say. My mother asks him what he's going to do when he doesn't have any more customers. "Milk, maybe. Or bread. Always something somebody wants delivered. Be getting a truck, though." She asks him something else, in a voice too low for me to hear. He answers in the same low voice. All I can hear are the words glue factory, which make him laugh and make my mother say hush.

My chunk of ice is burning in my hand and running cold down my wrist. I hold it flat on my palm the way I've seen the ice man do when he gives Billy an apple. Billy lifts the ice in his big front teeth and crunches it. Water dribbles from his lips onto the hot pavement. My mother tells me to stand back now, so the ice man can be on his way.

"Eee-up!"

"Why didn't we get any ice?"

"Because we don't need any, that's why." She sort of sings it, the way she sort of sings things on Christmas morning. "We're getting a refrigerator."

Billy starts to pull the wagon. I wait on the sidewalk the way I always do and watch him until he turns the corner out of sight— tail swishing, ears just barely showing above his back.

She stops writing. She knows without having to look that the horse is gone. She lifts her hand and wipes her face.

Freed of the weight holding it open, the notebook falls shut.

"Hello. Simon. How. Are you?"

He looks at her for a long moment before speaking. "I'm just fine Emily. And it's nice to hear my name. Except I think I'm going to miss being your boatswain."

She points with her left hand at her backside. "This one. Critical enough. For an All Saints. Pew?"

This time it takes him a little longer. "Next show's Sunday at eleven. See you there."

EMILY ~~WALKED TODAY~~ **is going home**

October Song

Dear Simon,

Thank you for inviting me to use your given name. (Perhaps it would be more in keeping with your station for me to say, your Christian name?) It shouldn't really have surprised me to learn that no one has addressed you as Reverend for several years. I am permitted books and newspapers and magazines, and I do have occasional access to television, so I am not entirely unaware of how casual the world has become.

But I have grown somewhat rusty when it comes to letter-writing, or indeed almost any form of social intercourse. For decades now, my only meaningful relationships have been with fictional characters. Even the so-called real-life figures in the news can seem to be the stuff of story. After all, I have no influence on them—can't argue with them or make suggestions or attempt to alter their path. So it was something of an event, I must say, to address a living correspondent. And to have him address me in turn, with a small suggestion of his own.

Nevertheless, Simon, would you think it strange or presumptuous of me to ask you to continue to address me on paper as Miss Vipond? It was a shock—albeit a pleasant one—to see those words on the envelope. My first letter in—well, my parents are no longer living, and I have no other family.

Here, to the ones who speak to me, I'm simply Alice. Have been for decades. It took me back, therefore, to see what was once my professional name. To hear it too, for I whispered it to myself. Miss Vipond. All at once I remembered the first time I ever chalked that name onto a blackboard. My hands were shaking. The chalk squeaked. "My name is Miss Vipond," I said. "Every morning I will say to you, Good morning, boys and girls. And you will say to me, Good morning, Miss Vipond." And they did. Good MOR-ning Miss VI-pond. Every morning. Without exception. Ragged, slightly off-key little sing-song. Good MOR-ning, Miss VI-pond.

Yes, I do think about my former students. Not constantly. But often enough. Does that surprise or offend you, Simon? You did encourage me to write about anything that was on my mind. And you assured me that you were trained and practised in accepting whatever you were told without judgement. But you must understand that I have had that sort of thing said to me many times over the years, with varying degrees of truthfulness. Even those of my minders who have strings of letters after their names can, for all their professional veneer, turn out to have an essentially prurient interest in who and what I am. So forgive me if, in our letters, I seem at times to be testing the waters.

I must say it caused a bit of a stir when I agreed to take part in this correspondence program. Why now, my minders wanted to know—especially the ones who come with their questions and write the answers down on their clipboards. (Refusal to answer is not an option. If you do refuse, they simply write the fact of your refusal down on their clipboards, making it, in effect, your answer.) Why now, they kept asking. Why would I finally be taking an interest, after decades of saying no to all their little plans and initiatives and experiments? The ones to which, at least, I was in a position to say no.

Well, it was very simple. They could probably have worked it out for themselves, if they had bothered to try. I needed something to think about. Something new. You can exhaust your own memory, you see. It does have its limits, like a town. Limits you inevitably reach. And if you're never allowed to leave that town, to go to different places, to do different things—well, then you have nothing from which to make new memories. Books, newspapers, television—for all they are my constant—indeed, my only—companions, have an unreality about them. They don't serve to push the boundaries back. So the memory-town stays the same size. No. It actually seems to shrink. There are certain corners of it you just get sick and tired of visiting, so you close them off. And there are others you can actually forget about. Until something jogs.

Which is what happened when I was told that you had not only been approved as a volunteer correspondent, but were actually willing to write to me. *Rector of All Saints Church*. In the city in which I grew up, no less. Such a coincidence. One of those corners of my memory that I'd neglected, almost to the point of forgetfulness. It was a bit of a shock, truth to tell, but not an unpleasant one. Though I should say that, for anyone in my circumstance, any new sensation, even a painful one, is welcome by virtue of being new. So you can imagine how gratifying it is for me to know that a letter of mine will be leaving this place and being received by someone not of this place. Someone who in turn will send a letter back, from a place that is not this place.

Oh dear. As you can see, I am coming to the end of my allotted pages. I am only allowed so many at a time, and I am watched as I write. My minders are afraid to leave me alone with these new treats—loose-leaf paper, and a pen I must hand back. It was years before they would allow me to read without supervision. I could assure them that I would only put the pen and paper to the use for which they were intended. But I learned long ago that trust is a privilege I must earn the hard way, in increments.

Still, I have a week of anticipation ahead! Whether or not you find the time in your busy day to reply, Simon, I will nevertheless enjoy composing in my mind what I will, in seven days' time, address to you.

Yours sincerely,
(Miss) Alice Vipond

*

Dear Simon,

So kind of you, not only to reply, but to take the trouble to find my name in the old parish records. Yes, I was indeed both baptised and confirmed at All Saints. I also attended the church school every Sunday until I was fifteen, at which time I became one of the teachers. I taught church school until I was eighteen and started normal school, as we called teachers' college then. But of course, you must already know that from your parish records. Not to mention the parts of my file that my minders will have shared with you.

If I may be allowed to boast a little, as a church school student, I received more perfect attendance certificates than any of the others in my class. But I really should attribute that to my mother, who had very high standards for such things. Attendance and punctuality—they added up to courtesy in her eyes, and duty and good citizenship. I was never once late for regular school either, nor my father ever late for work. We could not possibly have been, not with my mother there to feed us our breakfast and get us out the door.

She only came to see me once, after I was put in this place. She came with my father, who continued to come faithfully every month as long as he was able to make the drive. To this day, I wish she had not even come that one time, that my last sight of her had been other than her staring down at the purse in her lap, expressionless and silent for the entire hour, while my father struggled not to weep.

Oh, but I shouldn't be wasting my precious paper. I must remember that this is not a diary, but a letter that someone else will be reading. And that my reader is none other than Rector of All Saints Church.

Tell me—for it will soon be Thanksgiving—do you still decorate the church with vegetables and fruits and autumn leaves for the harvest festival service? And are the flowers on the altar an arrangement of yellow and russet chrysanthemums?

I must confess to being a little proud of myself for remembering that it will soon be Thanksgiving. It is very easy, in a place like this, to forget what time of year it is. When I was teaching school, I was constantly aware of the seasons. But then, there were so many reminders, everywhere I looked. Not just outside, but in the classroom too. Little sweaters hung on hooks in a row, then little coats, with boots lined up underneath. Problems with buttoning. Lost mittens. And the way we used to decorate the classroom. I'd have them cut shapes out of coloured paper to put up. This time of year, it would be red and yellow leaves and turkeys and pumpkins. Then, later in the month, black cats and witches. Little white ghosts. Oh yes, the seasons ruled the day when I was Miss Vipond. When I could casually look out through a window and watch the weather change.

Of course, in this place I'm kept away from windows. Under such circumstances, the seasons disappear. Or, more accurately, they meld into one long season without any specific beginning or end.

But that seems to be changing now, Simon, thanks to your letters. Just yesterday, when they were escorting me to the exercise room for one of my thrice-weekly walkabouts, I saw a brown oak leaf on the carpet. Must have blown in or been tracked in on one of the staff's shoes. I'm convinced I would not even have seen it, much less remembered it, save for the effect on me of our correspondence. It would merely have been an odd shape, soon forgotten. But since we have been writing to each other, since these letters—sent and received—have begun to punctuate my week, I have become so much more aware of what is around me. I pay attention to the taste of my food, to the different tones of my minders' voices. I notice now if a wall needs repainting. I can't say I exactly care, nor would I ever point it out to someone in authority. Nevertheless, I notice.

And now I notice that I am coming to the bottom of my last allowed page. I haven't even begun to address the questions you were so kind as to pose in your letter. Do forgive me. I will be more attentive next time. Though I am not allowed to keep your letters in my room, they are kept for me, and I may ask to review them, under supervision, whenever I wish. So that is what I will do. I will memorize the questions you have already asked, as well as any you may ask in any subsequent letters. And I promise you that I will answer them. Until then, I remain,

Yours sincerely,
(Miss) Alice Vipond

*

Dear Simon,

Again, my thanks for your prompt reply, and for that lovely compliment about my prose style. I must give the credit for that to other authors, however, particularly the authors of the classics, who have been my constant companions for most of my life. I've absorbed their diction, and have had little by way of conversation to dull its edges.

I confess I do envy you your freedom to write as much as you choose. And since, as I need not remind you, envy is one of the seven deadly sins, let me attempt to counter it with gratitude for your having written at such generous length. I feel very lucky to have you as a correspondent, Simon. I have no idea what kind of letters any of the others in this program receive. For my own safety, I have almost no contact with anyone but the staff.

But let me get on with answering your questions. You are curious about what All Saints was like when I attended it as a girl. I'm sorry to hear that your Sunday gatherings seldom exceed fifty in number. I remember a typical service attracting three times that, or more. But of course, this was decades ago, when so many things were so different. A woman, for example, would not so much as enter a church unless her head was covered. There were even little handkerchief affairs provided for her to put on with hair pins if she had managed to forget her hat. Which, as I am sure you can deduce from some of my comments about her, my mother never did. Any more than did her daughter.

From my reading of magazines and the bits of television I sometimes catch a glimpse of, I gather that one can now attend almost any function—even a church service—in very casual dress. Blue jeans appear to be the norm, and the only hats to be seen are baseball caps, frequently worn backwards. I would be interested to know your views about that, Simon. Be as frank as you please, even to the point of saying what you would prefer your parishioners not hear. After all, it's hardly going to get back to them, is it? My gossip circle here is rather small.

Oh, but there I go, talking about this place again, when I promised to focus on what you had asked me. So. Back to All Saints in the nineteen thirties and forties.

What I remember is a place of great correctness. Correct dress, correct deportment. Many conclusions, none of them flattering, would have been drawn about a man who loosened his tie before he was out the door of the church, even on a hot summer day, or a woman who wore white shoes and carried a white purse after Labour Day. And of course, any change in the liturgy, however small—even the choice of an unfamiliar hymn—was subject to great debate and condemnation. As a result, church was—yes, a bit of a bore. But also, in a way, comforting. There was a reliable sameness to it that one could, if not look forward to, at least count on.

And all that correct behaviour, all those rules religiously followed, the rituals from which no deviation was ever made, added up to—well, you might say anonymity. A sort of polite mask to put on. Everyone knew the mask was there. Everyone knew the identity and something of the nature of whoever was behind the mask. But that anonymity—both individual and corporate—was something we all agreed to and supported. Without, of course, ever speaking of it.

How the world seems to have changed. Though I have never and likely will never so much as put my hands on a computer, I understand from my reading that it is possible to share the most intimate details of one's existence with the world. I can't imagine wanting to do such a thing. Privacy, when I was growing up, was more than a right or expectation. It was a necessity, almost like air or water. You simply could not live in the world as it was then without keeping yourself to yourself and minding your own business. There were questions that you did not ask, not even of family. And there were facts of your existence, large and small, that you did not impose on anyone else. I remember my mother, for example, insisting that we come and go through the side door of our house, rather than the front door that faced the street. She never had to explain why.

I wish I had been more appreciative of that privacy and conformity, and the anonymity they granted. I never knew how much I needed that polite mask until it was ripped away.

You see, I never wanted to be famous. To be recognized. Known and talked about. That's just the conclusion everyone jumped to. But they were quite wrong. It all came as a bit of a shock, as a matter of fact. The notoriety. People writing letters to newspapers, saying they hoped I rotted in hell, that this place was too good for me, that hanging would be too good for me, that skinning alive would be too good for me.

It didn't so much frighten me as make me feel embarrassed. By the vehemence. The sheer energy. The level of attention. Almost as if I'd been given some extravagant compliment, or some huge, inappropriate gift. I felt I should give it back and say, I'm sorry. There must be some mistake. This can't possibly be for me. All of a sudden I had become THAT Alice Vipond. The one whose name people not only recognized but couldn't say without claiming to be sick to their stomachs.

It's odd, you know. I still feel like the person I always was. Before, I mean. The one nobody ever noticed. Or if they did, it was with a kind of guilty start, as if they realized they should have noticed me years ago. And so they would come out with one of those compliments. You know the kind. Isn't Alice marvellous, they would say. Shaking their heads with a rueful, wondering smile. Isn't Alice marvellous. Always there. Willing to do what needs to be done. Pick the costumes up off the floor where the little actresses have flung them. Sew buttons on. Scrub away at make-up stains. Yes. What would we do without Alice?

Oh no. Look what I've done. Used up my pages, talking about myself. Please write back, Simon. Please do not give up on me. I promise to be less self-centered next time.

Yours,
Alice Vipond.

*

Dear Simon,

Thank you so much for writing back and giving me a chance to redeem myself as a correspondent.

It is indeed, as you so kindly suggest, difficult to reach out to another, after years of being entirely self-referential. Almost like stretching cramped muscles, or trying to walk on bones grown fragile from disuse. Which may explain why it didn't even occur to me that the reference I made at the end of my last letter to picking costumes up off the floor for little actresses would be puzzling to you. Let me start by clearing that up.

But how does one clear something up? And where does one start? Everything is so intricately connected with everything else. I'm sure you'll agree with me there, Simon. You've no doubt given some thought to such things. Cause and effect. Crime and punishment. Sin and damnation.

Over the years, the minders who come with their clipboards have tried so hard to find out just exactly what it is about Alice Vipond. The key. The explanation for it all. Frankly, if there were such a thing, if I myself had been able to point to it and say, there—that's why—I'd have done it years ago. If only to stop them asking.

One or two of them seemed to think they had found the answer (and for a time I almost agreed with them) when I told them about a dream I used to have. It was a dream about being lost. Classic child's dream, or so I understand from my reading. I haven't had it for years—not since my mother's death, interestingly enough.

In the dream, I am, again, lost. Or at least, my mother is. I'm desperately looking for her. Through some fault of my own, we have become separated. I'm walking along a street that is a maddening combination of familiar and strange. My desperation grows, worsened by the knowledge that I am somehow to blame for my own plight. And then, all at once, there she is. My mother. Right in front of me. Not that she has been looking for me. Oh no. In fact, I seem to sense that until that moment, she hadn't noticed that I was missing. She is dressed for church. (In my memory, my mother is always dressed for church.) She looks at me—dishevelled and distraught as I am—and says, rather pettishly, "Oh, Alice!" Then she turns and starts walking quickly on her way, and it's up to me to catch up and make sure I don't lose her again.

Now, I assure you that nothing like that ever in fact happened to me. Still, it was all I had to tell the clipboard-wielding minders when they asked about unpleasant or frightening experiences I might have had as a child.

The truth is, nothing worthy of note ever happened to me. No uncle ever felt up under my party dress. Neither of my parents ever held my hands flat to the stove burner to teach me to be a lady. And I was never remarkable. In any way. At school, though I usually knew the answer to the teacher's question, I seldom raised my hand. If I excelled, it was in the areas of punctuality and deportment and neatness. When captains were choosing teams, they would pick me neither first nor last. And in the school play, I would be a face in the crowd. Or be given a couple of lines to say, just something to advance the plot. No stirring speeches. Nothing that would draw tears or laughter.

The one bit of applause I ever got—and this will explain my reference to picking up costumes—happened in junior high school. The play that year was *The Mikado*. Ambitious project. Lots of singing. Interesting characters. Naturally, it did not even occur to me to try out for a part. But the teacher who was directing the play insisted on including me, giving me a job. So she had me organize the costumes—make sure they were clean and in good repair and hung up on hangers, ready for the next performance. Costume Mistress, I suppose my title was. Or would have been, if whoever was drawing up the program hadn't forgotten to put me in it. Honestly, it was nothing. I didn't mind. Was hardly surprised, in fact. Kind of thing that happened all the time. And I certainly didn't complain. But on closing night, the director noticed. And I suppose she meant well. She was new, you see, and young. At any rate, once the applause had died down and people were starting to put on their coats, she stepped out from the wings and announced, "Ladies and gentlemen? There was an omission in the program. Alice Vipond organized the costumes backstage." Well. There was a silence. And then one of those ghastly little trickles of applause. The kind that happen when people aren't sure whether or not they should clap, but then seem to decide, Oh well. What harm can it do?

So now you know what I was going on about, Simon. And once again, I have filled up my allotted pages with self-indulgence. What a bore I must be to you, for all your patience!

The next letter you send (if, that is, you have not entirely given up on me) must be about yourself, and only yourself. I want to hear about your life. What you do all day as Rector of All Saints. Who your friends are. What you think about.

Not—I assure you—that I mean to intrude. But anything you could tell me—the smallest detail—would have the effect of an open window. Fresh, clean air. And would be so very much appreciated.

Yours sincerely,
(Miss) Alice Vipond.

*

Dear Simon,

Thank you for that delicious treat of a letter! You kept apologizing for the "boring" details of your life. Not so! For me, it was like a trip to the theatre to see the most intricate and fascinating of plays. How I enjoyed the little jokes you exchange in the morning with your secretary, Gail. How I commiserated with you when one of the "old guard" threatened to phone the Bishop and complain because the candles on the altar weren't lit. And how my heart beat like a girl's when you hinted at your growing affection for Kelly. Thank you for confiding that last detail, Simon. Of course, I understand that these things are delicate, she being a parishioner. But your decision to wait two years until you are retired to declare yourself to her gives me pause, if I may say so. Forgive my presumption, but I think you should tell her now. After all, anything can happen in two years. Even our own actions can surprise us. I assure you that I never envisioned the single act that would shape my life forever.

I never envisioned much of anything, truth to tell. At least, I can't remember a moment such as you describe experiencing as a young man, when it came to you that the central fact of your existence, the most significant thing about you, was your relationship with God. Nor did I ever have to struggle with such knowledge, as you depict yourself struggling with the notion of being a priest.

I don't even remember deciding to teach school. Choices were rather limited then, for young women. If you were nearing the end of high school with no engagement ring on your finger and no prospect of one, it was time to take stock and decide between teaching, nursing or being a secretary. Yes, young women sometimes did go to university. But though I had always been a solid student, I was not scholarship material, and my father could not afford to send me.

I didn't even actively decide to teach Grade Two. In normal school, I was told that Grade Two was the level on which I would be most effective. It was never spelled out, but I knew what they meant. I wasn't skilled enough to teach the basics to the Grade Ones, and I wasn't authoritative enough for the Grade Threes, who can be a bit of a handful. Grade Two it was, then. Ages six and seven. Edges rubbed off. Still inclined to obedience. Easy, in other words. Easy enough for such as me.

So I'm afraid you're not going to get the kind of answer I assume you may have been expecting or even hoping for, Simon, to your question about what is paramount in my own life. Though you will get an answer. As you can imagine, I've had some time to think about these things.

I would say the most significant thing about me is the fact of my having crossed a certain line. And I think you must know what I'm talking about. You mentioned that you still occasionally hear confessions. Most of them, I suspect, are about either crossing that particular line or wanting to.

The strange thing is, when we do finally cross the line, what we find on the other side of it is not strange at all. Everything that led up to that final step—all those years of doing exactly what everyone expected us to—that is what's strange. And we can't help wondering what took us so long. It's all so ordinary. Like coming home. Others think it must be extraordinary. But those of us who have crossed the line know better.

I have heard the words "unnatural" and "inhuman" and "monstrous" applied to me so often they have become all but meaningless. If I wish to give them meaning, I simply have to apply them to this place. No, we are not mistreated here. Far from it. Still, no torture chamber could possibly be worse. Pain, terror—they at least are events. Something on which to focus the mind. Something to anticipate, then remember. Make the time pass. But when the passage of time IS the event, the only event, and when all the mind has on which to focus is itself—

But people don't understand that. No one possibly could, unless they had been in a place like this for as long as I have. And so, in the eyes of the world, I have gone unpunished. Gotten off scot-free, as they say. But had I been publicly burned at the stake, which I'm told takes half an hour or so, would that have been better? True, those who wanted me to feel pain would have been satisfied; the monster within us all would have had a chance to howl; and I would be dead. But to what advantage?

Oh dear. I have once more come to the end of my allotted sheets. Simon, I know you will appreciate the fact that I have confided in you the way my minders have begged me to do for decades. And I know you will respect my confidence.

Yours sincerely,
(Miss) Alice Vipond.

*

Dear Simon,

Thank you for assuring me that I am indeed human. A creature of God, no less. Therefore loved by God. Therefore loved by you. "My Beloved's beloved," as you put it. Your own beloved once-removed, in other words.

I confess, Simon, that for the first time in our correspondence, I was tempted to tear your letter in two, hand the pieces to my watching minder and request not to receive anything further you might send. I do have that power—just about the only power I possess in this place—to end our correspondence.

Well. As this letter attests, I did not exercise that power. And I have gotten over the little fit of pique occasioned by your words. After all, what would I expect a clergyman to say?

On reflection, I have decided that it was not your reference to God that irritated me so much. I immunized myself years ago to such references, given that they usually portray me as God's deserving victim, subject to His torments for eternity. Sometimes I've wished I could debate those writers of letters to newspapers, who are so confident of God's attitude toward such as me. Would it not be reasonable, I would like to suggest to them, to see me more as God's partner than His victim? How do I differ from their God, after all? How do I differ from the One who does nothing while children starve to death in the millions, or are violated by men who wear the kind of collar you do, Simon, or are recruited as soldiers of war and forced to kill their own families? Is what I did more or less horrible than any of that?

But I digress. I was about to say that what in fact irritated me about your latest letter was your reference to love. Forgive me if I suggest that it is relatively easy for someone in your position to make casual use of that word. And you are, after all, a man in love, aren't you? And not just with God, either. Which means you may be everything I am not, have never been and never shall be. (I was tempted to add, "World without end. Amen." Yes, I do remember my *Book of Common Prayer*.)

You see, I was never in love. Nor, to my knowledge, did anyone ever feel that way about me. I did get a bit of attention now and then—there were what we used to call tea dances, and I didn't always have to sit out the whole time. It could even be said that, in my way, I was attractive. To a certain kind of young man. This would be the young man who—how shall I put this—needed a disguise. He had some slight physical weakness, some deficiency of character, that, if detected by the other young men, would cause him to be torn apart. Figuratively speaking, of course. Sometimes there would be some outward sign of this insufficiency—fingernails bitten down to bloody rims. Or a slight stammer. Or an unwillingness to meet one's eyes. Usually, it wasn't as blatant as that. He would seek me out—almost as if he had detected me across the dance floor—because he knew I would politely ignore whatever his outward flaw was, and be grateful to him, as he was to me, for the camouflage.

In those days, you see, a single woman had to somehow minimize her unattached state, as she might a deformity. It was such a two-by-two world. I understand from my newspapers and magazines that things have changed in that regard for young women, that being single has turned into something of a badge of honour. I assure you that it wasn't so, in my day.

The men, at least, could in time get to the point of joking about it and, in spite of baldness or a thickness through the middle, still be regarded as something of a prize. "Confirmed bachelor" had a ring to it, and managed to convey a sense of a choice being made. Not so "old maid." Even now, that sounds like something that has been done to one. Or not done.

Of course, by the time we got to the old maid stage, we didn't much need the confirmed bachelors any more for camouflage, for all we might sometimes yearn for them. We had found some way to earn our living, and could lose ourselves, virtually disappear into our work. It was a comfort, of a kind.

Still, sometimes I couldn't help wondering what my life would have been like if I had encouraged one of those camouflage boys. There was a line with them too, you see. A thigh pressing against one during a dance. A sweaty palm sliding from one's shoulder blade down to where a thumb might graze the side of one's breast. And you either crossed that line, by doing nothing and allowing whatever was happening to happen, or you stiffened in his arms and took a small but decisive step back. In extreme cases, you might even remove your hand from his, walk off the floor with an air of injured dignity and sit the rest of the dance out, ankles crossed. I never had to do that. But I did, on more than one occasion, take the small step back.

And now I am coming to the end of my allotted pages and time. My minder is glancing at her watch, no doubt looking forward to her coffee break. So I will write this last bit quickly. Simon, I sense there are things you want to say to me. Questions you want to ask. So I am going to extend to you the permission you granted me in your first letter. Say or ask whatever you wish. As long as you are writing from the place in you that is most genuine, I will not take offense, and will attempt to respond, in turn, as genuinely as I am able. Nor will I ever again consider putting an end to our correspondence. Though I feel I should warn you that you yourself might wish to do so.

Yours sincerely,
(Miss) Alice Vipond

*

Dear Simon,

Well. It would appear that our true correspondence has begun. Thank you for your question—the first of many, I hope.

I will address your question, Simon. But first I'm going to give you a little exercise to do. A bit of seat work, if you will. I want you to write down the names of your public school teachers—Kindergarten through Grade Six. In chronological order, if you wish. Or randomly, as they come to mind.

Done? Good. Now. There was one you hesitated over, wasn't there? One whose face or name emerged slowly, as if out of a fog. Because she was neither the first nor the last. Neither the kind one nor the cruel one. Neither the comedienne nor the crashing bore.

What you've forgotten is that when you were actually in her class, she was your sun. You revolved around her. If she smiled at you, all was warm and bright. When she was cross with you, your whole day darkened. Her knowledge was boundless and her word was law and the classroom you spent your days inside smelled of her cologne. You made offerings to her. Apples you had polished bright. Flowers you had snipped from your back-yard and whose stems your mother had wrapped in waxed paper. But then the school year ended. And when you returned after the summer, you were in the next grade up. Someone else was your sun. Your all in all. And so the years passed. Grade Six. Junior High. High School. Every now and then, in the grocery store or at a bus stop, you would catch sight of—who was she again? Oh yes. Miss Vipond. Look how much older she is. How much smaller. You would say hello and make some excruciatingly polite conversation, all the while praying for the bus to come and take her away. You would mind your P's and Q's. Avoid telling her anything personal, anything remotely interesting, for fear of offending her strange teacher's sensibilities. And above all, you would never ask her anything about herself, her own life. What could you ask, after all? And what could the poor thing possibly have to tell? In time, especially if you caught sight of her when you were with your friends, you would stop even saying hello. You would pretend not to see her. Then tell yourself that she hadn't seen you. As if she had gone conveniently blind. Or become possessed of some benign stupidity that kept her from knowing you were avoiding her on purpose.

But what, you are no doubt wondering, Simon, does all this have to do with what you asked me—that is, do I feel remorse for what I did? A true clergyman's question. And part of the ritual of confession, if I'm not mistaken.

In preparation for writing this letter, I requested to be escorted to the little lending library in the visitors' lounge. I needed to consult a dictionary. I suspected that remorse was more than just a matter of feeling sorry, or wishing one had not done something because the consequences had proven painful. And sure enough, according to the rather dog-eared dictionary I found, remorse is defined as a "deep and painful regret for wrongdoing."

Well. It would be a simple thing to say, in answer to your question, no. I do not now, nor have I ever felt any such thing. But I suspect the real answer is more complicated. Which is why I had you do that little exercise about your teachers' names. The word I kept snagging on is "wrongdoing." Is there such a thing as "rightdoing"? Or is there simply doing?

It's that line again, Simon. It's not so much a matter of crossing the line. Crossing the line is almost an afterthought. A formality. No, it's more a matter of having taken each of the steps leading up to it.

For example. You plan to have the class do a project on spring flowers. So you go to the public library to read up. That's one step. And while you're reading you come across foxglove. Pretty plant. And that clever shape. You've always been rather intrigued by it. So you read a little further and learn that it's not actually "fox" glove in reference to the animal. It comes from "folks'" glove. Folk as in fairy folk. And then you read a little further still. And you learn its Latin name. Digitalis.

That's one time when you could stop. When you are suddenly very aware of the line. But you don't. You take the next step toward it. You ask yourself where you've seen a clump of fox glove growing. Recently.

And that's when you could stop again. Because you don't have to try to remember. You could put it completely out of your mind. But you don't. You close the book. Put it back on the library cart. Smile at the librarian on your way out. She's known you for years and is always so helpful.

The steps are small. Easy to take. A book from the neighbourhood library. A clump of flowers growing nearby. A pair of kitchen shears. Some string. And then just a matter of time. While the bunches hang all summer in your kitchen, withering and greying and swaying in the breeze through the window.

It's time to stop now, Simon. But I will continue to ponder your question about remorse. And please do feel free to pose any additional questions in your next letter, to which I am already looking forward.

Yours sincerely,
(Miss) Alice Vipond

*

Dear Simon,

Thank you for attempting to help me with the remorse question. Yes, phrasing it differently, making it more concrete, does serve to make it clearer. But I'm not sure that it will bring us any closer to an answer. However, I will try.

You ask if I ever wish I could have that morning back again. Specifically, the moment before I began to pour the lemonade.

Simon, I really am not being deliberately obtuse here. But again, things are just not that simple. I might as well wish to have back the moment before I made the lemonade. Or the moment before I picked the foxglove. Hard to know exactly where the line is, isn't it? Maybe my birth was the line. My conception.

The theories put forth by the clipboard-wielders are endless. Did I perhaps hate the children? That's a favourite one of theirs. No. Of course I didn't. Why would I have hated them?

There's nothing to hate at that age. They're all eyes and fingers and questions. "Miss Vipond, may I? Can I, Miss Vipond?" Big heads on little shoulders. And so kind to each other. A half-awake, unseeing kind of kindness. They don't differentiate, the way older children will. They hardly distinguish between themselves and others. You, the teacher, are the only Other in their eyes. And you are wonderful in their sight.

It's in Grade Three that the growth spurt happens. Like an explosion. Some of them become unrecognizable. And they start to sort themselves into groups. Factions. They learn the cruelties of childhood. They see each others' weakness. Ugliness. And they turn back and see yours too. But in Grade Two, all that's still tucked inside. And you are still Miss Vipond. Their all in all.

Simon, it occurs to me that your question might in fact be masking a different question. I do not imply that you are being less that truthful. But I wonder if you yourself are fully aware of the unasked question to which I refer.

No, I'm not going to spell it out for you. The teacher in me knows all too well the value of your working it out for yourself. But here are a few things you might consider, as a help:

Think back to whatever motivated you to volunteer for this correspondence program. Of course, you are by nature and profession a compassionate person. But was your compassion pure? Or was it mixed with—one might even say tainted by—something else?

Secondly, try to remember first looking at the list of possible correspondents you were given to choose from—their names, and the paragraph or two that no doubt followed each name. You would, naturally, have recognized my name. You might even have remembered the news story breaking all those years ago, and some of the things your parents had to say about me. When you were surveying the list, Simon, you had a choice. To reject Alice Vipond, as all the others did. Or to accept her. Approach her. Engage with her. It might be useful now to review precisely what it was that moved you to make the choice you did.

And once more our time is up. As always, I look forward to your next letter, Simon.

Yours sincerely,
(Miss) Alice Vipond

*

Dear Simon,

Although I will keep my promise about welcoming and trying to answer your questions, forgive me if I pose one of my own first. I can't help wondering if you took my bit of friendly advice and have declared yourself yet to your friend Kelly. Again, though I understand the need for discretion, surely you can ask her to be discreet too. If she is everything you say she is, then she will want only what is best for you.

Forgive that little intrusion. I just felt that we needed to relax a bit before we tackled what seems to be the rather difficult task we have set ourselves. And since absolute truthfulness is part and parcel of that task, Simon, I must tell you that I am slightly worried about you. Your handwriting has altered somewhat, and there is, for the first time, something like desperation in your tone. I refer, specifically, to the way you ask whether or not I ever considered stopping, once I had started handing round the lemonade. Your sentence fragment, "So that at least some of the children would have had a chance" doesn't sound like you. You've always presented yourself in such a professional manner. This is the first time you've let that professionalism slip just a little. So I am concerned, Simon.

But let me get on with addressing your question. Which, again, is not as simple a matter as it might at first appear. Perhaps it would help if I were to reconstruct that morning for you, as faithfully as I can.

I always gave them their choice of a song to sing while they were having their little refreshment. I had established a mid-morning juice routine to pep them up. A cup of juice and a song—quite a treat at that age. And that morning, they were unanimous in what they wanted to sing. "The October Song, Miss Vipond! Oh please, Miss Vipond! The October Song!" Do you know it, by the way, Simon? The October Song? It starts, "This is Oct-o-o-ber, good old October, sing, oh children, sing!" I don't remember the precise lyrics, but it goes on about pumpkins and witches and leaves turning and so on. But back to your question: Did I even once consider putting a stop to what I had started to do?

Oh dear. I keep bumping my nose against the same difficulty. Because once again, it's a question of when, exactly, I crossed the line. Once you've done that, you see, you can look back. But you cannot go back. I remember looking at the closed door of the classroom. I'd told them I was closing the door so our singing wouldn't disturb the other classes. I suppose I could have run and opened it. Screamed for help after the first few sips. Maybe, if I had, some of them could have been saved. But again, by then I had crossed the line.

A few of them, the bigger ones, got as far as the second verse before they began to slur their words. I wonder if they thought it strange that their classmates were going to sleep so early in the day. One by one, they were putting their heads down. One by one, the plastic cups were falling from their hands and bouncing on the floor. The juice was making sticky little pools at their feet. After a while, I was the only one left singing.

Simon, I'm going to beg your indulgence. I didn't sleep well last night—bit of a digestive upset—and as a result I'm rather tired. So I'm going to sign off a little early this time. Please forgive me, and please rest assured that I look forward, as always, to your next letter. Which I promise to answer at greater length.

Yours sincerely,
Alice.

*

Dear Simon,

It was most gratifying to receive your letter, despite its being a week late. When seven days went by with nothing from you, I was more disappointed than I would have imagined myself capable of being. I requested to review all your letters, in order to try to winkle out what may have caused you to give up on me as a correspondent. And though I can fully understand that it may have been, as you say, simply a matter of being overwhelmed with work, I cannot help wondering if the reason is otherwise.

Again, Simon, your handwriting is deteriorating. In fact, I'm afraid I would have to apply the word "scrawl" to what I see in your final paragraph. I only mention this because it worries me on your behalf. Are you eating and sleeping as well as you should? Do you see a doctor on a regular basis?

Not that I expect answers to those last questions. Nor do I take offense at your request that we avoid discussing your personal life, particularly your relationship with Kelly. That is entirely up to you, Simon, and I will respect your wishes. In all fairness to myself, however, I really should remind you that it was you yourself who brought her into the conversation.

But now to your question. Which gave me pause, I must admit. Once again, it didn't sound like you. Indeed, I'm not sure it was even worthy of you. However, I will keep my promise and attempt to answer it.

You want to know why, if I was so desirous of killing someone, I did not drink the lemonade myself. I assume you mean, before I gave it to the children to drink. Afterwards, of course, there was simply none left over. At least, not enough to kill an adult. I had measured very carefully, you see. The only reason there was any at all left was that there was one child absent that day—Peter Aspinall. I remember looking at his name on the list as I took attendance. Peter Aspinall. Not thinking, "He alone will live," or "Why him and not some other," or anything melodramatic like that. No, just looking at it. Thinking it, well, curious that by sheer accident—a sniffle or slight fever—he would survive.

Odd little boy, as I remember. Bright enough. But a touch of the fay, as we used to say. I would look at him and wonder if he might grow up to be like one of those secretly damaged young men who used to ask me to dance.

The Grade Twos had begun to notice him too. His difference. Not in a cruel or teasing way. No, that would come in Grade Three. I might have looked out my window the next year and seen Peter Aspinall trapped inside a screeching, taunting circle of his peers.

But I digress. Let me get back to what I know you are in fact asking. And let me address your question by turning it around and posing it to you: If you were given a choice between killing someone else and killing yourself, which would you do? I think I know you too well to assume that, even as a man of God, you would automatically reply, "I would kill myself." Because it's not that easy, is it, Simon? We love our life, don't we? And though you might look at someone like me and ask yourself what I have to live for, let me assure you that I love my life as much as you do yours.

And in that vein, I am going to confess to you something that I have held back all these years from the clipboard-wielders. I know you will respect my confidence.

Once I was taken into custody, much weight was attached, by those who were to judge me, to what I did once I had finished singing The October Song. Once the last child had died, in other words. The official story is that I sat and waited for someone to discover what I had done, and to summon the authorities. This sitting and waiting was cause for much debate, as it seemed to some to indicate a sense of responsibility, hence sanity. To others, my doing nothing, when I still had every opportunity to run away and hide, indicated the opposite. And it was those others who won. As a result, I was sent to this kind of place instead of another kind of place. One where I very likely would not have survived.

But what was I really doing while I sat there, apparently waiting to have my crime discovered? For I was not at all concerned with others' assessments of my sanity or lack thereof. No, I was too busy revelling. Rejoicing. In the fact of my being. My sheer existence. You see, I WAS what I had just done. I still AM what I did, all these years later. For the first time, I knew myself. I can still feel the sensation of my dry lips moving, saying, This is you, Alice. This is you.

Everything that came later—the publicity, the notoriety—had nothing to do with what I was feeling then. I didn't need for the world to know who Alice Vipond was. I needed for Alice Vipond to know.

And with that, I'm going to sign off, Simon, since I feel I've left you with more than enough to think about. Looking forward to your next letter, as always.

Yours sincerely,
(Miss) Alice Vipond

*

Dear Simon,

I had an inkling, when I saw type-written sheets in place of that familiar (forgive me) scrawl, that your latest letter might be your last. And I am grateful to you for giving me permission to make one last reply.

For all my disappointment, I do appreciate your honesty in outlining your reasons for discontinuing our correspondence. It would have been so easy for you to blame overwork, or make vague references to family problems as an excuse. But if, as you say, you feel out of your depth, if the sight of one of my letters—waiting on your desk where your secretary Gail has left it—has started to make you feel something akin to panic, if your work and your relationships are being adversely affected by your corresponding with me, then it makes perfect sense for you to cease and desist.

Still, for all that, I would be less than honest and less than fair to both of us if I did not point out that, by allowing me this last missive, you are, so to speak, placing the ball in your own court. Another way of expressing it would be, you are placing yourself in my debt. For you will always owe me a letter, Simon. And I will never cease to wait for one. Again, you engaged with me. And as long as I live, you will not be able to fully disengage from me.

If I can do one thing for you, I would like to recommend that you forgive yourself. I suspect you're feeling as if you have let me down. Failed me, in some important way. Well, I think we both know that the only one you have let down is yourself. And not by being less of a clergyman than you might like to be—failing to guide me through the acts of confession and repentance. Bring me back into the fold, so to speak. No, that's not how you let yourself down.

Remember my suggesting that you ask yourself why you chose my name from the list of people to write to? I think you did ask yourself that question. And I think you answered yourself honestly. And I think that's why you want to end our correspondence.

Engaging with me meant crossing the line, didn't it, Simon? And we all know where our particular line is, don't we? We can see it. Very clearly. Just a little ahead of wherever our feet happen to be. We can measure the distance between our feet and that line. What it would take to cross it. What we would have to say. Or do. Sometimes we nudge one toe a little closer. But then we jerk it back, as if it's been singed.

And in the end, that is what you did. You couldn't cross the line because you were not willing to do it simply and purely. No, you wanted to carry suitcases with you, full of conditions: I will cross the line only if … I will cross the line in order to …

What would it have meant to you to get across with that baggage intact, Simon? To have made of me some kind of confessional trophy? Get me to spend the rest of my days as your penitent, with you as my spiritual advisor? What would success have done for you? More to the point, what has failure done to you?

The line is not without its terrors, Simon. And it is not for everyone to cross it. And that, I believe, is what is actually behind most peoples' reactions to my crime. To me. Nor do I blame them. It's a terrible thing, envy. It eats away at one.

So forgive yourself for wanting me dead, Simon. I know you do. To stop writing to me is to make me "die" in a way. And rest assured that in the not too distant future, you will see a notice in the paper of my death. Likely even a full-page article. I will not be allowed to die anonymously. Oh no. There will be reprints of the headlines that trumpeted my crime. And that photograph, which I'm told has become something of a news photography icon. The one in which, instead of trying to cover my face while I'm being taken into custody, I stare directly into the camera.

Oh yes, the whole story will be told again. The names of my victims listed. Family members interviewed. Perhaps even Peter Aspinall hunted down and asked what it was like to be the sole survivor.

But until then, Simon, I remain your willing correspondent, should you ever wish to pick up the threads of our conversation once again.

Yours sincerely,
(Miss) Alice Vipond.

Spare Change

Gail pushes her trowel blade down into the crack where the caked earth has shrunk back from the side of the pot. She always repots on a Monday, just before she waters, so the plants will be at their driest. But they still manage to cling. She nudges the blade round in a circle, prying, separating, feeling the snap of breaking rootlets.

She started hours ago with the ficus benjamina. It's the biggest, so once she got it repotted, she could promote all the rest. The philodendron moved into the ficus's old pot. The jade plant inherited the philodendron's. The aloe got what the jade left behind. The weeping fig went where the aloe was. Now there's just the English ivy.

She takes hold of the tangle of stems and gives them a slow, steady pull, rocking the pot, easing the plant out of where it's lived for—

There. Always the way. Resist, resist, then something just gives and there it is, exposed and exhausted-looking on the newspaper. The English ivy's root ball is more root than earth, the white fingers having circled round and round, reaching for what wasn't there. Potbound. Gail's been seeing signs of it in all the plants for weeks. Pallor in the leaves. Water collecting too fast in the dish underneath. Overall droop.

I can relate to that.

And there's Bob. Early today.

Morning, Bob.

She upends the bag of soil and shakes a couple of inches into the weeping fig's old pot. With one hand she balances the English ivy on its root ball, troweling more soil into the gap all around. She likes this part, when she can imagine the roots starting to loosen and stretch and discover.

There. All done. She sits back on her heels to rest for a minute, surrounded by her plants in their new pots. In the next few weeks they'll start thanking her with streaks of darker green, and little celebrations all over of new growth. She gets up and walks stiff-kneed toward the kitchen, careful to shake her feet before stepping off the newspapers.

You should have put down that old bed sheet. The dirt just moves around on newspaper and gets in between the cracks. But cloth has some traction, so—

Bob, if I'd wanted to use the old sheet, I'd have used the old sheet.

She lifts her kitchen shears down from the hook on the wall and takes them back into the living room. That's one thing she's never missed in twenty years of widowhood. The advice.

Okay. Which one? Quick, before Bob can suggest anything, she decides on the philodendron. Yes. They make for hardy cuttings. She picks up each of the plant's stems and snips a bit off the end, just a leaf or two and a single node. That's all it takes. The philodendron will hang sulky for a while, used to trailing along the ground. But in time it will replace its snipped-off bits, uncurling one leaf after another.

Back in the kitchen, she arranges her cuttings like a green bouquet in a drinking glass, then fills the glass with water and sets it on the windowsill to get the sun. In two weeks or so, when white rootlets begin to poke out of the nodes, she'll fill the English ivy's old pot with soil and press each cutting down into it. And there it will be. A child of the philodendron. A daughter plant. Is that the right term, she wonders. Daughter plant?

Bob?

Never speaks up when she wants him to. Some things don't change.

She lingers in the kitchen, enjoying the sun coming through the freshly-washed windowpane. She did all the windows yesterday, getting a jump on her spring cleaning. Once she moves the plants back where they belong, waters them and vacuums the rug, she won't have much else to do. The apartment's cleaner than it's been in years. At her last book club meeting, she insisted on being next month's host, just so she would have to clean again. Shop for goodies. Maybe even bake.

Gail, get yourself a cleaning lady. Rent a suite in a resort and host your book club there. Have it catered, for God's sake.

Back again. Thanks, Bob. You and Mr. Bay Street would get along great. You're two of a kind.

She goes back into the living room and starts returning the plants to their usual spots. Taking her time. Trying to think of another task. She usually saves her chores and errands for Sunday and Monday, her days off, because she's too tired when she comes home from work to do much more than eat supper and read her library book before bed. These last few weeks, though, she's been practically running home from All Saints at the end of the day, looking for jobs to keep her busy. Closets to organize. Brass to polish. Bookshelves to dust. She can imagine Mr. Bay Street shaking his head over her.

His name isn't really Mr. Bay Street. Gail can't remember his name at the moment, but she could get it from the business card she tucked into her wallet. Her five-year-old wallet. Funny, she thinks, lifting the weeping fig onto the fake marble pedestal by the dining-room window. She's started looking at things that way. Her ten-year-old couch. The towels she bought on sale three years ago.

She must be such a disappointment to Mr. Bay Street. She sensed as much, though he was perfectly courteous and patient, both times she sat in his office. "Don't make any decisions right now," he said the first time, handing her his card. All she saw was the thin gold cutline framing his name. "Take a few days to absorb what's happened. It can be a bit of a shock. Then come back and see me, and we'll talk about what's to be done."

She did go back after a few days. He had been recommended to her, after all, as someone who has helped a number of people in her situation. And she did need help. Somebody to tell her what to do. How to live. She was as bewildered as she'd always thought those people must be who crawl out of the rubble after an earthquake.

She wore her best suit, just two years old. Shoes she got last Easter. She climbed the steps again to the art deco entrance off Bay Street. Rode the absolutely silent elevator to the seventh floor. Padded the thick carpet to Suite 707. Politely refused the coffee, tea, water or juice offered by Mr. Bay Street's executive assistant. And proceeded to disappoint Mr. Bay Street all over again.

"Most people come with a list," he said, chuckling, but going a little pink in his carefully barbered cheeks. "Have you written a letter of resignation to the church yet?" When she shook her head no, he tried to explain again how much more manageable her taxes would be, if she simply stopped earning that not terribly large and now quite unnecessary salary. By manageable, Gail gathered that he meant avoidable. She wasn't sure she approved of avoiding taxes. She wasn't sure she approved of Mr. Bay Street, whose entire purpose seemed to be to help people in her situation avoid having to do things that most people—people in the situation she was in until a few weeks ago—had to do whether they liked it or not.

"If you're thinking in terms of a condo, real estate is always the best investment. And now is the time to buy outright. The recession has driven the prices down about as low as they're going to go. Not that you need to be too worried about that, of course."

Gail said she would think about it. Sitting on the edge of the leather wing chair facing Mr. Bay Street's mahogany desk. Clutching her four-year-old beige purse on her lap. Picturing the tall white condominium complexes that soar on either side of All Saints. In the last fifteen years, the church has had to sell off bits of its land. The grassy stretch with the oak trees, where they used to hold the Sunday School picnic, was the first to go. There haven't been enough kids in the congregation to warrant a picnic in over a decade. Gail hated looking out the office window and seeing those big old trees being cut down and cut up and dragged away. The tennis court went next, because most of the parishioners are too old now to play. The same developer who built the condos on either side of the church has approached the diocese about the land All Saints is still squatting on. Gail doesn't like to think of it that way, but she can't help it. Squatting. Like a brown toad huddled between two cranes.

"You could invest in art if you prefer," Mr. Bay Street was saying, his cheeks growing pinker. "Or set up scholarship funds. Look, why don't you just take a good long trip somewhere? That might help you come to grips with what's happened. Put things in perspective."

Gail said she'd think about it.

The plants are all back in place, looking good in the April light. She gets the watering can from the storage closet and fills it from the bathtub tap. Goes from plant to plant, giving each one a bit less than it normally gets. There's moisture enough in the new soil.

Whatever you do, don't feed them. The roots—

"I know, Bob. The roots are torn, and plant food is acidic and it will burn."

She stands still, watering can poised over the jade plant. Is that the first time she's answered him out loud? Or has she been doing it all along? She wets down the jade and moves on to the aloe.

The thing about going crazy, if that's what she's doing, is that you're not supposed to think you are. You're supposed to think everybody else is nuts, and you're the only sane person left. All right, she knows it isn't normal to suddenly start hearing your long-dead husband in your head as if he was beside you in the room. But at the same time, it all makes perfect sense to her. It feels completely natural. Not scary or spooky at all.

One morning, she clapped her hand down on the alarm, swung her feet out onto the floor and knew that Bob was there.

Not that she could see him or anything. *Less alone* was the phrase she settled on to describe it. She just felt less alone. And hearing his voice in her head was the same as imagining it, except she never knew what he was going to come out with.

Bob didn't explain himself, why he had waited twenty years to come back and haunt her, if that's what's happening, and she didn't demand an explanation. But it's been a few weeks now, and she can't help coming up with some theories. He showed up right after everything changed. So maybe she's experiencing—what did that shrink call it, the one she went to see a few weeks after Bob's funeral, because suddenly she couldn't make decisions, not even which shoes to put on? An adjustment reaction. Was that it? Or was it a reaction adjustment?

Bob?

No answer. Maybe he wants her to talk to him out loud all the time now. Or maybe he's sulking because she snapped at him.

She's done watering the plants. Gathering up the newspapers and vacuuming the rug will take fifteen minutes, tops. Then what? If most of her friends weren't at work, she could call somebody up, suggest lunch and a movie. That's the trouble with having Sundays and Mondays off, but that's what you get if you work in a church office.

She had always hated working Saturdays, right from the first. Beggars can't be choosers, though, and it wasn't as if they didn't need her. There used to be more drop-ins and calls to the office on Saturday than through the whole rest of the week.

She's not sure when things started to change. But the day came, late last year, when Simon had to break it to her that they might be cutting her Saturday hours. That night, instead of eating dinner she sat with a pencil and listed her expenses. Worked out how much of a pay cut it would be. Wondered how she would manage.

She picks up each sheet of newspaper in turn, shaking dirt onto the next one before folding it. She was so scared, just a few months ago, sitting right over there at the dining room table with her pencil and pad of foolscap. They haven't actually gotten around to cutting her hours. But it's just a matter of time. The church can hardly afford to pay her for four days a week, let alone five. And all they need her for now on Saturdays is to open up at eight to let the volunteer Lunch Ladies in, then again at nine-thirty for the guests.

She gathers up the last sheet of newspaper, the one with all the dirt, and carries it carefully into the kitchen, where she shakes it into the garbage. Guests. That's what everybody's supposed to call them. She bets the Lunch Ladies even think of them that way. And maybe if she was a nicer person, she would too. But if you're a guest somewhere, doesn't it mean that you want to be there, that you've chosen to come? Who wakes up in the morning and thinks, *Hey, what I'd really like is to be down and out and have to rely on a free lunch at a church.* She should feel sorry for them, at least. But on Saturdays she shuts the office door and works at the computer with her back turned. The smell of food and the clink of cutlery still come through from the room across the hall.

"It's our new congregation, Gail." Simon drops in sometimes on Saturdays to help. "We might as well do this on a Sunday. We'd get a bigger turnout."

But no more envelopes in the plates. She would never actually come out with that, even though she knows he's thinking the same thing. It's academic anyway. The old guard parishioners—the ones with the money—would raise hell if All Saints moved the lunch to Sunday. Her final task every Saturday is to spray Febreze around once everybody's left. The room they do the lunch in is the same one they serve coffee in after the Sunday service. Some people have complained to her about the smells—cooking smells, as they always hasten to clarify.

Just quit. It's not your problem anymore. Let somebody else spray the Febreze.

"Bob, there's more to my job than air freshener." She's glad they're talking again. But is she going to start answering him out loud on the bus? At work? And why is she just standing here? She folds the last sheet of newspaper and puts it in the recycle bin. All that's left is the vacuuming. But then what?

You don't have to be the best little girl in the world, Gail. You haven't done anything wrong.

"I know, Bob. I know. It's just that, unless I'm up and doing something, making myself useful, I feel guilty. As soon as I sit down and try to relax, all the stuff I could be doing or should be doing crowds into my head and starts yelling at me. And there's only one way to make it stop."

When she finishes vacuuming, she replaces the bag, even though the old one's not even half-full. Then she has to vacuum again, because replacing the bag makes dust. Everything makes dust, she thinks, wheeling the vacuum cleaner back toward the hall closet. Would she have to dust and vacuum in a brand new condo? Maybe somebody else comes in and does it. Maybe they have—what do you call it—concierge services.

Now you're talking.

"Bob, just leave it alone for a bit. Okay? I'm busy. I have to …" She looks around. Sees the crystal cabinet. "I have to polish the crystal."

She starts taking the goblets out of the cabinet and setting them on the dining-room table. They look like a little long-necked audience gathering to watch her—all clear, bland faces. When was the last time she used any of them? Book club, four months ago. They always have wine at the meetings. But she hasn't given a full out dinner party in years. The last time, even though Bob had been dead for ages, it still felt strange not to have him there before the guests arrived, telling her not to fuss, that everything would be fine. *Bob*, she always used to say, *we all have a purpose. I was put on this earth to fuss.* Then he'd pat her rear or squeeze her breast, saying, *I know why you were put on this earth, Baby,* and she would laugh and fight him off, struggling to get out of her apron because the doorbell was ringing.

She feather dusts the empty shelves of the crystal cabinet, erasing the pattern of dark circles the goblet bottoms have left. Then she takes a clean tea towel and polishes every piece, biggest to smallest. Red wine, white wine, sherry, liqueur.

She enjoys the squeak of the polishing and holds each piece up to the sunlight, imagining that it appreciates the attention.

She tried to start dating again, a year or so after Bob died. Her friends kept setting her up with this divorced brother-in-law or that single neighbour they were pretty sure wasn't gay. It wasn't that the men were complete jerks. They were nice enough. But they were—Gail had searched her mind for ages for the right word. Closed. Yes. And so was she. Something had closed over. Whenever she tried to imagine anything happening between her and the latest one, she saw the two of them bumping and rolling apart, like billiard balls.

With Bob, she could hardly tell where she ended and he began. The way they finished each other's sentences. And those episodes of her life that seemed to belong to him, that only he could report on. Like the time they went to buy a car, and got one of those bullshit salesmen who sat them down and leaned in all close and intimate and said that sure, he could just go ahead and sell them a car, but that wasn't why he was there. Bob loved telling the next bit, how Gail had leaned in all close and intimate herself, and said that sure, they could just sit there and listen to him not sell them a car, but that wasn't why *they* were there. Then she had gotten up and left, without even looking back to see if Bob was following her.

Gail has only tried to tell that story once by herself. It made her feel as if she was stealing Bob's material. She isn't much good at telling stories to begin with, and she kept waiting for him to interrupt. Remind her of bits she had left out.

One flesh. That's what they were. As if he did the breathing in and she did the breathing out. Or they only had one heartbeat, and he was *lub* and she was *dub*.

She gave up on dating. Told herself, Okay, that was it. You've had your big fat love. Anything else is bound to be thin and stringy.

She finishes polishing the crystal and puts it all back, trying not to clink each piece against its close-packed neighbours. The cabinet tinkles as if full of bells when she closes the door. Silence. Nothing left to do. And the rest of the day still ahead of her.

Maybe she should tell Simon about what's been happening to her. He is her employer, after all. He's bound to have noticed how driven she is lately, how she practically embraces anybody who comes through the church-office door these days, even the PPA's. Perpetual Pains in the Ass, as she explained to him when he first arrived. She's seen three rectors come and go, and she's tested each one with PPA. Simon laughed. And once he even deadpanned the code back to her, in the office, within hearing of a parishioner.

So maybe she should talk to him. Not make a big deal of it, not book an appointment or anything. Just, one morning when he comes down into the office to check his mail and touch base with her the way he does, say something like, "By the way, Bob's back." To which, if he's a little distracted, he might say, "Oh? Back from where?" To which she would not say, "The dead," but just wait a few seconds for the penny to drop.

No. She would never do that to Simon. It's still early days for him—not even five years. She's an old hand by comparison. He's probably still finding bits of Ruth here and there. A box in the back of a bathroom cupboard with one tampon still in it. A single earring down the back of a couch. They take their time taking their leave, the dead.

The first laundry she made herself do after Bob died, she found a pair of his shorts and two of his socks. He'd died early in the week, so there were no shirts or pants. She washed them and dried them and then wondered what to do with them. They weren't the kind of thing you donate. But they were too new to throw away. And she didn't want to keep them either. She had an old plaid shirt of his that she was sleeping in. But she couldn't imagine herself pulling his shorts on. Flopping around in his big old socks.

She put them in a shoebox. Watched herself cutting brown paper from the roll she always kept on hand. Wrapping it round. Tucking and taping. She wrote Bob's name and their— her—address on it. She was still in the house then. She took the wrapped shoebox to the post office and paid to send it regular mail. Three days later, the mailman knocked on the front door.

She accepted the package, closed the door, then went and sat down in Bob's easy chair. After an hour or two she took a black magic marker and wrote DECEASED across Bob's name. Then she went down into the basement to get the garden spade.

She hasn't thought about that shoebox in years. She wonders if the people who bought the house ever dug up the petunia bed and thought, *What the hell?*

Up till now, that's qualified as the craziest she's ever been. Maybe she should tell Simon about it, as a sort of preamble to telling him about hearing Bob in her head, giving her advice. Or maybe she wouldn't need any kind of preamble. Simon told her once that he wished he had a buck for every time somebody had pleaded with him not to tell anybody what they were about to tell him, because it sounded so insane. Then, when they finally came out with their awful secret, it was all he could do not to move his lips along with them. They were sitting beside a loved one's hospital bed, so the story went. Or they were at a friend's funeral. Or they were just riding the subway, worrying themselves sick about maybe losing their job. And all at once they felt a presence. They didn't see or hear anything. It wasn't like a ghost. It was just someone there. And somehow they knew that, whoever or whatever it was, it was on their side. Rooting for them. But please, please, don't tell anybody, because people would think they were nuts.

"I'm their priest, Gail. And they're begging me to try to understand that they may have experienced something of a spiritual nature. They're practically apologizing to me. As if what happened to them has nothing to do with what I've been going on and on about, week after week."

Gail would have to explain that what's been happening to her isn't quite in the same league. And before she even got to the part about Bob, she'd have to explain the context. The backstory, as they say.

She checks her watch. She's been standing in the middle of the living-room rug for twenty minutes. Staring into space.

This can't be the way it's supposed to be. There must be something the matter with her. Why isn't she out shopping in the kind of store she's always hurried past without even bothering to look in the window?

That's more like it, Gail.

"I just can't take it in, Bob."

She never really believed she would win, even though she's played the same numbers every week for years, and always asks the same nice young Korean man in the variety store on the corner to check her ticket. She's watched that young man grow up behind the counter of his parents' store. Maybe that's why it felt so odd—wrong, somehow—to hear the special little tune that plays when there's a big win, and to see him look at the machine, then at the ticket, then finally at her. As if he'd never seen her before.

She still hasn't told anybody. The only ones who know are Bob, Mr. Bay Street and the nice young Korean man. She hasn't gone back to his store since that day. Of course, the lottery corporation knows too. They charged her ten percent as a penalty because she refused to be photographed or to have her name published in the papers. She could tell they expected her to cave in when she heard how much she would be losing. But losing was as unreal to her as winning. If she tried to write down the amount on the cheque they gave her, she would probably have gotten the number of zeroes wrong.

She has to get out. Breathe fresh air. Get some exercise. Right. Like she hasn't been working her ass off all morning.

You could join a health club, Gail. Work out on those machines they have. Sit and sip margaritas in one of those hot tubs.

"Right, Bob," she says, pulling on her jacket and picking up her purse. "First take the weight off. Then put it back on. Sounds like a plan."

Outside it's a typical April day, a bit raw and smelling of mud. She heads up the street, taking long strides, trying to look as if she knows where she's going. She passes the cleaners. Does she have anything to pick up? No. And it's too soon to take her winter coat in, even though it could use a clean. April can always turn nasty.

Gail. Take your coat to the cleaners. If it starts to snow again, buy another coat.

"I'm not going back for it now," she mutters, and keeps walking. She hates to admit it, but Bob has a point. She doesn't know how to be rich. Now that she can have anything she wants, she can't seem to want anything at all.

But she's never been good at wanting things. Back before everything changed, when she used to think about how it would be if she won a fortune, all she could imagine doing was sleeping in. Not having to rush to get to work. Not having to work at all. Okay. So now she doesn't have to work. So why does the thought of quitting her job—

Every morning when she switches on the office light, the pieces of her day are waiting for her to assemble them. She gets the phone. Books rooms. Does the final tweak on *Saints Alive,* then prints it and posts it online. She revises the liturgical guide. Opens and files the paper mail. Replies to the e-mail. Answers questions when people drop in. Then there are the pew statistics to update, and the website to maintain. "I am the paperweight on the desk of life," she intones whenever Simon kids her about maybe drawing chalk circles around her stapler and her scissors. "Nobody notices me till there's a high wind. Then they want me to be everywhere at once." Still, nobody's indispensible. She could train a new person. Somebody younger. Just out of school. Up to their eyeballs in debt.

Except—

She stops in her tracks outside the grocery store. Damn it, she doesn't *want* to quit. Not that she loves her job. It's not about love. Or is it? Isn't love a matter of doing? Paying attention? The way she takes care of her plants? How often did she just stand still and *feel* herself loving Bob?

Not often enough.

She pulls a grocery cart from the line in the parking lot and wheels it through the IN door. She doesn't think she actually needs anything, but maybe once she's inside something or other will jog her memory.

There's another food drive on. She takes a brown paper bag from the stack, punches it open and makes a mental list: Dried pasta. Rice. Beans. Canned fruit. Canned vegetables. Peanut butter. Kraft dinner. Pabulum.

She turns first into the condiments aisle, looking for peanut butter. There is one part of her job that she loves, she reminds herself. She lifts down a jumbo jar of smooth and creamy. Puts it back. Takes a jar of chunky instead. More nourishing. She loves maintaining the archives. Scanning the old church records into the computer. Baptismal and marriage certificates going brown around the edges. Black and white photographs of Sunday School picnics and the Ladies' Auxiliary through the decades. Records of funerals and burials going back to 1858, when the place was built. She pauses, then reaches again for the creamy and puts it in the bag beside the chunky. What the hell. She can afford two jars of peanut butter. She wheels her cart out of condiments and into the canned goods aisle. She's very tender with those old bits of paper and film, letting them waft down onto the glass of the printer, then not quite closing the cover before pressing SCAN. All those people being born and getting married and having kids and dying. Touching base with All Saints at every milestone. Coming in, going out. As if the place was breathing. She lifts down a can of sliced peaches. Then one of mixed peas and carrots. The place *is* breathing, damn it. Maybe a bit shallowly, these days. But the little brown toad isn't dead yet. She reaches for a can of beans.

Still, it's never occurred to her to show up on a Sunday morning. Or go to any other church. People assume she must be religious because she works at All Saints. If they ask, she tells them she's United. Which is true enough. Bob was, and they used to go together, at Christmas and Easter. But after he died, the thought of singing *All Things Bright and Beautiful* made her want to throw up.

Kraft Dinner. Two packages. Why not?

That's right, Gail. Go wild.

When the food-bank bag is full, she settles it near the back end of her grocery cart and heads to the produce section. She doesn't actually need any fresh fruit or vegetables, but you can never have too much of that stuff. She can always blanch and freeze whatever she doesn't—

Dwayne?

It is Dwayne. Over there by the banks of lettuce with a shopping cart. Holding a list and frowning at it.

She stands very still, watching him the way she would some wild animal she had come across in a park. She's only ever seen him before at the Saturday lunch. According to the Lunch Ladies, he always looks in on the kitchen to make sure they're all wearing their aprons. Once one of them wasn't, and it set him off on a rant about how she was going to *spill soup all down her clean clothes!* He reminds the other guests to take their plates back to the counter, and barks "Quiet!" at anybody who's getting agitated.

Now he's picking up a head of iceberg lettuce. Turning it in one hand. Examining it critically.

Alas, poor Yorick.

Gail hisses, "Quiet, Bob!"

Dwayne knocked on her office door one Saturday morning. "You want to tell me what your procedure is?" he said when she opened it and saw him standing there. He spoke with such authority that for a moment she mistook him for one of the old guard. "I've been watching this waste receptacle for ten minutes now, and I'm starting to wonder just exactly what your procedure is." One of the Lunch Ladies crossed the hall from the kitchen and took him by the elbow. "Dwayne, this lady is busy. And we need you right now in the dining room."

There's a bag of carrots in his shopping cart, and three apples. While she watches, he puts the lettuce he was looking at back, then picks up another. Does he have a furnished room somewhere? Maybe he's gotten a book about basic nutrition out of the library. The few fresh things would make for some variety in a food bank diet. The Lunch Lady who rescued her that time told her that Dwayne drops into the local library every morning to check that the desk calendar on the front counter is turned to the right day. Then he inspects all the paper recycling bins to make sure nobody's put pop cans into them, or anything else they shouldn't. When he's done he goes and sits in the same chair in the corner, thumbing through cat and dog magazines. Glaring at anyone who talks too loud.

Shit. He's looking at her. He must have felt her staring. It's a piercing look, overhung by thick, gathering eyebrows. Gail turns away and pretends to be picking over the vegetables.

The banks of green, red, yellow and orange peppers look odd. Not like things to eat. They're too shiny and bright and colourful. She starts to reach for a red pepper. The automatic sprinklers come on and she snatches her hand back.

Is Dwayne still looking at her? She doesn't want to turn around to check, so she sidles over toward the fruit. Apples. There's something strange about them, too. Gail has never thought about how many different kinds there are. Macintosh. Granny Smith. Royal Gala. Delicious, red and golden. Spartan. Who names them, she wonders suddenly. Who decides these things? And oranges. Look at them all. Naval. Valencia. Mineola. Clementine. Blood. Somebody actually developed a blood orange. Why? For what? Does she need a blood orange? Does anybody? Grapes. Green. Red. Purple. All claiming to be seedless. But where do seedless grapes come from? Where could they possibly come from?

There's no way she can leave the store without turning in Dwayne's direction. She keeps going straight ahead to the deli section, her cart still empty except for the food-bank bag. Behind the deli counter, an employee is cutting slabs from a huge block of Monterey Jack. Cheese. Sure. She can always use cheese. Usually she chooses from a short list of favourites—Havarti with caraway, old Cheddar, Colby, Brie. But suddenly she's confused by all the cream cheeses and blue cheeses and cheeses with green veins running through them and cheeses with almonds embedded in their tops and cheeses with cherries lurking in their depths. The employee slicing the Monterey Jack turns suddenly and asks if he can help her. Gail mumbles, "Sorry," and wheels her cart away.

As she passes the produce section, she sneaks a glance. No. He's gone. All at once she wishes he was still there. So she could nod and smile at him and say, "Hello, Dwayne." She wheels her cart up and down the aisles, looking for him. No. No Dwayne. In the end she buys a second round of dried pasta, canned vegetables, canned fruit, peanut butter, Kraft dinner, Pabulum and beans. The cashier looks at her oddly and asks if she wants another brown paper bag for the food bank.

Don't do it, Gail.

"What, Bob? What exactly is it that I shouldn't do?"

She's sitting on a bench in a little parkette the city made out of an empty lot one block north of the grocery store. Philomena Blanding Parkette, according to the plaque she's walked past hundreds of times but never gotten around to reading. She's never sat on this bench before, either, or seen anyone else sitting on it. We are a city of charming little parkettes, she thinks grimly, that nobody ever visits. Named for local heroes that nobody remembers.

Don't give all your money away to some guy on the street.

"I can't, Bob. I'm broke." It's technically true. The second round of food-bank food, which she left in the bin at the front of the store, took all the cash she had in her wallet. She couldn't give a loonie to a panhandler if she wanted to. "And for your information, that was not some guy on the street. That was Dwayne. He has a name. And he was getting his groceries. In the store where I get my groceries. And now he's going to take them home. He lives somewhere. In this neighbourhood. And on Saturday he's going to come for lunch at All Saints. Where I work. For a while. Until the diocese sells the scrap of land it's taking up. So where's Dwayne going to go for lunch then? Where's he going to go?"

Oh, for God's sake. Who does she think she is? She's no kind of social justice advocate and she knows it. She's not even a nice person. A nice person would smile on Saturday mornings when she opens up to let in the lunch guests. A nice person would have gone up to Dwayne just now in the grocery store and said hello.

But this isn't about Dwayne. This is about Bob. It's him she's really mad at. For being dead. And for not even having a grave somewhere that she could visit at a time like this. "You selfish bastard," she hisses under her breath, amazed at how fresh her anger still is after all these years.

It was the only big fight they ever had. It was when they were drawing up their wills, in the lawyer's office. Bob came out with it so casually, so, oh by the way, that at first she couldn't believe he was serious. But he was. She just managed to keep the lid on until they were back inside the car. Then she let him have it.

He had told the lawyer, out of the blue, without having consulted her, that he wanted to donate his entire body to medical science. The whole thing. Nothing to bury, nothing to burn. No environmental impact. "Fuck the environment!" she screamed at him in the car. "What about me? You think I want to have to imagine you lying on some slab somewhere? People picking away at you? Slicing bits off?" They finally compromised on donating his organs and his eyes. Gail could have the rest, but not, he insisted, to bury. She could cremate and scatter him, if she wanted. "Put you out to the garbage, more like," she muttered, still mad.

But when the time came she scattered him. Up at the lake. Off the end of the dock of the cottage they used to rent. The wind shifted the very second she flung the ashes, and they blew back and stuck to her sunblock. She had to wade into the water and wash them off, laughing and crying at the same time.

"So where the hell are you, Bob? Why aren't you here? Now?" She's starting to cry again and doesn't care who sees her. She's a crazy rich lady, sitting on a bench in Philomena Blanding Parkette, with all the money in the world and no spare change.

Spare change, she thinks, rummaging in her purse for a Kleenex. *I'm a spare change person.* No Kleenex. Great. She wipes her face on the sleeve of her coat. *I am not a big bucks person.* Bob was. He'd have known what to do with big bucks.

He'd have never gone back to his job. He'd just have phoned in his resignation and hung up. Then booked them both onto a cruise.

"But that's not going to happen, is it, Bob?" she whispers. "Because you're dead." She sits on the bench until she starts to get cold. Then she gets up and walks home.

Inside the apartment, she makes the rounds of her plants. Do they really look a little greener? Already? Amazing what just one more inch of soil can do. The trick is to give them just enough. Not too much. It's like overwatering. Put a plant in too big a pot and it doesn't thrive, for some reason. It seems to need something to press against.

Gail has been fingering a leaf of the ficus benjamina. She drops it. Goes and gets the pencil and pad of foolscap she used that time when she was worried sick, listing her expenses. She sits down at the dining-room table and starts sharpening her pencil. *Okay, Bay Street,* she thinks. *You're going to get your list.* She smiles. That's what Bob would call him—just Bay Street. Or maybe even B.S.

At the top of the foolscap page, she prints, DONATION. Underneath that, CONDITIONS. Then she thinks back on what Simon told her about what he would do for All Saints if he could. "There's still some land out back," he said. "Or we could go straight up, the way the condos do." She remembers watching his mouth move. This was right after he told her they might have to cut her hours. All she could think was, how she would pay her rent if they laid her off completely? Who would hire her, even part-time, at her age?

"This place could become an abbey," Simon went on. "A place where you could come if you were poor or sick or some disaster had happened. You could get a meal. A shower. A bed for the night. Or longer than a night. Maybe some counselling. A decent outfit to wear to a job interview. Some pro bono legal help. Why not? It wouldn't be that hard. It doesn't take much, usually, to get somebody back on their feet."

Her list fills up a page and a half. When she's finished she prints, MUST BE <u>ANONYMOUS</u>. Right. No fucking little parkette named after her with a plaque nobody will ever read. Then, near the bottom of the page, SOMETHING FOR ME. IN A TRUST FUND OR WHATEVER. It won't have to be a lot. Just enough. Just so she can stay here in her apartment. And so her church pension will keep pace with inflation. When she can't work any more.

"That'll be the day."

Was that Bob? No, that was her.

"Bob?"

She sits listening to the quiet. That *less alone* feeling is gone. She's not sure she's going to miss it. Probably be too busy.

She reads through her list. Makes some changes. Checks her watch. Time to go drop in on B.S. Get this show on the road. When she phoned a few minutes ago, his executive assistant said he could just fit her in at four. Well, la-di-da.

At the door, while she's pulling on her jacket and checking her pockets for her gloves, she wonders how long it will be before Simon tells her the news. Some morning a few weeks from now, once he's picked up his mail and gone to his office, she'll hear him running back down the stairs. She'll have to arrange her face. Act surprised. Overjoyed. Relieved. All that stuff.

She's not much of an actress. But she's going to have to be. Unlocking the back door every morning to let the construction crew in. Putting calls from the architect through to Simon. Directing the cleaning staff to hang plastic sheets to keep the dust out of the sanctuary.

She makes sure she has her keys. Puts her hand on the doorknob. Stops. Then says, "Okay, Bob. This one's for you."

She's not good at this kind of thing either. But she'll give it a go. She starts by bouncing on the soles of her feet. Feeling silly. She makes it into a bunny-hop. Flaps her elbows. A grin splits her face. Becomes a giggle. She bird-dances back into the living room. Spins around, turning the plants into a green blur.

"I won!" she screams in a whisper. "I won! I won! I won!"

HEROES

BRIAN GOT A CRANE LAST WEEK *for his birthday. Peter was there when he opened the box. It has a big hook on a chain and he can make it pick up anything. So far this afternoon, he's made it pick up one of his dinky cars, his dump truck and the tin barn from his farm set.*

Now Peter watches as Brian trundles the crane toward a tomato box his mother gave him. He manoeuvres the swaying hook into the space between two slats, then turns the crank. This is the part that makes Peter afraid he might cry. It's something about how the tomato box tilts up and up until it's off the ground. Brian can take it anywhere now—clear to the other side of his room if he wants. Then he can set it down again by turning the crank the other way. He can even trundle the crane out into the hall and dangle the tomato box over the edge of the stairs, raising it higher, then lowering it, up and down, up and down forever, just by the way he turns the crank.

Peter's mouth is dry. His birthday was back in March. He could ask for a crane for Christmas, but it's only October.

"Can I make it do something?"

Brian frowns. "You have to go home soon. It's time for supper almost."

Ever since he got the crane, Brian has acted like he's older than Peter. But he's only seven, and Peter is seven and a half. No. He's way older than that. He must be. Look how big his hands are all of a sudden. And there are brown spots on them, like Grandpa's.

"It's just five o'clock," Peter says. His voice has gone all deep, like his father's voice. "I don't have to go home till five-thirty. Let me have a turn."

"I don't know." Brian shakes his head in a way that makes Peter want to give him a shove. "This crane is brand new. My dad says it cost four dollars."

"Please?" Peter thinks he might hate Brian. Even though they're best friends. "I'll be careful with it."

"No you won't. You'll break it."

Peter grabs the crane. Holds it high above Brian's head where he can't reach.

"Give that back! It's mine! Mom!"

"You can't have a mother anymore!" Peter crows down at Brian. "You can't have a crane either! You can't have anything! Because you're dead!"

He shouldn't have said that. It's not Brian's fault that he's dead.

"I'm sorry," Peter says, suddenly small and seven again and wishing he could give the crane back. But it's too late. Brian is in his coffin, dressed in his funeral suit and tie. His eyes are shut and his face is the colour of a candle.

Pete looks around the almost-empty coffee shop. There's a man about his age at a corner table. He's partly turned away, but the shape of the collar is visible. Tall, lanky guy, to judge from the width of his shoulders. Funny. The voice on the phone had conjured up someone shorter. Stockier.

He starts toward the man's table, padding like a cat. *He hasn't seen me yet. I could still turn around and walk out.* But the priest hears him. Turns.

"Pete? Simon. Nice to meet, finally." They shake hands. Simon gestures down at the table, his drained coffee cup. "Can I get you something?"

Pete wonders if anybody ever answers that question in the affirmative. Says, *Yeah, get me the large pumpkin latte special with extra nutmeg.* Then sits there and drinks it while the other guy drums his fingers. "No thanks. I'm fine."

"Maybe we should be on our way, then."

They step outside into the late October night. The streets are shiny black from recent rain, the sidewalks slippery with fallen leaves.

Pete feels a familiar trickling in his stomach. He used to tell the kids on opening night that stage fright was all about backstage, that the minute they got out under the lights, it would disappear. *Don't worry,* Simon had reassured him on the phone, *There is a script to follow. And the whole thing is very dignified.* A touch of irony in his tone, as if he was saying, *You're not being drawn into a cult.* Now Pete wishes he had gotten a coffee after all. Taken the time. He could have used a bit more preamble.

"It's been a mild fall, so far." He hates small talk, but the silence is spooking him.

"Yeah, but they say the winter's going to be a cold one."

Silence again, broken only by their footsteps whispering on the damp pavement.

Okay. Fine. I can be meditative too. As they walk along, Pete steals a look at the priest's still mouth, his profile. Character actor's face. Not pretty, but workable. Expressive. *This face you got. This here phizzog you carry around…* He used to give that poem to the kids to recite in the first class of September. It was funny, so it helped them over some of their self-consciousness. Got them thinking of their faces in terms of a mask, too. *You have an ideal actor's mask, Pete.* Sally, his one-time agent. *Perfectly even features. Could be anything.*

He must have been slowing down. Lost in thought. Simon has pulled a few steps ahead of him. Pete stops walking altogether. No idea why. It just feels right, like something in an improv.

Why did he agree to this? It all seemed so reasonable over the phone. Simon spoke calmly about the importance of ritual, the need for *closure.* Again that slightly ironic emphasis, letting him know he was aware it was a cliché. Pete was disarmed. Then intrigued. It couldn't hurt. Might even be therapeutic. And yes, he was curious. But now that the two of them have met and they're actually on their way—

Simon is a whole half-block ahead now, unaware that he's been walking alone. As Pete stands watching, the priest says something. Looks to the side. Stops. Turns. Then stands still himself and watches and waits. As if he understands perfectly what Pete is up to.

That makes one of us.

Simon has been thinking ahead, unconsciously speeding up. It has just occurred to him that they can't use the sanctuary tonight. Eduardo might notice a light on and come over and catch them. His office, then. Which means he'll have to dismantle the smoke alarm. Damn. He should have thought of that. He should have thought of a lot of things.

"Pete, do you have any experience tinkering with smoke alarms? Pete?"

What's he doing back there? He's such a small man. Boyish. Jutting ears. One of those faces that never get old, for all he must be pushing sixty. By the time he phoned, Simon had given up on hearing from him. Then Gail put the call through to his office. The voice—*Peter Aspinall here*—was deep. Resonant. Conjuring up a tall, craggy type.

Right now, standing all alone on the sidewalk, he looks like a scared kid. Simon can see himself walking slowly toward him. Taking him in his arms. One of those odd, dangerous notions he gets now and then. Completely inappropriate, yet strangely right. Like the first time he met Kelly. When they shook hands, he had to deliberately take his hand out of hers and grip the back of a chair, for fear of just pulling her into his arms.

Okay, Pete. Let's stand here and wait. For whatever we're waiting for.

Dear Mr. Aspinall, Simon's letter had begun.

I'm writing to determine if you are the Peter Aspinall who was a student of Miss Alice Vipond at Claredale Public School in 1957. You may have read about Miss Vipond's recent death in the newspapers. A year ago, I conducted a brief correspondence with her, and she mentioned a boy named Peter Aspinall who was absent from school the day of the tragedy.

Your name rang a bell for me. My late wife Ruth took a beginner acting course from a Pete Aspinall a few years ago and spoke very highly of her instructor. I hope you don't mind my writing to you care of the college. I considered e-mailing you through your website, then decided that some things are best not entrusted to the Internet.

The fact is, if you are the Peter Aspinall in question, I would appreciate having a conversation with you concerning Alice Vipond. This would in no way resemble an interview. I'm sure you've been pestered enough recently by reporters. I would not record or publish or make any inappropriate use of anything you told me. However, it would be very helpful for me to have some contact with someone who knew Alice—Miss Vipond as she would have been to you.

I was left somewhat affected by my association with her. The staff of the institution in which she spent most of her life have been thoroughly professional and helpful. You, however, have the advantage of having known her before the fact, if only for a short time when you were very—

Pete had stopped reading there. He was tired. The Brian dream had wakened him at three, and he hadn't been able to get back to sleep.

He took the letter over to his paper shredder and stood holding it an inch above the metal teeth. There had been phone calls from two newspapers. A microphone shoved into his face one day when he was leaving the college. Everybody curious to know what it was like to be the survivor. Default survivor, he wanted to correct them. At least that kid who went over the falls in the fifties and lived—there'd been a *Where is he now?* article in the paper a while ago—at least he did something. What did little Peter Aspinall do?

He could still hear his father on his way out the door that morning. *He's not sick again. You're spoiling him. Turning him into a little fairy. Make him go to school.* Did his father remember saying that? Afterwards? It hadn't sounded like him—the slow, careful use he normally made of words. The way he would answer questions over the counter about something like cough drops—taking the time to describe in detail how relatively effective each kind was, how pleasant or less pleasant to take.

But not that morning. *Little fairy.* Pete remembered ducking under the covers, curling up around his phony stomach ache. Wondering if he was already turning into a little fairy. With wings? Like Tinkerbell? Is that what happened if you lied about being sick because you wanted to stay home from school?

The shredder teeth were waiting.

Pete took Simon's letter back to his desk. Finished reading it. Put it face down in his IN box. Where it stayed for six weeks.

A week before he wrote the letter, Simon sat listening to a voicemail in his office:

Simon? It's Marylou Meister? You know, from the Philomena Blanding Institute? I guess you got the news about Alice Vipond, one way or another. The papers have been on it, God knows, and we've had all kinds of reporters phoning us here. I'm calling because, frankly, you're the only one from the outside who had anything to do with her toward the end. Well. For the last almost thirty years, actually. Her parents died back in the eighties. And she had no other family, or nobody who wanted to be bothered with her. So your letters were it. Sorry that whole thing ended under a bit of a cloud, but I don't blame you for putting a stop to it. Not one bit. Anyway, I'm rambling on here. We're going to have a short memorial service for Alice in the chapel on Thursday at two. We always do, whenever one of our residents passes on. It's for the family, but even if there is no family, it's good for the staff, too. I mean, you do get to know people, especially somebody like Alice who came here years before a lot of us were even born. And whatever you might think of her, she was a sweet old dear. Always did what she was told, never complained or gave us any trouble. And it could have been different, believe me, what with the level of surveillance we had to impose. For her own safety, as much as anything else. Anyway, Simon, if you can make it to the service, that would be great. There is one thing I have to ask, though. I need you to be very discreet about this. We're breaking the law, technically, by having even a little half-hour thing for Alice. Really. The powers that be made it clear that there would be no service, no marker, no disclosure of her grave site. They can do that, in cases like this. Because the last thing anybody wants is a media circus. Not that she'll be here in person. I had to turn her over to the coroner's office, so they'll dress her and put her in a box, all at taxpayers' expense of course. Then they'll bury her in what used to be called Potter's Field. And nobody will ever know where she is. Just as well. Lot of nutcases out there—worse than any that are in here, believe me—people who would turn her grave into a shrine, or dig her up and sell her on eBay or God knows what. Sorry, Simon. I'm rambling on again. Anyway, do come to the service if you possibly can. And I know I can trust you to keep mum about it. Take care.

Simon couldn't go. He had a wedding that day. He was distracted during the ceremony, came close to ruining it once or twice. Kept wondering in the back of his mind whether he would have driven up to the Institute if he had been free.

As soon as he could decently leave the reception, he got into his car and drove around the city. He had the feeling he was looking for something, but didn't know what. He ended up back at All Saints, in his office, where he opened the bottom drawer of his desk. Alice Vipond's letters were in a paper bag at the back.

He sat holding the package, breathing shallowly. The letters gave off a very faint institutional smell. Stale air with an overlay of chemical freshener.

AP—Notorious child-killer Alice Vipond is dead at the age of 89. She died peacefully in her bed Sunday night at the Philomena Blanding Institute for the Criminally Insane, where she had spent most of her life.

Alice Vipond was born in Toronto in 1922, the only child of Doris and Frederick Vipond. She attended Normal School and taught grade two for fifteen years at Claredale Public School, now the site of Claredale Condominiums.

On October 19, 1957, Alice Vipond murdered her entire grade two class by serving them lemonade laced with foxglove, the source of digitalis. There was one survivor, Peter Aspinall, who was absent from school that day. Mr. Aspinall, an instructor at Breadalbane College, was not available for comment.

Alice Vipond was found not guilty by reason of insanity. She was incarcerated in the Philomena Blanding Institute, where for her own protection she was kept under heavy surveillance.

Out of respect for any surviving members of the families of the murdered children, Corrections Canada has mandated that there will be no memorial service for Alice Vipond, and that her gravesite will be unmarked.

Too soon, Simon stops walking and says, "Here we are."

The church has just appeared out of nowhere. They were going past the grounds of a big new condo building, presentation centre modelled after the Parthenon, when all at once there was this little brown—thing.

"I know," Simon smiles at Pete's expression. "Not the greatest example of Anglican church architecture. First time I saw it, I thought somebody had slapped a bell tower on top of a garage."

Pete stands looking at the recessed entrance, fists balled in his pockets. He still doesn't know what he was doing, stopping and waiting for Simon to notice he was gone. The priest had turned, seen him and just stood, his expression neutral. After what was probably less than a minute but felt like ten, Pete had shrugged and closed the distance between them.

Simon had made no reference to the incident, had kept the talk light as they walked along. So Pete was retired from teaching high school? *Yes.* How long? *Five years.* But he still keeps his hand in, teaching courses? Like the one Ruth took? At the college? *That's right.*

Listening to himself, his terse replies, Pete had wanted to slap his own face.

"You know," Simon begins, "a lot of people have associations with churches that aren't great. I've had folks phone me and ask if they can talk to me in a library or on a park bench. Anyplace but *in there.*" When Pete says nothing, he adds, "And this collar does come off." He pulls his dickey away from his neck and tucks it inside his jacket. "I only wore it so you would recognize me in the coffee—"

"It's not about the church. Or your collar. It's—I'm sorry. I don't know what it is. So can we just—" He gestures toward the door.

"Sure. Did you bring your report card?"

Pete pats his lapel. "I've got it here."

"And I've got the letters. So. Here we go." Simon leads Pete down a laneway to a smaller entrance. "I'm going to take you up to my office. I'd rather do this in the sanctuary, but we have to be careful."

At some point during the six weeks between reading Simon's letter and talking to him on the phone, Pete decided he was having a breakdown.

It didn't feel like something he was allowed to have. Nervous breakdowns were for grown-ups, and Pete had given up on ever thinking of himself as one of those. He knew how to pass for one. He went about his day like a mature person, a citizen, a taxpayer. But he felt like a fraud. Not qualified to do something as grown-up as breaking down.

It was easy to deny it at first. He always went a bit strange in October. Touch of depression. Stomach upset. Trouble sleeping. And the Brian dream, of course. Stir in the news of Alice Vipond's death and things were bound to be a little turbulent for a while. But Alice had been in her grave, wherever that was, for weeks. And the anniversary of the crime had come and gone. Things should have settled down by now.

So he reminded himself that he had had a lot of stress, what with moving into his present living space just a few months ago and Jean divorcing him last year. He still thought of both things in those terms. His present living space. And the divorce as something Jean had done all by herself.

She had engaged one of her colleagues as their lawyer—a man who kept complimenting the two of them on the most easy and amicable divorce of his career. And she had moved Pete's stuff into their guest room so he could stay in the house while he was looking for an apartment. Then, when he found one, she had all but organized his move for him.

Pete was used to things being taken out of his hands. He must have proposed to Jean, but couldn't remember doing it. What he did remember was her arranging the marriage. Lining it up. Facilitating it, the way she would a corporate merger—all very much to his advantage, as he surely could not fail to see. The teaching thing—that's how she had referred to his career—wouldn't have to be forever. He could even quit right away if he wanted. Start seeing agents. Become the actor they both knew he wanted to be.

She never said so, but Pete knew Jean was embarrassed to be married to a man who taught high school. She wanted him to have a name and a face that her colleagues might recognize. At the very least, she wanted him to be a little strange and interesting—someone she could show off at company gatherings like an exotic pet.

That was hindsight talking. At the time, Pete had believed he wanted to be an actor instead of a high-school theatre arts teacher the way he had believed he wanted to marry Jean. And when the schools started to downsize, he looked forward to being offered a retirement package. He was two years away from the requisite length of service. All he had to do was hang in. Pray they wouldn't pick him off early. For the first time in his career, he wished he was teaching something like math or science—something people thought of as hard and necessary.

But in the end, it was all taken out of his hands.

Mr. Aspinall? Do you think there's any point—Like—I mean, it's probably a stupid idea. Long pause. Then, in a rush—*Yale Drama School?*

Brendan. Not a child. Seventeen. But not quite an adult, either. Brilliant young actor. Not beautiful. Bumpy nose, bit of an underbite. But a voice. And a body.

They filled out the Yale application together, Simon correcting Brendan's spelling and writing a letter of recommendation. Then the audition—the boy flew down with his mother. Then the wait. Then that day.

Running steps behind him. *Mr. Aspinall! Mr. Aspinall!* Pete turned. Saw the boy's tears. Prepared to be strong. Calm. The teacher, who would help his student find something to learn from this disappointment.

They want me! I'm in!

He didn't have time. The boy-man was on him. Arms wrapping his shoulders. Spiky hair tickling his throat. Chest, damp through the T-shirt, heaving against his. Then the kiss. Not on the mouth, of course. More like the way he would have kissed his father. But.

There had been nothing before that. No dreams. No crushes on other men, not even when he was a student. And he was married. To a woman. And they had sex. Not a lot, and not fabulous, but often enough and good enough.

"That's wonderful news, Brendan." Gently disengaging himself. Pitching his voice, arranging his mask into teacher mode—kind but not too friendly. Praying the kid would not glance down at the erection he had miraculously missed feeling. "Let's take a look at that acceptance letter."

He told Jean he couldn't do another two years. He was burned out. And the package wouldn't be that much smaller anyway. Then he burst into ridiculous tears at the exit interview, was handed a box of Kleenex and assured that lots of people cried. Retirement was a big step, after all. Even when it was exactly what you wanted.

Obedient to Jean, he made the rounds of agents. Found Sally, who had been in first year university when he was in fourth, and had seen him play Laertes. *You should have been Hamlet, Pete. I remember thinking that.* He refrained from saying, No, I should have been a teacher. I should still be a teacher.

Sally sent him out on auditions for TV, film, stage, voice work. *You're perfect, Pete. You look great, and you're at the age when men start being very rare in this business, and very valuable.* He started to get jobs. A few TV commercials. A one-line film role. A couple of parts in plays in small theatres. *It'll take a couple of years to sell you, Pete. But once you're in, you'll be in like Flynn.*

For the first time, he felt that Jean respected him. He had always assumed that she loved him, but in a rueful, *oh well, what can you do* kind of way. As if he were some sort of lovable nincompoop. Now she was shy around him. Even a little frightened. Not long after being taken on by the agency, he had requested separate beds. Used his bad back as an excuse.

Sometimes he thought about Brendan. What had that been about? Why had he panicked and run? He hadn't done anything wrong. And it wasn't as if he couldn't trust himself to keep his hands off the boy. Off the boys who would have come after him. Sometimes Brendan did show up in his dreams. But when he did he was more like Brian. Brendan/Brian and Peter. Two little guys playing together.

It was just a matter of time before he started scribbling lists of figures on foolscap. Estimates of monthly expenses. Food. Rent. Separate insurance. And it was just a matter of time before he started leaving those sheets of foolscap lying around where Jean was bound to see them.

Once he had scraped together enough credits to get his Equity and Actra cards, he quit the agency. (*But you were just hitting your stride, Pete!* Sally, wailing. *You were starting to get known! Saleable!*) He applied for and got a part-time teaching position at Breadalbane Community College. Two regular classes, plus some continuing ed work in the evenings. With his high-school teacher's pension, it would be enough to keep him.

"This is the story of Pete."

It was an exercise he used to give his high-school students. Tell the story of your life as if you were talking about somebody else. Act bits of it out. Story theatre.

He missed theatre games. His students at the college were more focussed than the high-school kids had been. They were either there to craft a career, full of questions about technique and the business end of things, or they were retirees, taking an acting course to make friends, perk up their marriages, whatever. He missed the younger kids, missed playing with them. Yes, he had been their teacher—but a teacher who sat on the floor and mimed peeling an orange.

Now he sat on the couch, resting his scotch on the arm. Addressing a non-existent audience.

"When Pete was in Grade Two, Grade Two disappeared. No more teacher. No more classmates. Yellow sticky tape criss-crossing the door of his classroom. So where could Pete go to school?"

He got up from the couch, grabbing his scotch as it sloshed. Was that his second? Already?

"At first, they gave Pete a desk at the back of the Grade One classroom."

He went and sat on a dining-room chair, heels tucked up on a rung, looking down at the floor as a giant would look down on a tiny village.

"But the desk was too small for him and it made him feel big and stupid, as if he had to do Grade One all over again, even though the teacher visited him back there now and then to give him Grade Two work to do."

He unfolded himself from the dining-room chair and went and flopped down in his big armchair, clutching his scotch.

"So then, for a while, they put Pete in a desk at the front of the Grade Three classroom."

He looked fearfully up and all around, like a mouse on the floor.

"But the desk was too big, and all the kids sitting behind him were big kids and he couldn't understand the work they were doing and he cried, even though the teacher told him he didn't have to do it, and that when she had a moment she would help him with his Grade Two work."

He slumped back in the armchair. Jesus Christ. It was his third scotch, matter of fact. Is this the story of Pete? Divorced. Retired high-school teacher. College instructor by way of aborted acting career. Getting drunk every night. Playing theatre games by himself. In his present living space.

By the time Simon's letter arrived, there were still no pictures on the walls. He hadn't unpacked the pictures. Or much of anything else. Months after the move, he was still edging his way around stacks of sealed brown cartons. They had a curiously Soviet look—identical save for the stickers with Jean's impatient dashings in black Magic Marker: BOOKS, AUTHORS R—T, DIPLOMAS, TOOLBOX .

When he first moved in, he had managed to excavate the sheets, towels, coffee maker, a couple of plates, some cutlery, a frying pan and a pot. Just the stuff he needed to get through the day. He had been getting through the days with that same stuff ever since.

He went to work. Taught his classes in voice and TV acting for the young pros, beginner stagecraft for the retired boomers. Drank scotch. Cooked balanced, if bland, meals for himself. (SPICE RACK was still packed with SALAD SPINNER and MUG TREE.)

Every now and then, he would approach one of the cartons with a pair of scissors gripped in his hand. Sometimes he would get as far as sliding a blade under a strip of packing tape. But then he would pull the blade free and scurry away from the box. Run to the bedroom. Shut the door. Curl up on the bed, still clutching his scissors.

It was stress, he would tell himself again, once he had managed to uncurl and get up and put the scissors back in the kitchen drawer, forcing himself en route to look at the box he had tried to open. It hadn't tipped itself over. Nothing was heaving at the flaps, trying to get out. Stress.

Yes. Change of career. Divorce. Moving. Those were three of the big ones.

The day he decided he was having a bona fide breakdown was the day he fished Simon's letter out of his inbox and picked up the phone.

"There. I think that should do it."

Simon is standing on a chair in his office, disabling the smoke detector. It's not as hard as he thought it would be, but he's taking his time. Stalling. Now that the two of them are actually here, ready to start, the evening's agenda is embarrassing him.

"Thank God there's no sprinkler in here." He sounds over-hearty even to his own ears. "I wouldn't have a clue how to turn one of those things off." Behind him, Pete says nothing. Simon steps down and carries the chair back to his desk.

He wishes Kelly were here. Missing her has subsided into a distant ache, but every now and then it comes back fresh and sharp, like her voice in his ear. *You've got to do something, Simon. You've got to—I don't know. You tell me. You're the closure expert.*

They became lovers shortly after he started writing to Alice Vipond. They didn't have time to get past the awkward stage in bed—too eager or too hesitant, apologizing, assuring each other there was nothing to apologize for.

Kelly was his first since Ruth's death. They had talked and e-mailed back and forth for a year before touching each other. There had been a feeling of inevitability, much like what Simon thought people in arranged marriages must feel during their engagement—as if the two of them were riding a wave of expectation and implied blessing. There was no point trying to swim against it, and no need to hurry. "Do you think we should slow down?" Kelly had joked when he finally kissed her for the first time after a long talk on a bench in a graveyard. "At this rate, by Christmas we'll be holding hands."

She had been interested at first in his correspondence with Alice Vipond, had Googled the old newspaper articles, could hold her own when Alice and her crime came into the conversation. "Hearing from you must be the high point of her week." He savoured that comment of hers, running it through his mind again and again.

He should never have let Alice know about Kelly's existence. But when she wrote asking for details of his life, she made the request so humbly that he was moved. What could it hurt to give her a few bits and pieces, something to focus on through her long institutionalized day?

So he told her about his routines. Jokes he exchanged with his secretary. Odd requests he got sometimes for wedding ceremonies. A red flag did go up in his mind when he started to write about Kelly. But he kept things light, casting her as a parishioner he was starting to get fond of. Someone he might approach. Once he had retired from All Saints, needless to say.

He should have known that Alice would smell the half-truth. The second he dropped the first letter containing Kelly's name through the slot of the mail box, he thought, *She's got me.* It wasn't a rational fear. He hadn't told Alice anything she could use against him. Even if he had, she was not allowed to keep his letters in her room and had no access to the Internet. Besides, what credibility could she have—a criminally insane mass murderer of children? What could she do to him?

It started with Kelly making rueful jokes—*Other women have guys who are into Internet porn. Me, I'm competing with an old lady in a loony bin.*

Then—*Do you think we could talk about something besides Alice Vipond?*

Then—*She's between us, Simon. She's in our bed. I can see her. I can see you thinking about her.*

Could he have called Kelly tonight? Told her what he was going to do? She had said it was all right to call now and then. Tentatively, wary of hurt, he lets himself imagine picking up the phone. Hearing her voice. She might have joked with Pete, made him smile with one of her quirky sayings. Mitigated between the two of them. Because God knows, they could use some common ground. Besides Alice.

Fuck Alice.

He sits back down in his chair. Picks up his prayer book. Opens it.

Fuck Alice.

Great attitude to have toward the dear departed, he thinks, making himself smile at Pete.

Pete has been watching Simon, consciously taking in details, as if he might have to describe him to the police or pick him out of a line-up. Well, there is something clandestine about what the two of them are doing here tonight.

There's no point in wondering what Jean would have to say about it. Not that he misses her. But she was there. Somebody to talk to. Dump on at the end of the day.

He watches Simon step down and carry the chair back behind his desk. The man is graceful, for all his rangy build. Sports in his background? Basketball? Dance, even? Now he's opening a small book. Running his finger down the contents page. Turning to a place near the back.

"I thought we'd use the traditional *Book of Common Prayer*." Simon hands a second copy across the desk to Pete. "It's the book Alice would have grown up with. She went to church here at All Saints, as I think I mentioned to you. She was a Church School teacher, in fact, back in the 1930s when she would have been in her teens. Quite possibly sat once or twice in your chair. Sorry. That's a bit creepy."

"It's okay," Pete says. But he does look down at the chair. Oak. Thin black leather padding on the seat and armrests. Metal studs. He needs to focus on something. That odd stage fright is back. Except now it's more like the dread he feels when he's inside the Brian dream.

"Maybe we should just start." Simon is sounding a touch impatient. "The service begins on page 591."

Pete opens his prayer book. Finds the place. Reads, *The Order for the Burial of the Dead*. Stares at the words. Closes the book. Puts it back on the desk.

"I'm sorry," he says. "This seemed like a good idea when we talked. But right now I can't remember why I said yes to it."

Simon closes his own prayer book. Waits for a moment. Then says, "Do you remember the kids Alice killed?"

Pete looks at him. "Of course I do. I was almost one of them."

"Do you remember their names?"

"Some of them. Most of them, probably." *Brian.*

Simon pulls a pad of paper toward him. Picks up a pen and clicks it. "Please tell me all the names you can remember."

"You want their names."

"Please. It might help. Both of us."

Oh, what the fuck. Pete puts himself back inside his grade two classroom. Sees the coloured paper cut-outs—autumn leaves, pumpkins—scotch-taped to the window. The blackboard. Miss Vipond's big desk up at the front. All the little desks in rows. He starts with the first row.

"Okay. There was Sharon Fulton. Andrew Stenkowski. Douglas Little."

Brian.

Simon finishes writing. "Any more? Take your time."

"Hendrik Vandeven. Diane—Look, maybe this isn't—"

"Please. I think it's important that we say their names."

"All right. Where was I?"

Simon looks down at the pad. "You said Diane."

"Diane. Diane Verway. Gail Darby. Allan Ramsden. Jimmy Suzuki. Linda Miller. Eddie Avolio. Sammy Goldsmith."

Brian Bellingham.

"That's all. All the names I can remember."

Simon puts his pen down. "Okay. What if we were to incorporate their names into the service? Would that make this possible for you?"

After a second, Pete nods.

"Is there anything else we should do? Anything that I should do?"

"Yeah. There is. You can tell me what's in this for you."

"For me? Well, as we discussed on—"

"Yes, I remember our phone conversation. You and Alice wrote letters back and forth. You didn't like the business about there being no religious service for her when she died. You feel obligated to do something. Because she was a human being and you're a priest. Okay. Fair enough. I guess. But you could do that all by yourself. Why bring me into it? Why do you need me here?"

All Simon can think of is the dream that woke him that morning. He was a boy again, in his childhood bed. Slowly, as he came awake, he had to remind himself that his sister was not in her room across the hall and his parents not in their own bed downstairs. Then he had to remember that he grew up and became a priest and married a woman named Ruth. But Ruth died. And now there's another woman. Named Kelly. Except there isn't. Because they aren't together any more.

Pete doesn't wait any longer for Simon's answer. "Look. This is just a guess. You tell me if I've got it wrong. I think Alice did something to you. And whatever it was, you can only talk about it to somebody else that she did something to. That sound right?"

Simon nods.

"Okay. How about I tell you exactly what she did to me. And then you return the favour."

After a moment, Simon nods again.

Pete props his elbows on the arms of the chair. Leans forward, looking into Simon's eyes.

"First of all, I haven't been inside a church since I was married. And before that, I hadn't been in one since I was a kid. We used to go. Everybody did back then. I went to Sunday School. The whole bit. But we stopped. After." His last word hangs in the air.

"Your parents lost their faith?" Simon prompts. "As a result of—?"

"What my parents lost was my father's business. Aspinall's Pharmacy. The big chains were starting up then. Maybe one of them would have swallowed Aspinall's anyway. Who knows? But the thing is, nobody whose kid has been murdered wants to have a prescription filled by a neighbour whose kid narrowly missed being murdered. And that's the thing. We were neighbours. The schools were zoned. The kid next door could be in your class. And at the end of the week you might see him again in church. It's not the greatest thing, being the only seven-year-old left for blocks and blocks around. I remember sitting one Sunday morning between my mother and father. Hearing the minister offering prayers for the bereaved parents in the congregation."

Pete falls silent. All this stuff he hasn't thought about for years. *Do you want to see him, Peter?* His father's voice. Gentle, but insistent. *It's entirely up to you, son.* No it wasn't. He knew what the right answer was, the one his father wanted to hear. The one that wouldn't make him sound like a little fairy.

He straightens up. Clears his throat. "Sorry. Wool-gathering. Where was I? My father. A lot of his regular customers started going to other pharmacies—miles out of their way. So that was it for Aspinall's. Dad went to work behind the counter of a Rexall's. And he survived. Made a pretty good living. We all survived. I guess that's what's so remarkable—the sheer normalcy of the lives we ended up living."

The smell of flowers. Like a taste he couldn't get out of his mouth. And that light trained on the box Brian lay in. On his face. No matter where you were in the room, you couldn't help being drawn to the still mouth, the shut eyes. *Come and say goodbye.* His father's hand engulfing his. Tugging, gently but insistently. Taking him closer and closer—

"Okay. That's me. Bare-assed. You know exactly what Alice did to me. So now it's your turn. What did she do to you?"

Simon looks down at his hands. "She just about destroyed my faith."

"In God, you mean."

"No. That's the funny thing. God remained. Everything else went to hell. I could hardly do my job. My—relationships suffered. I went through the motions. But there was no—"

I couldn't get it up.

He and Kelly would be making love. All at once he would flash on that iconic photograph of Alice Vipond being taken into custody. Instead of trying to cover her face she is staring straight into the camera, as if daring it to blink. Staring straight into his eyes.

Pete says, "What was in those letters she sent you? I mean, you already knew what she'd done. It's not as if she could shock you. Or could she?"

"No. She couldn't shock me. But she could play me like a fish. She could read between the lines. Suss out my weaknesses." He shakes his head. "It was my own fault. I was supposed to be just a friendly outlet for her. A pen pal. A connection with the world outside the institution. But that wasn't good enough for me. So I started by trying to analyze her. I wanted to find the hurt little girl at her centre—the reason she did what she did. And when that didn't work, I tried to get her to confess to me. Show some contrition. So that I could forgive her." He snorts. "Well, she got me confessing to her. Probably had a big old laugh doing it, too. And she taught me a very good lesson. One I should have learned back in Theology 101."

"What was that?"

"If Alice Vipond had a black hole where most of us have some kind of moral sense or conscience or empathy, whatever you want to call it, that was just the way God made her. And the reason why was none of my damned business."

He stops talking. Pete lets the silence hang between them—a friendlier silence.

"So you were right," Simon goes on. "This isn't about being a priest. This is about getting my woman back." He smiles wearily. Some of the strain has gone out of his face. "And that's me, as you say. Bare-assed."

"What's her name? Your woman friend?"

"Kelly."

Pete nods, thinking *Brian. Brian Bellingham.* He can feel the name on his tongue, nudging against the inner seam of his lips. There's a box of Kleenex on Simon's desk. Do people still sometimes come to a priest instead of going to see a psychiatrist? He can imagine Simon being detached, professional. He can see him putting an arm around someone, too. Pulling them close. Pressing their face into his shoulder. "Could I say something?"

"Please do."

"Maybe what happened to you—and to me—is just part of the story. That's something I used to say to the high-school kids I taught. They'd tell me stuff—a drama teacher hears all kinds of things. Stuff about their parents fighting. Heading for divorce. Or the love of their life dumping them for their best friend. All the hell of being a teenager. And when they were done, I'd tell them to look at their life as a story. They're the protagonist. They don't know how the story's going to end. Or even what's going to happen next. And they can count on a certain amount of shit, because it would be a pretty boring story without it. But no matter what happens, they're still the protagonist. They're the hero."

"Thanks. I don't feel much like a hero at the moment. But thanks."

Pete picks the prayer book back up. "Maybe now we can get started?"

Simon nods and opens his own copy. "We've got a couple of stage directions up front. '*Unless there be special cause to the contrary, the first part of the Service shall take place in the Church.*' Well, I'd say we have special cause to the contrary, so here we are. Just let me grab some holy hardware." He stands and goes across the room to a cabinet. Pete watches him. All of a sudden he's very attuned, sensually. The slope of Simon's shoulder. The hardness of the chair seat. The smells of varnish and incense.

Simon comes back, carrying a brass bowl. "This is what we put the ashes in on Ash Wednesday."

Pete takes a faded brown envelope out of his jacket pocket and puts it in the bowl.

Simon looks at it. "I have to ask. What kind of marks did Miss Vipond give you?"

"Have a look."

Simon picks up the report card and opens it. "Well, your reading and spelling were pretty good. Your arithmetic not so much. Oh, here's something. *Deportment excellent.*"

"That means a lot coming from Alice Vipond."

Simon reads aloud, "*Peter sometimes gets upset about rather unimportant matters.*"

"Yeah. I was a little perfectionist. Still am."

Simon smiles, slipping the report card back inside its envelope and putting it in the bowl. "These are the letters I got from Alice," he says, pulling a brown paper bag out of his bottom drawer and tipping the contents into the bowl. He looks at Pete. "Do you want to—"

"Read what she said about me? I thought you'd never ask."

Simon sorts through the letters, checking the dates. He unfolds one of them and hands it to Pete.

Pete reads the passage silently. "*There was one child absent that day—Peter Aspinall. I remember looking at his name on the list as I took attendance. Peter Aspinall. Not thinking, "He alone will live," or "Why him and not some other," or anything melodramatic like that. No, just looking at it. Thinking it curious that by sheer accident—a sniffle or slight fever—he would escape.*

Odd little boy, as I remember. Bright enough. But a touch of the fay, as we used to say. The Grade Twos had begun to notice him too. His difference. Not in a cruel or teasing way. No, that would come in Grade Three. I might have looked out my window the next year and seen Peter Aspinall trapped inside a screeching, taunting circle of his peers."

"Jesus Christ," Pete breathes. He looks at Simon and says, "Sorry."

"It's okay. I say all the words."

Pete folds the letter back up, remembering the big brothers and sisters of the vanished Grade Twos. *Why you, Pee-ter?* In his ear. *Yeah, why you, you little sissy?* In his other ear. Circling him. He turns to one but now they're behind him. And the one that was behind him—

He puts the letter in the bowl.

Simon looks at his prayer book and says, "The service continues over the page. What say we do this next part responsively?" He reads aloud: "We brought nothing into this world, and it is certain we can carry nothing out. The Lord gave, and the Lord hath taken away; blessed be the name of the Lord."

He nods to Pete, who reads the next passage: "I am persuaded, that neither death, nor life, nor angels, nor principalities, nor powers, nor things present, nor things to come, nor height, nor depth, nor any other created thing, shall be able to separate us from the love of God."

Simon responds, "Out of the deeps have I called unto thee, O Lord; hear my voice. O let thine ears consider well the voice of my complaint. If thou, Lord, wilt be extreme to mark what is done amiss, who may abide it? But there is forgiveness with thee; therefore shalt thou be feared."

He stops reading and turns two pages. "I'm cherry-picking a bit here. What follows is a bunch of pretty orthodox stuff. Death and resurrection and the last trumpet and all that. I haven't believed any of it for years. What happens when we die. Whether there's an afterlife. Reward and punishment. I used to think I had some answers, but now it's all just as mysterious to me as it is to anybody else. And I'm pretty sure Alice would have made mincemeat out of it too. So I think we should cut to the chase. When we come to the bit about those we love but see no longer, I can read out the names of the kids, or you can, or we can alternate, or maybe—"

"There's one more name."

Simon picks up his pen.

"No. I'll write it. Just—give me a minute. "

Simon puts the pen back down. Waits. *All I've learned,* he thinks, *in all the years, is when to shut up and listen.*

Pete begins, "We lived next door to each other. Walked to school together. Played with each other at recess. Our desks were close enough to pass stuff back and forth."

But there was more. There was the way Brian would be waiting for him on the sidewalk every morning, too. His eyes would go round and his whole face would lift when Pete came out the door. And they would rub and bump and jostle each other as they walked side by side—not deliberately, just letting it happen. And now and then Brian would catch sight of something, and grab Pete's hand and say, *Look! There!*

"We had a fight. After school at his house. The night before. Just a stupid little-boy fight over his toy crane that I was jealous of. I was still mad at him in the morning so I played sick. That's why I'm alive. Because I picked a fight with my best friend, then lied to my mother."

"Have you ever told anybody else that you weren't really sick?"

Pete shakes his head.

Simon pushes the pad and pen across the desk. After a long moment, Pete picks up the pen and writes, *Brian Bellingham.*

"Lord, we beseech thee," Simon reads again from the prayer book, "look with compassion upon those who are now in sorrow and affliction; comfort them with thy gracious consolations; make them know that all things work together for good. Give rest to thy servants, where sorrow and pain are no more. We pray to thee for those whom we love but see no longer."

He puts the prayer book aside and pulls the list of names back toward him. "Sharon Fulton. Andrew Stenkowski..." He reads the whole list, ending with "Sammy Goldsmith." Then he looks up at Pete. Would you like to say this last one?"

Pete nods. Says, "Brian." His mouth is dry. He clears his throat. "Bellingham."

Simon puts the list of names in the bowl along with the report card and letters. He did not reread Alice's correspondence prior to this meeting. He has her last words to him memorized. *By allowing me this last missive, Simon, you are, so to speak, placing the ball in your own court. Another way of expressing it would be that you are placing yourself in my debt. For you will always owe me a letter. And I will never cease to wait for one. You engaged with me, Simon. And as long as I live, you will never be able to fully disengage from me.*

He rummages in his desk drawer for a book of matches, strikes one and touches the flame to the corner of a letter. "Should maybe have scrunched things up a bit," he says. "Made some air spaces." But the paper blackens and catches, then spreads its flame to the rest.

He reads aloud again from the prayer book, "Forasmuch as it hath pleased Almighty God of his great mercy to receive unto himself the soul of our dear sister here departed: we therefore commit her body to be consumed by fire." He and Pete sit breathing the last of the smoke, watching the mass burn down.

When nothing but ash remains, Simon says, "There's a tiny old graveyard out back of the church. Bring your prayer book And don't forget your coat. Oops. Flashlight. I'm a fine one to talk." He rummages in his desk.

They leave the office, go back down the steps and out into the dark. The air smells damp. Pete can just make out the shapes of small white gravestones tilting at different angles.

Simon puts the bowl on the ground, trains the flashlight on his prayer book and reads, "We commit her ashes to their resting place; earth to earth, ashes to ashes, dust to dust."

He hands the flashlight to Pete, who reads, "Rest eternal grant unto her, O Lord, and let light perpetual shine upon her."

Simon picks the bowl back up. Offers it to Pete, who takes a pinch of ash and scatters it into the dark. Simon scatters some, then Pete. They take turns until it's gone. Then Simon upends the bowl and taps it gently. Pete turns the flashlight off. They stand side by side in the dark and the silence.

Lines from a poem go through Simon's mind—*The grave's a fine and private place, but none, I think, do there embrace.* He feels again that odd compulsion to take Pete in his arms.

Pete is trying to remember if he and Brian ever hugged each other or kissed, the way little boys sometimes do. He is very aware of Simon beside him. His height. The way his own face would just fit against the priest's shoulder.

"And here comes the rain," Simon says, looking up. Pete looks up too, feeling the cold drops on his face. He raises his hand to wipe them away, then lowers it. He just stands, eyes closed. Letting it come.

Acknowledgements

I wish to thank Biblioasis, *The New Quarterly*, The Porcupine's Quill and Thomas Allen Publishers for recommending this collection of stories for Ontario Arts Council Writers' Reserve grants. I am also grateful to the Ontario Arts Council for a Works In Progress grant.

Many thanks to the friends and colleagues who read the book in manuscript form: Kim Aubrey, Mike Barnes, Elaine Batcher, Mary Borsky, Melinda Burns, Andrew Leith Macrae and Richard Tanner. Finally, I owe much to Dan Wells and John Metcalf of Biblioasis, for their good faith and good humour.

ABOUT THE AUTHOR

K.D. MILLER is the author of three previous short story collections, *Give Me Your Answer*, *A Litany in Time of Plague*, and *The Other Voice*, as well as an essay collection (*Holy Writ*) and a novel (*Brown Dwarf*). Her work has twice been collected in *The Journey Prize Anthology* and *Best Canadian Stories*, and she has been nominated for a National Magazine Award for Fiction. She lives and writes in Toronto.